THE RANGE
WOLF

THE RANGE WOLF

ANDREW J. FENADY

PINNACLE BOOKS
Kensington Publishing Corp.
www.kensingtonbooks.com

PINNACLE BOOKS are published by

Kensington Publishing Corp.
119 West 40th Street
New York, NY 10018

All Kensington titles, imprints, and distributed lines are available at special quantity discounts for bulk purchases for sales promotions, premiums, fund-raising, educational, or institutional use. Special book excerpts or customized printings can also be created to fit specific needs. For details, write or phone the office of the Kensington special sales manager: Kensington Publishing Corp., 119 West 40th Street, New York, NY 10018, attn: Special Sales Department; phone 1-800-221-2647.

PINNACLE BOOKS and the Pinnacle logo are Reg. U.S. Pat. & TM Off.

ISBN-13: 978-0-7860-3471-0
ISBN-10: 0-7860-3471-8

First printing: April 2014

10 9 8 7 6 5 4 3 2 1

Printed in the United States of America

First electronic edition: April 2014

ISBN-13: 978-0-7860-3472-7
ISBN-10: 0-7860-3472-6

With a grateful bow—

for my two *compadres*
on the trail of
THE RANGE WOLF

JACK LONDON
and
DUKE FENADY

and, of course,
for MARY FRANCES

PROLOGUE

The chronicle of Wolf Riker, who was more often called the Range Wolf, began long before we came across each other. Actually, he came across *me* and cared little, or not at all, if I lived or died.

The Range Wolf had infinitely more important things on his wefted mind than the life or death of a piece of human flotsam. After decades of bruised fists, smoking guns, and iron will against insuperable odds, he was on a perilous venture that meant ultimate fortune or ruinous failure— and death.

But this wolf did not run with the pack. He ran the pack. A predator who sometimes devoured even those who were fated to follow him—as was I.

The saga of the Range Wolf, as far as I later was able to weave it together, might well have had its beginnings when two young brothers rode west to Texas. It was after Sam Houston had avenged the Alamo and defeated General Santa Anna at San Jacinto, declared the vast territory of Texas a Republic, then led the movement for Texas to become the 28th state of the United States of America in 1845.

Two brothers, Dirk and Wolf Riker, united by blood, but thereafter divided by ambition, conceit, caprice, gloss—and yes, greed.

Destiny, fate, or chance, made a fist and gripped one of the two brothers, Wolf Riker, and me— Christopher Guthrie.

It was a different world, and I was a different man, part-time writer, critic, and full-time dilettante—and Wolf Riker was a hell-beast I came to know and fear like nothing on heaven or earth. His command, his mood, his every whim, was the law, without mercy—and there was no higher court of appeal.

At that time Wolf Riker was at the peak of his physical power, a dark Viking with broad shoulders and deep chest, dressed in devil's black from head to heel—thick raven hair, sapphire eyes of fire and ice, and a scar that ran across the left side of his forehead into his hairline and more than likely into his brain.

He was the master of his domain, and at that time, the most valuable asset of that domain was moveable. A herd of more than seven thousand Texas cattle—but only if he could move them to Kansas. In Texas that herd was worth less than a dollar a head—in Kansas, more than twenty times that much—over $140,000.

But Kansas was nearly a thousand miles away with floods, fever, Kiowas, Comanches, border raiders, and a brazen brother in between.

The odds against him were unyielding.

So was Wolf Riker.

What led up to my first sight of him—and what followed?

I have set down, through the course of that bleak passage, the men, women, and events as best I can remember.

But a man I can never forget is the one they called the Range Wolf.

CHAPTER I

I never fancied myself as an officer and a gentleman—only as a gentleman. Maybe that's why I, as did many other gentlemen of the North, bought myself out of serving in the army.

The fact is, I didn't buy myself out; my father, Douglas Wendell Guthrie, Esquire, did. He had graduated from Harvard Law. It was his wish that I do the same. So I did. It was his wish that I, his only progeny, go to work in his firm. So I did. It was his wish that I did not go into the army. So I did not.

I was not a very good lawyer. I was not a very good anything.

But my father was a very good everything.

Douglas Wendell Guthrie was a formidable force. No one ever called him Doug, not his mother or father, even when he was an infant. Not the children at school, not the students at Harvard. Not his two law partners, Oliver Talbot and Galen Flexner, of Guthrie, Talbot and Flexner. Of course they were not equal partners. No one was Douglas Guthrie's equal. No, no one ever called him Doug, not even my mother whom I don't remember. She died while giving birth.

What did I call him? A lot of things. But not to his face. To his face, I called him "father."

Dutifully, I went to the law office every workday. But I didn't work. I dabbled. Poetry. Short stories. Even plays. I thought of myself as a budding Edgar Allan Poe—sans drink or dope. My father overlooked my frivolity, hoping that someday I would change—and become more like Douglas Wendell Guthrie. But in his heart he knew that no one could be quite like him. Especially me.

Somehow I managed to idle my way through the dreary days, stay awake and seemingly attentive during conference room conferences. The one thing I was rather good at was entertaining clients, especially rich—very rich—clients and most especially young, attractive female clients, who sought advice on how to spend the earnings from inherited trust funds. Lunches, carriage rides, theatres, suppers—I provided good company and occasionally even good advice—good enough so that other young, attractive female inheritresses sought the services of Guthrie, Talbot and Flexner—and particularly of Christopher Guthrie.

All in all it was a comfortable, if rather confined,

circle of existence, and I paid hardly any attention to matters outside that circle, not even bothering to vote when someone named Abraham Lincoln was elected President of the United States representing something called the Republican Party.

Abraham Lincoln stood for a strong Union and was against slavery—and most of the country stood with Lincoln. A swelling rumble of discontent erupted into gunfire at Fort Sumter on April 12, 1861—Confederate gunfire, aimed at the heart of the Union, and no longer could anyone, even those within my cloistered circle, fail to be affected by current events.

That's when my father paid handsomely for another fellow to don a Union uniform in my place. At the time, as usual, I did nothing to contradict or counteract my father's action. This, by the way, was not an uncommon procedure among those in a position to pay for a substitute soldier of the North.

But as time went by and the clash of resounding arms brought forth a clash of conscience, even I was compelled to no longer stand idle.

When I announced to my father my intention to enlist, there was another clash. There was a white man, a fellow Harvard graduate friend of mine, Robert Gould Shaw, who was forming a negro brigade, the Fifty-fourth Massachusetts Volunteer Infantry, but with white officers. It was my intention to be one of those white officers.

It was my father's intention to disinherit me if I so did.

But I did so anyway.

Howsomever, after my enlistment I found that instead of the Fifty-fourth Massachusetts Infantry, I had been arbitrarily transferred to Washington and the War Department's Bureau of Military Justice and Corps of Judge Advocates.

I knew damn well this was the result of my father's less than subtle influence, and I also knew that there was not a damn thing I could do about it.

So, once again, I became a lawyer—this time for the U.S. Army—and a damn poor lawyer, who, for the duration of hostilities, never heard the sound of gunfire—and never won a case. Well, *never* may be a slight exaggeration. But for the most part if I was assigned as counsel for the defense, the prosecution won. If I represented the prosecution, the defense was acquitted. Half the time even I couldn't decide whether my clients were guilty or innocent, so how could I expect the court to decide?

But I am sure that due to my courtroom skills, or rather, lack thereof, the scales of justice often were tipped awry.

In spite of my litigious record, or maybe because of it, the army saw fit to promote me from the rank of lieutenant to captain. Later, someone told me that the army had an officer quota to meet.

Toward the very end of hostilities I was dealt a blow, a blow that stunned me as I had never been stunned before—and affected me more than I could have ever imagined.

I received word that Douglas Wendell Guthrie had died of a massive heart attack while delivering a summation to a jury. And, of course, even in death, my father won the case.

After the funeral—and being mustered out of the army—at the reading of his will, I learned that he had not written me out of the will, but left everything to me, including a trust fund involving more than I could spend in several lifetimes.

The law firm of Guthrie, Talbot and Flexner would go on being the firm of Guthrie, Talbot and Flexner, but without Douglas Wendell Guthrie—or Christopher Guthrie.

Along with the former slaves, I was free.

But free to do what?

To be idle?

Yes.

But bone idle?

No.

I pursued my literary aspirations.

And to my, and others, surprise, quite successfully. I published a slim volume of romantic poetry, several short stories, and even a humorous novel entitled *The Conquering Coward.*

A friend of mine, Charles Furseth, who was a dramatic critic for Horace Greeley's newspaper, the *New York Tribune,* fell ill (drunk) one evening and asked me to write a review of the play called *Forever and a Night.* I obliged—and to my surprise it was received approvingly by Mr. Greeley himself, and to my further surprise, Mr. Furseth told Mr. Greeley that I had written it—and to my ultimate surprise, Mr. Greeley offered me a part-time position reviewing other theatrical offerings.

I accepted and made quite a name for myself in my critical endeavors—for a time. In fact, my reviews often were discussed for a longer period of time than the reviewed plays ran.

But there came a time several months later when Mr. Greeley and I, after one particular review, for reasons of my own, parted company, and I found myself a part of the swelling human tide—actually a mere ripple in that tide—moving West.

For nearly two centuries America's rivers had carried life blood to the continent's heartland.

The great mass of earth between the Atlantic and Pacific oceans had been conquered by pilgrims, pioneers, settlers, and speculators, by way of water first and then by land.

Villages, towns, and cities sprang up primarily along the navigable rivers, and later, the Erie

Canal linked the eastern seaboard to the entire Midwest.

The nearby land was developed—homesteads farmed and formed into communities in a crooked land chain that reached out toward America's Manifest Destiny. That crooked land chain was then linked by stagecoach, wagon train, and finally by railroad.

Even as I traveled West, two great railroad companies, the Central Pacific and the Union Pacific, were forging ahead, one from the East, the other from the West, to meet somewhere in between and unite the country by rails of steel and engines of steam.

But until that happened, I had to be one of those wayfarers who traversed the continent via the Erie Canal, then the Mississippi to Baton Rouge.

From Baton Rouge it had been my intention to board a stagecoach to Houston, transfer to a series of other stagecoaches and span the continent until the continent ended at the "Athens of the United States"—a city christened San Francisco.

But intention is one thing, fate is another. And the fate of Christopher Guthrie, and several others, took a strange twist—a twist that entailed a tortuous deviation and led to someone called the Range Wolf.

Up to that time I had begun a journal—long

since lost—that was to chronicle the glories and romance of the westward movement—something I knew nothing about. What a fool I was, but probably no more a fool than countless others who had the same naive notions.

An uncertain number of those hardy fools are buried along the way. Those who survived helped in forging the future of a great nation. In truth, I fall into neither category; nevertheless, it was my lot to become at least a small part of a quantum conflict that could happen only in the American West.

Until I reached Baton Rouge, I carried with me, among other things, an essential wardrobe, five hundred dollars in currency, my mother's diamond ring on a thin gold chain around my neck—a ring my father left me in his will—and a deck of playing cards, at which I had become quite adept between losing litigations in the service of the Union.

The scars from the Battle of Baton Rouge, won by Union Commander Thomas W. Cahill and lost by Confederate Major General John C. Breckenridge in August of 1862, were a long way from healing. That might take years—lifetimes—forever.

I stayed at the Grand Palace Hotel, which was neither grand nor palatial, but in Baton Rouge it was considered the city's first-class resort. In

New York it probably would have been located somewhere in the Bowery.

However, the accommodations, including the food and beverages, were tolerable, and there was an area designated as the card room where citizens and travelers might while away the time in a friendly game of poker.

Having made an entry in my journal, taken a tub bath, donned a starched shirt, sliced my way through a satisfactory steak, seasoned with a local McIlhenny pepper sauce called Tabasco, and downed a double bourbon, I joined a clean-cut quintet of card players.

For an hour or so the game was pleasant enough—neither winning nor losing enough to matter—until one hand came down to a portly gentleman named Gaylord Brisbane and me.

I was looking at three deuces, a king, and a six.

I bet a hundred dollars.

Brisbane saw the hundred dollars and raised two hundred.

I saw the raise, discarded the six, and took one card.

I didn't know it, but Brisbane held three aces, a six, and a seven. He discarded the two numbers and drew two cards.

I looked at my draw cards and saw what I wanted to see. But so did Brisbane when he looked at his hand.

I bet my remaining three hundred.

There was a pause. A long pause.

"See it," said Brisbane. "And raise another three hundred."

I removed the gold chain and diamond ring from under my shirt and placed it on the table in front of me.

"Table stakes," said Brisbane.

"The ring is on the table," I said.

"I'm not a pawn shop," Brisbane said with a smile.

"I'll redeem that ring for three hundred, or three thousand, dollars at any time," I countered.

"How do I know you're good for it?" he said, and smirked.

"Here's how." I pulled a bankbook from my vest pocket, opened it to the balance page, and placed it on the table.

The balance showed 40,450 dollars and 68 cents.

"I'll have the money telegraphed in the morning. Is that good enough?"

"Good enough," he smirked again, and turned up his hand. Three aces—and two queens that he had drawn. Full house, aces up.

I spread out the four deuces and collected the pot and my diamond ring.

I returned the original $500 to my breast wallet, placed it back in my inside coat pocket, folded the currency from the winning wager, placed the wad in my left trouser pocket, then rose.

Another thing I didn't know at the time was that there were several people in the vicinity who were interested in my activity.

I repaired to the bar area, stood at the counter and ordered another double bourbon. As the bartender complied, a rather attractive young lady with rather too much applied makeup approached.

"I saw the game," she nodded. "Congratulations."

"Thank you."

"You're welcome."

"Would you care to buy me a drink?"

I didn't care to create a scene by refusing, so I motioned to the bartender.

"I'll have what the gentleman is having," she smiled, then added, "What is the gentleman's name?"

"Guthrie," I said. "Christopher Guthrie."

"Name fit for a duke." She sipped her bourbon. "I'm Francine DuBois; I take it you're new in town. Would you like me to . . . show you around?"

I hadn't had much experience with saloon girls and didn't know whether she worked for the hotel or for herself. But I had heard stories about big winners in card games. The upstairs rooms, the ladies in waiting, the drinks called Mickey Finns, and waking up with a turbulent head and empty pockets. Francine DuBois, if that was her name, was attractive, but not that attractive.

"I said, would you like me . . ."

"Look, Miss DuBois, please don't take offense, but . . ."

"Oh, oh, I think I know what's coming . . . and what's not."

"I'm sorry . . ."

"So am I. The night is young and I have to move on, but I took a fancy to you, I really did, so listen to me. Thanks for the drink, and I'm sorry we met like this. You take care of that poke you won . . . and so long, pilgrim."

As she moved away I almost had second thoughts . . . almost.

Instead, I finished my bourbon, lit a cigar, and walked outside to cool off and breathe a little fresh air while I smoked.

Not far from the entrance I heard voices. First a female voice.

"It must be here . . . I felt the chain break and . . ."

Then a man's voice, a distinguished voice.

"For heaven's sake, Flaxen, I'll buy you another one. I don't propose to hunker here all night."

"Oh, hello," she said as she looked up at me.

Even in the dark I could discern a lady of quality—her mien, her dress, her voice, and especially her face, a face of natural beauty and aristocracy.

"Good evening," I replied.

"We have lost Louie," she shrugged. "He's an

elephant, not a real elephant of course. An ivory charm, with a diamond for an eye."

She held up a broken chain.

"You see," she continued, "the chain broke and Louie's lost. He's always been such good luck."

I dropped my cigar, stooped, and squinted.

"Shouldn't be that difficult to find an elephant," I remarked.

"Find him, my friend"—the man with the distinguished voice ran his hand along the boardwalk—"and name your reward."

"One million dollars!" I said as, smiling, I held up Louie.

"The banking business is good"—he smiled back and rose—"but not that good."

He was tall and somewhat frail, gray haired, and obviously a gentleman of quality, but I was studying the young lady.

"Then I'll settle for an introduction," I said. "I'm Christopher Guthrie."

The man held out his hand.

"Reginald Brewster. My daughter, Flaxen."

We shook hands, then I extended the charm to Flaxen. In the exchange our fingers touched for a moment.

"And this," I smiled, "of course, is Louie."

"Yes," she nodded and laughed.

"Well," I responded, "now that we've all been properly introduced . . ."

Suddenly, two burly specimens appeared.

"Not quite all," one of the men barked. "Sergeant Baker and Officer O'Bannion, Baton Rouge Police." Sergeant Baker produced a badge.

"My congratulations," I said. "And what can we do for you?"

"Nothing," Sergeant Baker bellowed, "but we're going do to something for you."

"What, may I ask?" I inquired.

Both men moved quickly and efficiently. Officer O'Bannion grabbed Reginald Brewster and pinned back both arms. Sergeant Baker reached into Mr. Brewster's coat pocket.

"Get your wallet back," he said.

And he did indeed bring forth my wallet and handed it to me.

"Mr. Brewster?!" I blurted and glanced at his daughter.

"*Booster* is more like it," the sergeant said, "and they're about the best team in the business. We've had our eye on 'em for some time, and if you'll testify, this time they'll both go to jail."

"Please . . . please, Mr. Guthrie," Flaxen Brewster pleaded, "you won't testify against us. It'll mean prison. My father and I will . . ."

"Your father and you will get exactly what you deserve." I restored my wallet to where it belonged.

"We'll book 'em and let you know when the

trial will be set to take place," Sergeant Baker informed.

"How long might that be?"

"Maybe next week, maybe next month, but they'll both be in the cooler until then. Judge Crockett's got a lot on his docket."

Crockett's docket to the contrary, I had other plans, which I didn't intend to change.

"Sergeant Baker, may I speak to you privately?"

"Sure," Baker said. "Step over here."

"Sergeant," I whispered, "I'm leaving town tomorrow."

"Not if you want to see these two grifters go to jail."

"It is more urgent that I get to Houston. I've made arrangements for connections from there and I can't change those arrangements. I'm sorry."

"Damn! Too damn bad," he said just above a whisper. "You sure?"

"I'm sure."

"Well, then I'll have to do the next best thing."

Sergeant Baker led us back to the trio.

"You two grifters are damn lucky," he said. "The gentleman has decided not to testify against you . . ."

"Thank you, thank you, Mr. Guthrie," Flaxen Brewster sighed with genuine relief.

"But that doesn't end it," he went on. "Unless

you're out of my jurisdiction before the sun sets tomorrow, I'll make up some reason to slam you in the cooler anyhow. Now get out of here before he changes his mind. Let go of him, O'Bannion."

O'Bannion did, but roughly, so roughly that Mr. Brewster nearly lost his balance.

"We're grateful to you, Mr. Guthrie," Flaxen whispered. "Eternally grateful."

Father and daughter made their way to the entrance of the Grand Palace with amazing dignity, under the circumstances.

Sergeant Baker took something out of his pocket and handed it to me.

"Here's my card. If you change your mind, stop by the station. I'll be there."

"I'm much obliged, officers. Thank you again and good night."

As the two minions of the law walked away, I could hear the sergeant grumble, "Damn grifters."

Inside the Grand Palace, as I moved past the bar area, I saw Francine DuBois engaged in amiable conversation with a young gentleman who had an anticipatory look on his flushed face.

At least, I thought to myself, with Francine DuBois, unlike with Flaxen Brewster, you could judge the book by its binding.

* * *

Upstairs, I entered my room and closed the door. The room was dark, dimly lit by gaslight. As I moved toward the fixture to adjust the light and make an entry into my journal, the room abruptly got darker and I descended into that darkness from a blow across my forehead.

Stunned into semi-conscious, I could barely make out the figures of two men. The blow giver stood by while his accomplice flung open my coat and removed my wallet.

I suppose if I had mustered some sort of valiant effort I might have managed to put up some sort of resistance, maybe even overpower one of the intruders, but under those circumstances, I neither could, nor wanted, to muster anything resembling any effort, valiant, or otherwise.

One encounter with whatever battered my skull would suffice. I feigned complete unconsciousness and hoped for the best, whatever that might be.

It turned out to be a wise decision.

Without further ado both figures quickly left the room and left me still stunned on the floor.

How long I remained there I didn't know— or care.

When I finally managed to get to my feet, weave and wobble to the bed, I realized that the bandits were not entirely successful.

The winnings from the poker game were still in

the left pocket of my trousers and the diamond ring and necklace around my throat.

But the bastards had made off with the $500 and my initialed Morocco wallet.

It's strange, the thoughts that buzz through a body's brain when that body has been disoriented by an unexpected concussion. Thoughts such as: what in the hell am I doing far from the trappings of civilized society in a benighted backwater called Baton Rouge, the victim of a series of scams and slams, perpetrated by female beauties and male beasties? And which and how many of those perpetrators were responsible for my current condition?

The list of possible conspirators included: an amiable, portly loser at poker, one Gaylord Brisbane—a rather attractive, over made-up denizen of the saloon, who called herself Francine DuBois, and who might well have had a couple of accomplices in her nocturnal operations—a lady of quality and her distinguished forbearer, Flaxen and Reginald Brewster, respectively, who were not what they seemed—and much to my dismay, even a brace of oversized minions of the law, Sergeant Baker and Officer O'Bannion, one, or both of whom, well might employ the sort of sap with which to coerce criminals, or pick up a little side money on their rounds—and then there might be some anonymous observers, whom I did not observe, but who preyed on simpletons such as I, who were lucky at cards.

After such random thoughts, after how long I lay there I do not know, I decided that the riddle was too complicated and not worthy of pursuit in the time I had left before the stagecoach departed for Houston in the morning.

I would chalk up my losses to experience and the warning of the West, and get the hell out of Baton Rouge while the getting was good.

The next morning I was in no mood to make an entry in my journal. That would have to wait. After a hearty breakfast, I paid my hotel bill and made arrangements to have my baggage delivered to the stagecoach depot in time to board and continue my westward trek.

To my great surprise, at the depot, standing beside the stagecoach, were two familiar individuals, Sergeant Baker and Officer O'Bannion.

As I approached I saw another fellow passenger step into the carriage, but neither the lawmen nor I paid any attention to the traveler.

"Good morning, gentlemen," I greeted. "It was very nice of you to come see me off."

"Good morning," Sergeant Baker said. "That's not why we're here, but"—he pointed to the bruise on my forehead—"what happened to you?"

"Oh, I ran into something." I smiled. "Nothing serious."

"You ought to be more careful," Officer O'Bannion suggested.

"Good advice." I nodded, and as I did, I noticed two people standing across the street.

I hadn't noticed if they had arrived together or separately, but for the moment they stood like a pair of bookends—and those bookends were looking across the street at me.

The bookends were Francine DuBois and the portly gentleman loser, Gaylord Brisbane.

"Good luck, Mr. Guthrie," said Sergeant Baker and offered me his hand.

We shook hands, then I repeated the gesture with Officer O'Bannion. Both had hands befitting Paul Bunyan.

At that point Miss DuBois and Mr. Brisbane parted company and moved away in separate directions, perhaps having ascertained that I was leaving town without further consort with the police.

As I started for the stagecoach it occurred to me that the watchdog duo had told me why they weren't there, but not why they were.

So I thought I'd inquire of Sergeant Baker.

"If not to see me off, do you mind telling me why you're at the stage depot?"

Sergeant Baker pointed his thumb toward two other passengers who were already inside.

Flaxen and Reginald Brewster were seated on the rear seat of the stagecoach, looking straight ahead.

"You're gonna have a couple of familiar companions," Sergeant Baker added.

"So I see," I said.

"Ought to make for an interesting trip," he remarked.

Truer words were never spoken East or West of the Hundredth Meridian.

CHAPTER II

And so I boarded and bade a silent farewell to the community of Baton Rouge.

But before we departed the two teamsters who were to deliver us to Houston poked their respective heads through the windows of the coach and introduced themselves.

"I'm Slim," said the driver.

The description might have been accurate years ago, but his present girth belied that delineation.

"Baldy," chimed the fellow with the rifle.

Whether that was the case I could not determine at the time, since his pate was covered by a sun bleached crown.

But it didn't much matter since both seemed competent and confident.

"We've got a ways to go"—Slim spat out a load of tobacco juice—"and the road'll get bumpy at times, but we've been there before and we'll do 'er again, so sit there and get acquainted for the next few days.

"Now me and Baldy'll only take you as far as Houston. From there, if you're aimin' to go on, you'll connect to points west as far as San Francisco. Now Butterfield's been in business since '58 and has the best record of any line anywhere. We'll be stoppin' at the way stations for food and sleep and relief of the innards, but if you're in need of relief along the road just bang on the side of the coach and we'll accommodate."

I couldn't help but notice Flaxen blanch a bit as Slim spoke and then let fly another stream of tobacco juice.

As we rolled past the outer limits of Baton Rouge, the fourth passenger tipped his hat and smiled toward Flaxen and her father, who was sipping from a silver flask and trying to stifle a cough.

"Amos Yirbee, ma'am. Pleased to make your acquaintance." He spoke with a noticeable Southern accent.

Clean-cut, in his early thirties, well wardrobed in a dark suit, coal-black flat-brimmed hat, white shirt, and black string tie.

There was an awkward pause.

"Flaxen Brewster . . . my father, Mr. Brewster."

Amos Yirbee turned to me and smiled.

"Christopher Guthrie. Glad to meet you, Mr. Yirbee."

That was the extent of the "get acquainted" conversation for quite a while.

Mr. Yirbee removed a Bible from his inside coat pocket and commenced to read to himself.

Mr. Brewster, between coughing spells, went to work on his silver flask, which seemed to have an inexhaustible supply of liquid, while Flaxen and I stole silent glances at each other as the stagecoach proceeded on its bumpy way west.

During those silent glances I couldn't help but recall a line from the Bard. Would that there'd been some "art to find the mind's construction in the face"!

Her face was perfectly constructed, beauty, delicacy, elegance, innocence—lustrous yellow hair, luminous blue-green eyes, and with delicate hands fitted with white traveling gloves—not the face and form of a grifter.

The overnight stops at the way stations were mostly devoid of conversation except for Slim and Baldy, who I finally discovered was indeed devoid of hirsute atop his shiny dome.

But on the third night after supper, as I lit a cigar and Mr. Yirbee opened his Bible, I did make comment.

"Sir," I said, "you seem to be quite interested in that volume."

"That's why they call it the Good Book."

"Did you grow up with it?"

"Only since the war."

I couldn't help notice that Flaxen Brewster was listening.

"That's when you found religion?" I asked.

"Salvation. After the carnage at Yellow Tavern I swore I'd never carry a gun again. Instead I'd carry this." He touched the open Bible.

"North or South?"

"South. You?"

"North, but . . . not on any battlefield. Washington. Military justice."

"They also serve," Mr. Yirbee said and smiled.

"What part are you reading?" I pointed to the Good Book.

"'My lips shall not speak wickedness, nor my tongue utter deceit.'"

"That's Job, isn't it?"

"It is."

"He had his troubles."

"But it turned out all right. The Lord gave Job twice as much as he had before. 'Job died, being old and full of days.'"

"You a preacher, Mr. Yirbee?"

"I will be in Prescott. There's a small congregation waiting for me."

"Congratulations."

"Thank you." Mr. Yirbee rose, still holding his Bible, and retired to his quarters.

Flaxen Brewster sat for a moment or so finishing her coffee, until she heard her father coughing in another room, then she also rose.

"Good night," I said, half lifting myself from the chair.

"Good night . . . and Mr. Guthrie . . ."

"Yes?"

"On this trip . . . please, please don't interpret my silence . . . or that of my father, as a sign of our ingratitude for what you did for us in Baton Rouge. He's a sick man now . . . and I . . . I . . ."

"Miss Brewster, I expect no explanation. Many things happened in Baton Rouge that I'd prefer to forget. I suggest we both do just that."

"Very well, Mr. Guthrie."

When she left the room I sat there with my cigar until there was little of it left.

It occurred to me that none of the passengers on the stagecoach carried a gun.

Only a Bible.

CHAPTER III

"If I rise on the wings of the dawn, if I settle on the far side of the sea, even there your hand will guide me, your right hand will hold me fast, O LORD."

At the sound of the voice I turned in my bunk and saw Amos Yirbee, fully clothed and on his knees at the side of his bunk across from mine.

"Oh, I'm sorry, Mr. Guthrie," he looked up, then rose. "I didn't mean to wake you."

"I've been awakened worse ways. Psalms?"

Yirbee nodded.

"Have you ever been held in the right hand of the Lord, Mr. Yirbee?"

"I have, sir, at Yellow Tavern."

"What about the hundreds who bled and died there? Where was His hand for them?"

"'Mysterious ways.' They're in God's hands now."

"I see. Well, I'd like to wait a little longer if it's all the same to you . . . and Him. Let's see what's for breakfast."

CHAPTER IV

"This is the chanciest part of the trip," Slim said as he spat out part of his morning mouthful of tobacco—just as we were all getting ready to board.

"In what way?" I inquired like a damn fool.

"All ways. Terrain. Dusters. Bandits. Redskins. Comancheros. Border raiders. You name it and it's out there."

"But don't fret," Baldy cackled. "Not with the three of us up top."

"Three?" I inquired. "Who else beside Slim and you?"

"Henry." Baldy held up his rifle. ".44 caliber rimfire metallic cartridges. Load it on Sunday and shoot all week. Our best friend and our enemy's worst enemy. 'Course a lot depends on who's shootin'."

"Baldy can shoot a flea off'n your ear twenty yards away," Slim said.

"It's not fleas I'm concerned about," I noted. "Not after that little speech you just made."

"Oh, that . . . well, that's just to add a little color to the trip since we're about to cross into Satan's Orchard."

"What the hell is Satan's Orchard?" was my next question.

"Texas." Slim smiled. "Well, let's get to gettin'."

Texas. Dull, flat, monotonous in places where the Lord had stomped the dust off his boots—spectacular, craggy, and colorful in other parts—jagged cliffs and red stone monuments—a battlefield since time remembered—claimed and conquered by Indian tribes who fought each other with arrows and tomahawks. Kiowa, Comanche, and Apache. Then came the conquerors with gunpowder—Spaniards and Mexicans—and then the lusty procession of Americans, determined and unyielding.

I was one of those Americans, but hardly determined or unyielding. I was only determined to pass through Texas, and the primary passage was across the Red River.

Our Concord stagecoach could not forge across—too deep and too treacherous. But there was a way.

That way was a flat ferry, sturdy and large enough to carry the six horses, unhitched, and the coach itself, with the passengers standing alongside, looking down at the swirling, wine-colored water, while we held our breath, and the teamsters betrayed their amusement with wry smiles at our apprehension.

To my surprise, the only mitigation was that throughout the crossing, whether she realized it or not, Flaxen took hold of my hand and didn't let go until we were on dry land at a place called Texas.

As the Concord continued west, the glances between us became more frequent and lasted longer.

Somehow, at the way station, Mr. Brewster must have renewed the supply of liquid in his silver flask. The intervals between sips became shorter and the coughing spells longer. At one point Flaxen made a half-hearted attempt to confiscate the flask, but Mr. Brewster brushed her hand away.

Amos Yirbee continued his concentration on the Bible as the team of six horses kicked up ever more Texas dust into the carriage.

During, and between, glances, I knew not what Flaxen was thinking, but I often had to remind myself that she was a common criminal—well, maybe not common, but, nevertheless a criminal.

I thought back to Sergeant Baker's words, ". . . if you testify, this time they'll both go to jail."

I couldn't imagine Mr. Brewster lasting very long in jail. He must have mustered just about all his energy and acting ability to command such a distinguished performance that evening, to say nothing of his dactyl dexterity in removing my wallet.

And to think of Flaxen Brewster in prison surroundings and confinement was next to impossible.

I found myself wondering how far west they intended to travel—and also having to admit that my thoughts were not entirely pure.

I even considered making polite and casual conversation regarding their destination, but before further consideration, it happened.

And it happened so fast and with such impact and effect that the occurrence is a blurred whirlwind in my mind; but to the best of my recollection and summarization—there were shots, first from a distance, then from atop the carriage—riders—three or four from each side of the coach—Indians—only one in the lead with a rifle—the others with arrows—one of the arrows struck the throat of Amos Yirbee, who dropped his Bible and fell to the floor—there were wild yells and cries from the attackers—the coach picked up speed—two of the attackers fell from Baldy's Henry—another arrow pierced the inside of the coach without hitting a living target—Flaxen screamed, then again—more gunshots—

some from above, others from the Indian with the rifle—Baldy fell from the wagon and bounced like a dead cat—the rifled Indian shot the lead horse smashing it to the ground, and the rest of the team stumbled and twisted crashing into each other, ripping traces and overturning the carriage with us still in it, bouncing against the sides and doors.

What happened next is even more of a blur—dazed, nearly senseless—but somehow barely aware—the horses and stagecoach on its side came to a stop in a swirl of dirt while the raiders went about their business—killing Slim—cutting the horses loose—picking up Baldy's rifle—and then before they had a chance to get to the passengers, dead or alive, inside the broken Concord—more shots from a distance—and other riders—maybe a half dozen, saddled and well armed—charging toward the coach as the Indians scattered—but not before I saw the leader of the rescuers fall from his horse—and that's the last I remembered as I fell into a black pit, which at the time, I thought could be death.

But it wasn't.

CHAPTER V

How much later I did not know.

From out of the stillness, depth, and darkness of what I had thought was death, slowly through a vinculum—sounds, erratic, divergent, unintelligible, but foreboding—animal noises, hooves moving—and human voices murmuring—then one voice in particular—not murmuring—cursing.

At me?

I wasn't sure.

And didn't care.

"Stupid son of a bitch . . . bastard . . . charging in like some crusading cavalier . . . risking your life and the lives of my men and for what . . . damn idiot . . . Donavan, you damn fool."

I finally managed to open my eyes, but the world was out of focus.

I closed my eyes, then tried again. Better. I was on the ground and near me lay Flaxen unconscious, her dress tattered, her breast smeared with blood.

More than a dozen of the fiercest specimens of mankind in an uneven semi-circle, and at the front stood the man who cursed at the fallen rescuer who had led the charge.

Bending over him was another man, trembling.

One word came to my mind as I gazed at the man who cursed.

Power.

At least six feet tall, but from my position, he was a giant.

Dressed in western garb, all black—but it might as well have been a suit of armor—and smoking a cigar black as his boots.

A face carved out of granite, eyes without a soul, a mouth without mercy. A serrated scar on his forehead just below the brim of his black hat. Boulder shoulders, a broad chest tapering to a narrow waist with a holstered gun strapped on his right side. The belt that sustained the gun was black and the brass buckle that sustained the belt was oval with the raised letters CSA—a buckle worn by officers of the Confederate States of America.

The man, even while standing still, exuded energy.

"Well . . . *doctor*?"

"Ba . . . bad . . . very bad . . . I don't think . . ."

"You don't think! Never mind thinking, you damn drunk. Do something!"

"Too . . . too far gone, Mr. Riker, I . . ."

Mr. Riker kicked the fallen man viciously with his pointed boot.

"Damn him and you, too, *Doctor* Picard."

There came a painful gasp from the wounded man.

I had managed to move closer to Flaxen, touch her, and determine that she was alive—then struggle to my feet.

"Sir. Mr. Riker . . . she, she's badly hurt. Can't the doctor . . ."

"No!" Riker bellowed. "The doctor stays with Donavan."

"But surely . . ."

"Surely my trail boss is more important than some . . . piece of fluff."

"Mr. Riker . . ."

He reached out and roughly, but effortlessly, slammed me against the wheel of a wagon.

There was a last coarse gasp from Donavan. His chest heaved, his eyes rolled upward, and his head fell to one side with a flush of finality.

"He's dead," the doctor said without looking at Riker.

As Donavan had died, the sun settled beneath a distant saw-tooth peak, and darkness spread across the plain.

I regained my balance and composure and staggered toward Riker.

"Sir, there's nothing more the doctor can do for that man, may I . . ."

"What are you, a preacher?"

"I am a gentleman," I replied. "And that is a lady and I demand . . ."

"Wolf Riker makes the demands on this drive. You'll learn that soon enough." He turned toward the dirtiest of the drovers. "Won't he, Cookie?"

"That he will. That he will," Cookie cackled. "Rest of 'em's all dead. One with an arrow in his Adam's apple and the old geezer with a broken neck. All dead but him and her."

He pointed to Flaxen.

"All right, Doc," Wolf Riker motioned toward Flaxen. "Get her into a wagon where there's some light and see what you can do."

Riker inhaled from his sloe-black cigar and walked away followed by an older man who limped.

I had seen the look of naked lust in the eyes of Cookie and the rest of Riker's men gazing upon the exposed form of Flaxen as she lay on the ground.

In case she survived, I wanted to afford her some semblance of dignity and if possible, protection from that look and what might come after.

I managed to get to her before the others and in the dark, break off the chain from my neck, remove Flaxen's glove, and place the diamond ring on the third finger of her left hand.

CHAPTER VI

The inside of the wagon was lit by two lamps illuminating the faces of Wolf Riker, Dr. Picard, me, and Cookie, whose filthy, scrawny hands still quivered from the feel of having helped to carry Flaxen, now lying on a makeshift operating table, still unconscious, and only partially covered by her torn and disarrayed dress.

I placed a sheet over her body and breasts.

"There's not much I can do," the doctor said.

"You could sober up," Riker remarked.

"I'm . . . I'm afraid," the doctor stammered, "she's not going to survive."

"You say that about all your patients," Wolf Riker nearly smiled.

"She's lost a great deal of blood . . . there's a splinter lodged near the pulmonary artery . . . one slip and she'll die."

"She'll die anyway," Riker shrugged. "She's a lady, delicate . . . not one of the hearty breed."

"Doctor," I pleaded. "If there's any chance at all . . ."

Dr. Picard held up his right hand. It was trembling.

"Just pretend," Riker said, "that she's one of those corpses you practiced on at medical school." He left the wagon.

"Cookie," Pickard ordered. "You can go now."

Cookie left after one last look at Flaxen.

"Doctor," I breathed. "Please."

"I'll try," Dr. Picard whispered.

CHAPTER VII

The dawn spread slowly across five fresh graves.

I had spent the night in the wagon which had served as a makeshift operating room, with Dr. Picard and of course Flaxen Brewster.

The doctor's hand had steadied as he removed several instruments from a scuffed medical bag. A look of determination crept across his face. And it seemed as if a different set of reflexes took over his brain and body after Wolf Riker left the wagon.

If Dr. Picard had not become a sober man, then I had never seen one.

I watched, fascinated, as he went about the intricate procedure: removed the splinter—actually splinters—stanched the bleeding, and sewed the wound.

We kept vigil through the night, sometimes nodding off, while Flaxen Brewster teetered between life and afterlife, until the scale seemed to balance in her favor. When I stepped out of the wagon into the dawning camp I beheld the strangest sight I had ever seen—up to that time.

Five freshly dug graves, several men with picks and shovels, the belongings of the dead in a pile nearby, and most of the drovers from the drive standing by, some drinking coffee from tin cups, others smoking morning cigarettes, pipes, and cigars.

And as far as the eye could see—cattle—cattle—cattle—grazing and moaning.

The names of most of the men were unfamiliar to me then, but names and men I would get to know—and mostly to distrust and decry—besides Cookie, there was Leach, Smoke, Chandler, Simpson, French Frank, Dogbreath, Reese, Latimer, Drago, a pair of Mexicans known only as Morales One and Morales Two, others, including one I got to know better than most of the others—not a drover, but a driver called Pepper, who limped and drove Wolf Riker's wagon—and of course Wolf Riker, smoking a cigar, with a look of impatience in those deep-set eyes.

He spoke to me without removing the cigar from his mouth.

"We don't know their names except for Donavan, that damn fool, but we'll give them a Christian burial anyhow."

"That's very decent of you, Mr. Riker."

"It wasn't my idea, but I went along with it, so long as we can still get an early start."

"Whose idea was it?"

"Mr. Reese's and a couple of the others. What about the lady? Do we bury her, too?"

"She's still alive."

"In spite of Dr. Picard?"

"Because of him."

"Miraculous." He looked around at the drovers. "Any of you Christians have a Bible or prayer book?"

A man stepped forward.

"You, Reese?"

"There was a Bible among the belongings of one of the passengers, Mr. Riker."

"Yes, well, we won't waste the time. I'll just say the part of the service that's relevant."

As the sun rose higher, Wolf Riker spoke the words while still smoking his cigar and without removing his hat.

"We come into the world with nothing and we leave with nothing. The Lord giveth and the Lord taketh away. Amen."

When he finished, I took a step closer.

"Mr. Riker."

"What is it?"

"I've got to get back to civilization."

"Are you so sure"—Riker arched an eyebrow—"you're away from it?"

"I mean someplace where I can make connections with a stagecoach. I can pay for an escort. I'll pay you a hundred dollars—two hundred."

"Two hundred, huh. Well, I can't spare anybody to escort you anywhere. You stay with the drive. What do you do for a living?"

"I . . . I have an income."

"Who earned it?"

"From an estate, mostly. My father . . ."

"I thought so. You stand on dead man's legs. Let me see your hands."

Roughly, Wolf Riker grabbed my hands in his hawser grip.

"And dead man's hands have kept yours soft. Maybe good for cook wagon work, cleaning and peeling, eh, Cookie?"

Cookie nodded and smiled as Riker dropped my hands, turned toward, and spoke to the one called Pepper.

"And speaking of wagons, he can give you a hand with yours if you like."

"I don't like—and I don't need a hand or a foot or anything else from him or you, or anybody else, Mr. Riker."

To my surprise Wolf Riker did not take umbrage to the man's surly remark. Instead he smiled and replied.

"Duly noted, Mr. Pepper."

Then Riker addressed the rest of the drovers without a trace of smile.

"All right, before we start, listen to this. Now

that Donavan's gone to his reward, we're one man short, so there are going to be some promotions. Chandler, do you know anything about trail bossing?"

"No, sir," the man with a walrus mustache and face to match, except for the tusks, replied.

"Well, never mind, you're the trail boss anyhow, except that I'll do the bossing. And you, Leach, you're no longer Cookie's helper. You're promoted, too. You'll tail the drive."

"I don't want no part of tailin', Mr. Riker."

"Oh, our young prison graduate is particular, huh? Why not, Leach?"

"I didn't sign up for tailin', Mr. Riker . . . eatin' all that dust all day and . . ." Leach's lips seemed twisted into a permanent snarl.

"You'll eat anything I say."

"I don't want no tailin' in mine. I signed . . ."

Riker's fist slammed into Leach's midsection, buckling him onto the ground.

"Well, Leach, are you tailing the herd?"

Leach gained enough breath to rise, his face ashen, barely able to whisper.

"Yes . . . Mr. Riker."

Riker turned to me.

"That makes you . . . what's your name?

"Guthrie. Christopher Guthrie."

"All right Guth, that makes you Cookie's helper. Thirty a month and bonus when we finish the drive. This is going to be good for you. To earn an honest wage."

"But . . ."

"No buts! You see that herd out there?"

"Yes, of course I see it."

"Well, that's not a herd. It's an empire. All branded with a Double R. My empire, and I'm going to turn it into cash in Kansas. Nothing in this world or the next can stop me. Besides, who is that quail in the wagon?"

"The lady's name is Flaxen Brewster. She's my . . . fiancée."

"Well, just in case she does survive, you wouldn't want to leave her behind with all these . . . drovers, would you, Guth?"

"No, Mr. Riker, I wouldn't."

"Good then. Cookie, take Guth along. Show him his duties."

Cookie nodded and smiled as Riker continued.

"The rest of you saddle up and get these beeves moving."

The men scrambled to carry out Riker's orders.

Cookie half bowed and pointed to the kitchen wagon, then slammed the heavy frying pan he carried in his hand hard across my back.

So began my introduction to a cattle drive . . . and to Wolf Riker.

The Range Wolf.

No man was better named.

CHAPTER VIII

There was no doubt as to who ruled the strange, savage, new world that I now inhabited.

Wolf Riker was the ruler—and no one questioned his authority, at least in a voice that could be heard. He was the sovereign and his saddle was his throne. During the day he was mostly in the saddle on a monumental horse he had named Bucephalus.

But soon I was to find out that he also had kingly quarters. The closed wooden wagon where he often slept, but I had yet to see the inside and contents of that wagon—the wagon driven by Pepper, the man who limped and canted to the left—of indeterminate age, fifty—sixty—well worn, but still bone hard, with cord-like fingers made for the trigger of the low-slung .44 strapped to one side of his lean frame and a sheathed knife strapped to the other. A man who said things to Wolf Riker that no other man dared utter. There

seemed to be an unspoken bond between them—
even beyond brothers.

There were others among the hierarchy in the
drive—as on a sailing ship. The trail boss was first
mate and Cookie, my immediate superior, held a
lofty rank, that of vice tyrant, as far as I was concerned.

He was obsequious and servile to Wolf Riker,
but condescending and blasphemous to everyone
else—especially to me. And I was to find out that
he was something else.

In this new world that I now inhabited there
was also a new language that I was soon to learn—
words and phrases that I had never heard—"cutting
out"—"booger"—"hog leg"—"maverick"—"over-
hack"—"remuda"—"roistered"—"night hawk"—
"skookum"—"suggans"—"waddy"—an entire
dictionary of the trail.

And then there were myriad definitions for
those who held the position of my immediate
superior—"bean master"—"belly cheater"—
"dough puncher"—"grub worm"—"gut robber"—
and dozens more, appellations that have no place
in polite society, but then a trail drive is anything
but polite.

That first day on the drive is among the worst
experiences of my recollection up to that time—
but somehow, though in a daze, I managed to
survive—and to serve. Through kicks and curses
as the herd traveled north, I somehow carried out

Cookie's orders as we completed what passed for breakfast, the noon meal, and supper for the drovers.

Humiliation is too soft a word to describe the experience.

Humiliation and exhaustion, but somehow, I made it into the night, mostly avoiding Wolf Riker, who had more important things on his mind.

I was informed that often Riker ate alone, or with Dr. Picard, in his wagon, but luckily for me, that day he dined with the drovers, otherwise serving him would have been included in my duties.

When we weren't preparing or cleaning up after meals, I rode on his wagon next to Cookie, whose odor was barely bearable.

I did manage to look into the wagon with Dr. Picard and his inert patient, my "fiancée," Flaxen Brewster.

"How is she doing, doctor?" I asked.

"Hard to tell, until, and *if*, she regains consciousness."

"If? What do you mean, '*if*'?"

"If is a conjunction, my boy, meaning in simple terms, maybe she will, and maybe she won't. I can't predict either way, even though I'm sober for the time being, and . . ."

"And what?"

". . . plan to stay that way—at least until the

outcome is determined by a higher authority, and I don't mean Wolf Riker, thank God, although, if it were up to him we'd move faster, much faster, to the promised land—Kansas."

"I've never met anyone like him."

"There is no one like him—except maybe, his brother is close."

"Brother?"

"His name is Dirk," Picard nodded, "and join me in praying that we don't meet him—at least not until this drive is over."

"Why not?"

"Not because the world wouldn't be better off without the two of them—but God only knows how many of us they'd take with them. However, after the drive it would most likely be just the two of them."

"How did it start?"

"How did it start with Cain and Abel? It's a long story and I don't know all of it, nobody does. I guess Pepper knows more of it than anybody, and . . ."

"And what?"

"I'm tired. Haven't had much sleep. Maybe some other time."

"Good night, doctor, and—thanks for all you're doing for Flaxen."

"You're welcome . . . and I am doing it mostly for her . . . but also to show Wolf Riker that . . . well, never mind."

As I left that wagon and proceeded to my quarters, I witnessed from a distance something I didn't need to remind me of Wolf Riker's prowess.

Riker was on his mount, Bucephalus, when French Frank rode up next to him and spoke.

There were only a few words exchanged by the two men, words I could not hear, when quicker than a cobra's strike, Wolf Riker slapped French Frank with a backhanded blow that sent the man literally flying off his saddle and hard upon the ground.

For less than an instant, even though dazed, French Frank moved his right hand toward his holstered gun.

Riker looked down with contempt. In that microsecond it seemed that French Frank's future would be over.

But his hand froze in mid-motion—then trembled.

Wolf Riker could have killed him, and might have—if he didn't need him and all of us—for the drive.

Without any apparent signal from the rider, Bucephalus turned and slowly moved away.

As Wolf Riker approached, then went past me, I wanted to avoid looking at him, but was unable, impelled by fear and fascination.

He went by as if I didn't exist.

And I wasn't so sure that I, or any of this, did.

Maybe I had already passed through the gates of hell.

I barely managed to make my way to my quarters, if you could so identify the area beneath the cook wagon. At least it was far enough away so that I did not have to suffer the odor from Cookie, who slept inside the wagon.

That night I dove into the deepest sleep of my life, half hoping that I would never awaken.

But awaken I did, from a kick by Cookie, to discover that the money in my pocket was no longer in my pocket, which had been turned inside out.

Besides being my immediate superior, it was evident that Cookie was a thief.

CHAPTER IX

I had neither the time, nor the inclination—I guess the cowboys would call it "guts"—to confront Cookie while we were preparing breakfast and particularly while the drovers were within sight and hearing distance. The truth is, I was afraid the outcome might prove embarrassing—or worse—to me.

I didn't like the way Cookie handled the knives he worked with—or the surly look in his eyes when they met mine—even though I did my utmost to avoid eye contact while we labored, carrying out my part of the procedure:

Setting a blazing fire along a trench—placing the heavy Dutch ovens and lids where they would heat—dropping in hunks of beef tallow—cutting the steaks—building the biscuits while the fragrance of hot coffee rose from the large fire pit—and then serving the grub while the drovers sat or squatted down and devoured their morning meal.

As each man finished, he dropped his dirty plates and implements into the wrecking pan, saddled up, and repaired to his assigned section of the herd, urging the cattle along as Cookie and I washed and dried the dishes.

During all this time I had seen no sign of Wolf Riker.

Since Cookie and I were alone, I thought it time to broach the subject of my missing money.

I wasn't sure of the exact amount. I had won just over four hundred dollars, however, there were expenses—the hotel bill and other incidentals. But I knew the roll in my pocket had included two one hundred dollar bills, several twenties, fives, and singles—more than three hundred dollars.

"There's something I'd like to talk to you about, Cookie."

"All right, but make it fast and keep working."

"Very well. It's about a financial matter."

"How's that?"

"When I retired last night there was a roll of bills in my pocket, over three hundred dollars. This morning the pocket was turned inside out and the money was gone. I'd like to . . ."

Before I finished he had picked up a dirty, wet towel and, with a swift stroke, slapped me hard across the face.

And in his other hand, he held a gleaming carving knife pointed against my breastbone.

"You button up, Guth! 'Cause if I ever hear you say one word about it to anybody I'll rip you from belly to brisket. You understand!?"

I could feel the point of the blade pressing into my flesh and thought it best to pursue the matter no further—at least for the time being.

"I . . . I understand."

"Good. You finish up here while I hitch the team."

As he walked away I could hear him grumble.

"Miserable specimen of human scum. Pukin' weasel . . . callin' me a thief."

For an instant I thought about picking up one of the other knives and . . .

But the instant and the thought passed with my doing nothing.

CHAPTER X

"Mr. Guthrie." It was a strong, yet sympathetic voice, and it belonged to the one I had heard called Simpson. A big man, rugged, but with gentle eyes and a Scandinavian complexion.

He had obviously seen, and probably heard, much of what had just occurred between Cookie and me. He was tightening the cinch on his appaloosa.

"No," I replied with resignation. "I'm 'Guth,' Cookie's assistant."

"You're a man. The same as you've always been."

"Wolf Riker's right about one thing. I've never been much of a man."

"You never will be if you don't stand up to him. Him and Cookie and the rest of them. The more they can take advantage of you, the more they will."

"You expect me to beat the entire bunch of them?"

"You don't have to. Just Cookie, at first. If they see you do that you will have earned some respect. Stand up to him. Don't let him break you. That's what he's trying to do, because you're better than he is, better than all of them—and smarter. Fight 'em any way you can. You've got an advantage"—Simpson pointed to my temple—"your brain. Never give up . . . Mr. Guthrie."

"Yes." I did my best to summon up at least a patina of acknowledgment, if not bravado. "Well, no matter what happens, thank you, Mr. Simpson."

Before I could do or say anything more, he had mounted with ease for such a big man, and rode toward the herd on his Appaloosa.

The herd. I watched as it began to stir and move—as it was made to move by riders at the point and flanks and too far away for me to see, the drag men who prodded the trailers onward. Wave after wave of ignorant beasts. Teaming tons of bawling beef between hoof and horn, heading north to their doom if Riker succeeded in his obsessive mission to deliver his moveable empire to Kansas—and me along with it. If Wolf Riker succeeded they would be slaughtered, methodically sectioned and sliced, shipped to feed hungry bellies hundreds of miles away. That was their fate and destiny, if they reached their destination—Kansas.

But what of the fate and destiny of Christopher Guthrie? A so-called gentleman among bitter, war-beaten brutes, led by the bitterest brute of them all?

Kansas or Canada? What difference did it make? A thousand miles or five thousand miles? It might as well have been as far away as the moon. What chance did I have to survive—or to escape?

And if I did escape, what about Flaxen Brewster? If she survived her wounds, what was the fate of my nominal fiancée, who was actually a thief—or at least a thief's accomplice, even though he was her father?

What was my moral obligation to her?

All this flashed through my mind in a mad moment before I realized that my first, if not only, obligation was to myself.

To survive.

As Simpson said, to fight them any way I could. To use my brain. To never give up.

But it was easier for Simpson to give advice than for me to take it; however, I did appreciate his good intention and concern. Even though I didn't know the intentions or concerns, or, in some cases, even the names, of all the drovers, I had begun to separate those whose society I cared to share, from those whom I preferred to avoid. The latter category far outnumbered the former.

In my estimation, Dr. Picard had proved himself a good man, so, it seemed, had Simpson. I would have liked to know what French Frank had said to Wolf Riker that provoked our leader to slap him out of the saddle and come close to killing him. There was something about Reese that set him apart from the rest. I had noticed that he had pocketed the Bible from which Riker did not read over the graves of the buried bodies. As for Leach, I had heard Riker refer to him as "our young prison graduate," but . . . just then I saw something—someone—who stopped me short in my appraisal.

Wolf Riker, not far away, smoking his black cigar, astride his horse Bucephalus, and looking in my direction.

I wondered how long he had been there and how much he had seen and heard.

Within that instant I dismissed all of my brave words and thoughts—and started to go back to my duties as Cookie's lackey.

But this time something else stopped me—a sound—sounds—terrifying. Inhuman. Beastly. Born of pain and frenzy. I did not know it at the time but morning is one of the most dangerous periods on the drive. The cattle stirred from the night's sleep, each animal seeking its own space for the long miles ahead, irritable, stumbling and still half asleep, prodded, tottering, crashing into each other with long razor sharp horns ripping into hide and flank.

Instinctively, I turned to the direction of the sound and fury.

One of the larger beasts, bellowing, screaming, bucking, its horns ripping into whatever other beast it could strike in its madness.

One of its eyes had been ripped out of its socket by the dagger-like horn of another steer and hung loosely across the face of the crazed animal.

By now several riders including Riker had moved closer to the commotion, so had Pepper and several others on foot. I wondered why one of them did not shoot the animal out of its misery and end the damage it was inflicting, but at the same time realized that a gunshot might instantly send the herd into a stampede.

All the drovers knew well enough not to fire a shot as the crazed animal ripped at anything that moved within striking distance, but none knew what he could do about the raging animal—none but Riker.

He flung away his cigar, spurred his horse alongside the snorting beast, leaped from his saddle, landed with both hands on the horns, twisted its huge head with the great power of his bull shoulders and body until the steer crashed hard onto the ground.

"Pepper! Knife!" Wolf Riker's voice tore the air.

He lifted his right arm high above him—held the beast at bay with one hand and the force of his body—as Pepper slapped the handle of a unique knife into Riker's palm, then Wolf Riker plunged the salient, glinting blade again and again into the throat, then brain, of the trembling beast. One last spasm, and it trembled no more.

Neither I, nor, I dare say, any of the other men, had ever witnessed such a feat of raw strength and confidence, ever in our lives. Reese, French Frank, Simpson, Leach, Chandler, and the rest.

We stared in awe as Wolf Riker rose, handed Pepper his bloody knife, and took a steady step toward Cookie.

"We'll have the son of a bitch for supper," Riker said, then walked toward his wagon.

I looked down at the twisted heap, with one eye still dangling from its vacant socket, and thought to myself, not I.

I'm not having that son of a bitch for supper.

CHAPTER XI

That night, after the herd had been driven more than twelve miles north over not too unfriendly terrain, I was just about finished helping Cookie serve the meat from the animal Wolf Riker had slaughtered for supper.

Through the day, while carrying out my kitchen chores, I had been privy to bits and pieces of comments and conversation from the drovers. Comments mostly lamenting the outcome of the encounter between two beasts—one human and the other horned. The boldest remarks came from the young prison graduate, Leach, and French Frank—bold, but well out of earshot of Wolf Riker, and the trail boss, Chandler, who wasn't doing much bossing.

Riker now sat away from all the others, except for his driver and knife provider, Pepper. The two of them had finished eating. Riker smoked one of his cigars, and Pepper was working on a cinch with that knife of his.

I carried a plate of meat and beans toward one of the wagons, the path to which took me past Riker and Pepper, when I heard that unmistakable voice—and stopped.

"Guth."

"Yes, Mr. Riker."

"I see you've quite a good appetite."

"This is not for me, Mr. Riker."

"No? Who then? Your fiancée?"

"No, sir. She's not conscious yet. But I thought Dr. Picard might . . ."

"Very thoughtful, Guth. I presume he's going to provide his own whiskey."

"Dr. Picard hasn't had any whiskey since . . ."

"The operation? Well, we'll see how long his state of sobriety lasts. I'll wager not as long as his patient. I've seen it happen before."

"Yes, sir. But there's always a first time."

"Not always."

Pepper stuck the knife into the ground and tugged at the cinch with both hands.

I couldn't help but glance from the plate of meat I carried to the knife sticking out of the earth.

And, of course, Wolf Riker noticed my glance.

"Ever see one like it before, Guth? The knife, I mean."

"No, Mr. Riker. I haven't."

"It's known as a Bowie knife. Quite a story behind it. This one was given to Pepper by Jim Bowie himself. You must get Pepper to tell you about it sometime, if you'd be interested."

"Yes, I would."

"Well, on your way, Guth. We don't want to keep you from your good works."

"Thank you, Mr. Riker."

Not once during that conversation had Pepper even glanced up at me. But still, I somehow got the impression he was watching me.

After walking several yards away—another voice—this one out of the darkness.

"Mr. Guthrie."

I stopped and turned.

"Reese. Alan Reese."

"Oh, yes. The man with the Bible."

"Do you want it? I have it with me."

"No, Mr. Reese. You might as well keep it. You and the rest of them, along with everything that belonged to us."

"That's what I wanted to talk to you about. The others gambled for the belongings from the stagecoach. But I did manage to put aside a suitcase with your initials on it and one that's obviously the lady's. Both still with their contents. They're in the utility wagon. That's all."

"Mr. Reese, wait a minute. That was very kind and thoughtful of you, and I truly appreciate it. Thank you."

"You're welcome."

"You say they gambled for the rest."

"It's not the first time that happened."

"On this drive?"

"Oh, no. All the way back to Calvary."

"The Centurions . . . for His robe?"

"Good night, Mr. Guthrie."

He walked back into the darkness.

CHAPTER XII

She lay breathing softly by lamplight. A patrician profile befitting a Ruritanian princess asleep in a palace by a verdant hill.

I sat silently looking at her for how long I was not aware.

But she was no Ruritanian princess and this was no palace by a verdant hill. And I certainly was no prince. We were in a shadowy wagon that creaked from a vagrant wind, though that wagon stood un-moving in the midst of a forgotten Texas terrain.

Dr. Picard set his empty tin plate on the floor next to him, then let the knife and fork drop into it.

I turned at the sound.

"Thank you for the repast." Picard smiled. "I'd almost forgotten what it was like to eat."

"You can thank Wolf Riker for the repast. He killed your supper with Pepper's Bowie knife—and his brute strength."

"Yes, I know. I looked out at the commotion and caught sight of the contest."

"Not exactly Saint George and the dragon."

"Not exactly. But it had to be done, and he was the only one who could do it."

"You sound as if you admire him."

"There's little about Wolf Riker that I admire, but his strength is undeniable and . . ."

"And what?"

"There's much about Wolf Riker that's not evident—at least at first. Like an iceberg, there's much more beneath the surface."

"Doctor," I said, glancing at Flaxen. "What do you think are her chances?"

"The positive part of the prognosis is that during the day, the herd and this wagon are not moving very fast. She's resting in relative comfort. Even speaks a word or two now and again."

"What does she say?"

"That I can't discern. Not yet."

"You think . . . she'll make it?"

"I think the odds are better today than yesterday. How long have you been engaged?"

"What's that?"

"You and Miss Brewster. How long have you been engaged to be married?"

"Oh . . . not very long."

"Have you set a wedding date?"

"I'd say that now it very much depends on two people."

"Two people?"

"You . . . and Wolf Riker."

"Well, there's not much more I can do. Most of my effort on her behalf is already done. As for Wolf Riker, I'd say that's largely between you and him."

"Do you think I have a better chance than . . ."

"Than what?"

I pointed to the empty plate.

"There's a fundamental difference between you and that beast. You have brains."

"You're the second one who's mentioned that to me."

"Who was the first? Surely not Cookie."

"No. It was Simpson."

"Well, that's good counsel. I hope he takes it, too."

"Tell me something, doctor."

"More counsel?"

"No. How is it that someone like you . . . educated . . . skilled . . . a doctor, is in the company of a man like Riker on a drive like this?"

"Your description omitted one word . . ."

"What word?"

"Drunkard." He went on speaking in a colorful monotone. "You're here quite by accident—you and your fiancée. Mine is a different story. A long story."

"I'd like to hear it. If you don't mind."

"No. I don't mind. I said it's a long story. But I'll give you the abbreviated rendition if you're sure you care to listen."

"Yes, Dr. Picard. I would."

"Then it begins during the war. Dr. Miles Picard, the city of San Francisco, prestigious, prospering, if not yet prosperous. Never more than a drink or two during the evening—and after years and years of study and sacrifice, and yes, loneliness, in love with a beautiful, young lady, Catherine Graham, engaged to be married, like you and Miss Brewster.

"But the war was going badly for the North, so badly that the Confederates, led by Lee and his generals, mostly West Point graduates, seemed invincible, winning battle after battle: Fort Sumter, Lexington, Belmont, Shiloh, Fort Royal, Bull Run—with Union casualties mounting every month and week and day and hour, without nearly enough doctors to save the lives of the sick and wounded.

"I believed that even one more doctor could make a difference. I also believed that a woman would wait, but a war wouldn't. Catherine begged me not to go, or, at least to marry her before leaving. But no, I felt that would be unfair to her if I didn't come back.

"And so I enlisted as a doctor in the Medical Corps.

"Sherman said that 'war is hell.' No one knew that better, or more bitterly, than a battlefield doctor tending hundreds of causalities on both sides, amputating arms, legs, sometimes arms and legs, trying to stop the bleeding amid screams of agony and the smell of death in so-called operating rooms at the front lines. And sometimes there were no lines. Yesterday's victory turned into today's defeat.

"But as time went on there were more victories than defeats for the Union. Still the casualties mounted and the doctors sought relief for those casualties and for themselves. Analgesics. Morphine. Whiskey. Anything to get the wounded and the doctors through the endless operations.

"And then the letter came. Another casualty. This one not in the battlefield. More than a thousand miles away. A deadly fever had struck San Francisco and her family wrote that Catherine was among the dead.

"And in a way so was I.

"If I had been there I might have saved her—and others. There weren't enough doctors.

"Somehow I found enough strength or courage or determination to go on. But unfortunately, I found that strength or courage or determination in a bottle, until, near the end, the hand that held the scalpel was no longer steady and the brain that guided that hand became unclear and unreliable.

"So Dr. Miles Picard received a medical discharge even as Grant received Lee at Appomattox and the war ended. *That* war—while Dr. Picard became a derelict, who for some reason still carried a medical bag and found himself in a flyspeck of a saloon in a flyspeck of a Texas town called Gilead—not far from what was left of a once proud ranch owned by a man named Wolf Riker.

"Unfortunately, I still wore remnants of a Union uniform from which I withdrew my last Yankee dollar and ordered another drink. And even more unfortunately, there were three pig ugly brothers who entered and sat at a nearby table.

"The bartender brought a bottle and set it in front of me. I reached for the bottle but another hand beat me to it. A hand that belonged to one of the pig ugly brothers.

"'This town don't serve Indians, niggers, or Yankees,' he growled. 'We saw enough of your kind during the war.'

"Another brother grabbed my medical bag from the table and snapped it open.

"'Let's see what the bluebelly's got here.'

"He held up a couple of scalpels.

"'Knives,' he grunted.

"'Put that back, and leave him alone,' a voice commanded from the bar.

"The voice, I was to find, belonged to Wolf Riker.

"The three brothers didn't care who it belonged to.

"'He's a goddamn Yankee and we're gonna . . .'

"That brother never finished. It all happened so fast they never knew what hit them—and neither really did I.

"He sprang from the bar, both fists thundering into faces and bodies until the three brothers lay in three crumpled heaps on the sawdust of the floor.

"One of those three stirred and started to lift his head until the heel of Riker's boot stomped it hard back into the floor.

"Then Riker turned to me.

"'You are a doctor, aren't you?'

"'According to a certain medical institution, I am.'

"'Then grab that pouch'—he pointed to the medical bag on the table—'and come with me.'

"I pointed to the three unconscious victims.

"'Those fellows could use some medical attention.'

"'I don't give a damn about them. Come on!'

"I grabbed the bag and the bottle and followed him out the door.

"As I sat next to him in the buckboard on the

way to wherever we were going, I couldn't help occasionally glancing at the man who looked straight ahead, and who had rescued me from the post-war wrath of three unreconstructed belligerents, and who had suffered the wrath of a human whirlwind.

"A granite face atop a wide shouldered chest and with heavy hands that held the reins. A man who for his size moved with the grace and power of a panther.

"He said nothing until I uncorked the bottle of whiskey and took a deep swallow.

"'Go easy on that until we get there.'

"'Get where?'

"'My ranch.'

"'How far?'

"'Not far.'

"'You don't waste many words, do you, Mister . . .'

"'Sometimes . . . Riker. Wolf Riker.'

"'Miles Picard. Dr. Miles Picard. Can you tell me what this is all about . . . this time?'

"'Somebody's sick. Fever. Sick in bed. I came into town to get a doctor.'

"'Did you expect to find him in a saloon?'

"'I didn't know it, but the doctor left town, left Texas; I stopped for a drink.'

"'Lucky for me . . . I think.'

"I started to take another drink from the bottle. He spoke without looking at me.

"'Part of the Hippocratic Oath is that a doctor will do no harm, *Doctor* Picard.'

"'Whom am I harming?'

"This time he did turn and look at me. The penetrating glare in his eyes answered my question without his saying a word.

"'All right, Mr. Riker, Dr. Picard will drink no more until after tending to the patient.'

"'There it is.'

"'What?'

"'The ranch.'

"From a distance it looked like a huge stone bridge over dry land, arching high and wide across the narrow trail we had been following. But it was not a bridge. It was an entrance. A proclamation. Across the top of the arch were carved two 'R's' back-to-back. A brand.

"'Two R's,' I said. 'Riker and Riker?'

"'Not anymore,' he replied. 'Riker's Range.'

"Farther ahead, the main building was an imposing Spanish-style two-story structure with a tile roof and wide veranda. Nearby, corrals and small buildings, bunkhouses. A stable. Nothing in the condition it once must have been . . . and should be.

"Dozens of ranch hands, some on horseback, most on foot, none of whom waved at, nor greeted, Riker, nor did he acknowledge their presence.

"As the buckboard pulled up to the main building, Riker loosed the reins, looked toward the porch, stroked at the scar on his forehead and spoke . . . but not to me.

"'I'll be goddamned. You son of a bitch!'

"Standing on the porch, leaning to the left, smoking the stub of a black cigar, a well-worn cowboy rubbed the stubble of a speckled beard, squinted and smirked.

"''Bout time you got back,' the cowboy said.

"'Pepper, you son of a bitch.'

"'What's wrong?' I managed to inquire.

"'Wrong?! That's your patient. He was on his deathbed when I left.'

"We both got off the buckboard as the cowboy limped off the porch and closer to us.

"'Well,' I remarked. 'He doesn't seem to be dead anymore. What happened to the fever?' I asked.

"'It just decided to go away, so I just decided to get up and smoke one of Mr. Riker's cigars.'

"'It happens to patients sometimes,' I said to Mr. Riker. 'Partly they die and partly they revive. May I take a drink before I leave?'

"'You can drink the whole damn bottle, doctor . . . and stay as long as you want. Pepper, this is Dr. Miles Picard—and to paraphrase the Bard, 'At journey's end . . . present mirth hath present laughter.'

"Well, Mr. Guthrie, you asked how Riker and I met. That's how. As to why I stayed, the truth is I had no place to go and no money to get there . . .

and I was fascinated by the so-called Range Wolf, a man who could beat three men senseless without compunction or conscience . . . and at the same time care for an old crippled cowboy while quoting Hippocrates and Shakespeare. And in spite of his primitive nature he seemed to enjoy the interchange of views with a sometimes sober doctor. He pays me a pittance, enough to provide for a limited supply of spirited libation.

"As for my medical duties on the ranch, mostly I set an assortment of broken bones of wranglers with a degree of success, but not in the case of a young wrangler, who was thrown off a horse and suffered a broken neck.

"And now, Mr. Guthrie, enough of my autobiographical rambling. You must tell me the story of your life some time . . . some other time.

"I'm tired and sleepy."

CHAPTER XIII

"Where the hell you been?"

That was Cookie's salutation as I approached the campfire, where quite a few of the drovers were gathered.

"Visiting a sick friend," I answered.

"Humph!" He responded and went back to watching the contest.

After a grueling day's work, twelve or more hours in the saddle herding recalcitrant cattle, the drovers sought diversion of any kind before calling it a day.

I paused also to watch.

On either end of a small table two men sat engaged in an arm wrestling contest.

One was Simpson, the other, a Negro called Smoke, both of about the same size and muscle. Both sweating and straining by the gleaming light of the campfire, cheered on by the onlookers, most of them cheering for the Negro.

Just when the black arm seemed to gain advantage, the white fist and arm slowly drove the black arm to an upright position . . . both quivered, but neither gave way.

Locked and shuddering for a long time and for what must have seemed a much longer time to the two opponents, neither receded nor gained advantage.

First, the black man smiled, then the Scandinavian . . . both still straining.

"You ain't shy of muscle," Smoke gritted.

"Neither are you," Simpson managed to nod.

"What say to a draw?" Smoke smiled.

"I say done!" Simpson smiled back.

Each man let loose of his grip.

Protests.

Epithets.

"Bastards."

"Quitters."

"Assholes."

Two of the biggest protesters, neither of whose names I knew, advanced. One close to Smoke, the other to Simpson.

"We got money bet here," one shouted.

"Then nobody lost," Simpson said.

The protester grabbed Simpson's shirt.

"I say you finish . . ."

Simpson hit the first protester and knocked him to the ground.

Smoke hit the other and knocked him next to the first.

"I'm finished," said Simpson, and looked at Smoke. "Are you?"

"I are," Smoke nodded.

"There'll be no more fighting on this drive unless I say so," came a voice out of the darkness, and Wolf Riker stepped into the light of the campfire with Pepper standing next to him. "I need every able-bodied man to be able to do a day's work until we get to Kansas. Now call it a night. We're going to get an early start."

Wolf Riker looked down at the two men on the ground who had begun to stir.

"That goes for the pair of you lilies, too."

Riker walked away followed by Pepper as the pair of lilies managed to stagger to their feet while drovers dispersed.

It occurred to me that if I wanted to write about the untamed West, there was no better—or worse—place to start.

CHAPTER XIV

We did get an early start the next day. Before first light I already had managed to go through my suitcase in the utility wagon and secure clothing items more suited for the trail and for my current occupation.

This was followed by the usual abuse from the kitchen commandant. I had found that the best defense from such abuse was to avoid eye contact, and any other form of contact from the smelly son of a bitch while performing my assigned workload.

In the morning this included standing as far away as possible from Cookie while the two of us passed out plates loaded with breakfast and cups filled with coffee to the drovers lined up in front of the two of us near the kitchen wagon.

While so doing I glanced some distance away and discovered that Mr. Wolf Riker talked to horses—at least to one horse. The one he called Bucephalus. And not just a word or two.

Riker stroked the animal's huge head with one hand, patted its flank with the other, and leaned in close, whispering only the two of them knew what.

I watched, half expecting the horse to talk back, when I heard Pepper's voice.

"Are we standing in line for morning meal, or what?"

"Oh, yes, excuse me, Mr. Pepper. I was just noticing that Mr. Riker is having quite a conversation with that animal. Bucephalus. Isn't that his name?"

"They got a lot to talk about, and that is his name. Him and that horse go back a long way—but not as long as him and me. Quite an animal."

"Which one of them do you mean?"

"I mean you'd best watch your smart remarks."

"You're right, of course, and I apologize."

"More'n seventeen hands high. Powerful as a locomotive. And never bestrided by anyone else. The horse, I mean."

"I can believe that. Would you like me to fix a plate and coffee for you to take over to him? Mr. Riker, I mean."

"I don't fetch for Mr. Riker and he don't fetch for me."

"How far back do you go with Mr. Riker?"

"Maybe I'll tell you sometime. But that ain't as pertinent as how far ahead we got to go."

"'And of all best things upon earth, I hold that a faithful friend is the best.'"

"Is that your opinion, Mr. Guthrie?"

"A poet's opinion, Mr. Pepper. But I'd wager it's yours, too."

"What're you two palaverin' about?" came Cookie's voice.

"Something you wouldn't understand," I replied.

Pepper smiled, took his plate and cup of coffee, and hobbled away.

George Leach, the "prison graduate" as Wolf Riker had termed him, elbowed his way in front of the drover who stood in front of Cookie's line.

"Come on, Cookie, goddamn it, I'm in a hurry." Leach growled.

"You can hurry to the back of the line, you bastard. First come first served."

"But I got to ride all the way back to the rear of the herd and . . ."

"You can ride all the way back to the rear of hell, far as I give a damn. It's first come first served."

George Leach was not an overly large man, with a pinched face, black olive pits for eyes, and short cropped hair I'd guess he cropped himself. And it was obvious he had a short cropped disposition.

But so did Cookie.

"You get to the back"—Cookie brandished his knife and pointed it close to Leach's throat—"or you'll lose your Adam's apple!"

"Here, Leach," the one called Dogbreath, who had just received his breakfast from Cookie, shoved his plate and cup into Leach's hands. "Take mine. I ain't in no hurry."

There was a dark pause.

Then Leach took a step back, holding on to Dogbreath's offering, and snarled at Cookie.

"You ain't heard the last o' this!"

"Then I'll keep listenin' . . . with this."

Cookie thrust the knife blade into the table as Leach strutted away.

"You want me to go to the back of the line?" Dogbreath asked.

"Just shut up, you asshole."

It seemed the crisis had passed . . . at least for the time being.

However, I noticed that the confrontation had not escaped the notice of Mr. Riker and Mr. Pepper, who stood not far away.

After Cookie and I finished the breakfast chores, and before we boarded the kitchen wagon to head north ahead of the herd in preparation for the noon meal, I managed to pay another visit to Dr. Picard and his patient.

"I see you've had a change of wardrobe," he noted.

"Yes, thanks to Alan Reese. I brought you some

breakfast, doctor." I set the tray on the table. "Is there any change in . . . the patient?"

"Not noticeable, Mr. Guthrie, not noticeable. I wish I could be more encouraging, but your fiancée has lost a lot of blood. She's weak. It could still go either way. But I'm doing all I can."

"I know that, doctor . . . and appreciate it."

"Thank you, Mr. Guthrie. I haven't received much appreciation . . . lately. Not that I deserved it."

"You deserve it now. Even Wolf Riker would have to concede that."

"Wolf Riker has never conceded anything. Not even the loss of the Confederacy."

"I notice he still wears his Confederate belt buckle.

"Oh, yes. And he still has his sword. His unsurrendered sword."

"That scar on his forehead. From the war?"

"From before the war. A different war. A war he's still fighting."

There came a sound from Flaxen, an effort to say something. Unintelligible to me.

"Doctor, can you understand what she's saying?"

"No. No more than you can . . . or she can. She's still unconscious. I think you'd better go now and let her rest."

"I *have* to go now . . . or undergo another tirade from grease belly."

"Grease belly?" Dr. Picard smiled.

"Yes. I'm acquiring the nomenclature of the cattle drive . . . and there's something *you* have to do now, doctor."

"What's that?"

"Eat." I pointed to the plate and cup on the table. "That's *my* prescription."

"And not a bad one at that. *Doctor* Guthrie."

As I left, I reflected on Flaxen's good fortune. If Dr. Picard had not been on this drive, Flaxen Brewster already would have been dead and buried in the dry sea of Texas.

But in spite of him . . . she still might.

CHAPTER XV

Less than four hours later Texas was anything but a dry sea—at least this part of Texas.

Without warning the sky turned black before noon and brought forth a saturating torrent.

There came the sound of unseen cannon thundering in the distance—then closer, followed by jagged patterns of lightning crisscrossing just above the barely visible horizon.

What had been a dry, baked cake of soil turned into a massive sponge absorbing a cascade of soaking flurry.

Where minutes before were gnarled cracks in the earth suddenly were rivulets, then surging streams.

It was what Texans call a goose drowner—but, of course, there were no geese. No birds or animals of any kind—except those that were a part of the drive. Thousands upon thousands of moaning, snorting, dripping, blinded beeves.

But I found out that cattle are unpredictable creatures—partly because sometimes, they themselves don't know how they're going to react under the same circumstances. On some occasions the clap of thunder, like the crescendo of gunshots, will trigger a stampede. On other occasions, such as this one, when, at the same time, the sky unleashes a shower of pelting rain, the animals are stunned, uncertain, and scatter tentatively in multiple directions.

Hooves and horns were moving every which way.

Almost a hundred riderless horses that made up the remuda, battered by the pouring rain, tried turning their backs against the onslaught.

Oxen that pulled the loaded wagons were barely able to draw the wagon wheels through the sudden mud.

One of the wagons carrying supplies twisted and overturned in a glutted gully, spilling its cargo onto the rain splattered barranca.

Chandler, Reese, Smoke, Simpson, Dogbreath, Latimer, Drago, Leach, Morales One, Morales Two, and the rest, along with Wolf Riker, drenched drovers all on horseback, cursed through the downpour, desperately trying to maintain order, or doing their damnest to at least prevent chaos.

I imagine that Cookie's cursing was the loudest and most blasphemous, but then, he was the nearest to me, and I assume the nearest he'd come to a bath in some time.

And then as abruptly as it began, it was over.

A sudden summer storm quelled by an unseen hand—and the sky a blanket of blue gloss.

The immediate task was to round up the scattered cattle and the horses of the remuda—a task that would consume the rest of the day—and by Wolf Riker's order, cancel the noon meal.

For the rest of the day Wolf Riker seemed to be everywhere. At the point, on the flanks, at the tail, barking orders, and pointing in all directions at the broken herd, making sure that the gaps were closed and that Leach and the drag men pressured the stragglers into place.

With empty bellies and soaked skin, the drovers never even thought of dismounting until the task was finished.

Another task was to assess the damage. Surprisingly no one was seriously injured, not even the driver of the overturned wagon. The teamsters, including Cookie and me, assisted in turning the wagon upright and replacing a broken wheel.

Precious supplies had been scattered, soaked, and spoiled, lodged in mud.

Through all this, my main concern was for Flaxen, and as soon as I was able, I went to Dr. Picard.

He seemed unperturbed, and if anything, grateful for the respite.

"She's sleeping like a baby," he said, "though most babies I've come across don't sleep as reposefully."

She was indeed asleep and breathing more evenly than before.

"Anybody badly injured out there?"

"Hard to believe, but the answer is no."

"Macho bastards wouldn't admit it unless a bone was splintered and hanging out—just to prove how durable they are."

"Well, no bones were visible as far as I could tell."

"And how about you, Mr. Guthrie? Any worse for the wear?"

"No, not really . . . and I'm not what you'd call 'macho.'"

"Maybe not, but I'd say you're doing all right . . . for a tenderfoot."

"So are you, doctor. In more ways than one."

"At another time," he smiled, "I would have said, 'I'll drink to that.'"

As I stepped out of the wagon I heard a voice.

"How's she doing?"

I turned toward Pepper.

"Seems to be doing all right, and so is Dr. Picard."

"Still sober?"

"Stone cold."

"You never can tell."

"About what?"

"About anything. Take you for example."

"What about me?"

"Some of the boys were bettin' that Cookie'ud have you quiverin' by now."

"How did you bet, Mr. Pepper?"

"Me? I'm not a bettin' man, but . . ."

"But, what?"

"If you ever want to borrow my Bowie . . . let me know."

"I will. And thanks, Mr. Pepper . . . for asking about Flaxen, I mean."

That night around the campfire, the drovers made up for the missed noon meal by devouring double portions of supper.

Not all the drovers. Some had eaten earlier and were riding slowly on horseback, curling around the regrouped cattle now asleep, and still damp from the day's cloudburst.

I had heard that cowboys, at the end of a hard day's work, would relax and smoke and yes, sing the songs of the range and lost loves. What I had heard was confirmed that night. Several of the serenaders, led by Smoke's deep baritone, were vocalizing one of the favorites.

> *Oh, Shenandoah, I hear you calling,*
> *Away, you rolling river . . .*
> *Oh Shenandoah, I'm going to leave you*
> *Away I'm bound*
> *Across the wide Missouri*

"That's enough."

Wolf Riker stepped forward into the light of the campfire, followed by Pepper.

"I've got something to say."

The singing stopped and all faces turned toward Riker.

I, as well as most of the drovers, I think, believed at the time that Wolf Riker was going to take the opportunity to voice a few words of commendation for a day's work well done during the unexpected storm and what followed in its wake.

Riker inhaled a lungful from his cigar and let the smoke drift away from both nostrils.

"This drive has little more than just begun— and we're behind schedule. Whose schedule, some of you might ask. I'll tell you. Mine. And that's the schedule we're going to stick to come hell or high tide.

"What happened today is nothing to what's ahead for a thousand miles, from here to the Red and to Kansas.

"I made my speech before you signed, and all of you did sign . . ."

Wolf Riker looked toward me.

". . . except for Guth over there . . . and by the great Lord Harry, you're going to live up to that agreement, if you have to die trying.

"We lost some supplies today, so after tonight we're going to be on shorter rations, and I don't want to hear any grumbling from any of you brush poppers. Most of us here lost a war—or so they say. This is a different kind of war, and I promise you one thing—we're not going to lose this one.

"We're going to make up for the time we lost today—and then some. This outfit's going to move and keep moving.

"Now you can go on singing, or turn in and get all the rest you can, because you're going to need it."

Wolf Riker stuck the stub of the cigar back into his mouth, turned, and walked away.

Pepper stood for a moment more, scratched at his beard, then limped after the Range Wolf.

So much for Wolf Riker's words of commendation for the day's work well done during the storm and what followed.

There *was* some grumbling among the brush poppers, none of it very audible except from Leach. He concluded by turning to Alan Reese who was nearest to him.

". . . who the hell does he think he is?"

"Why didn't you ask him?" Reese responded.

"I'll do more than ask . . . when the time comes."

"Sure you will," Cookie cackled. "About the time you get your third set of teeth."

"I'm turning in," Dogbreath said. "I've had enough of this bullshit."

"Me, too," said Morales One.

"Me, too," echoed Morales Two.

So ended another day and night on the prairie.

CHAPTER XVI

But in a way it wasn't the end of the night, not for me. Exhausted as I was from the events and exertions of the day, as I lay on the blanket atop the still damp earth, the component my body craved and silently cried out for—sleep—eluded me, trumped by conflicting speculation and contemplation of the future—if there was a future.

My mind, a scrambled bedlam, would not let go of the faces and events of the foregoing weeks, days, and hours.

Christopher Guthrie, *bon vivant*, elitist even among the cognoscenti of New York society, wallower in the lavish comfort of a Park Avenue residence, diner at the most expensive restaurants on the continent, escort about town of assorted spoiled, but desirable debutants, attendee and critic of the city's finest theatrical productions—including my rave review of Edwin Booth's triumphant return to the stage as Hamlet at the

Winter Garden Theatre, little more than a year after his brother, John Wilkes, had assassinated the President of the United States.

Booth's voice, his soliloquy as Hamlet still echoing in my mind.

> *What a rogue and peasant slave am I . . .*
> *What a rogue and peasant slave am I . . .*
> *What a rogue and peasant slave am I . . .*

And I had become little more than a peasant slave.

From an existence of ease, comfort, and leisure, to the fierce, pitiless society of quasi-civilized vulgarians—Cookie, Leach, Dogbreath, French Frank, and Latimer—to name the worst, most of them dregs of the Confederacy, now without country or conscience, commanded by the most forceful, contradictory character it had ever been my misfortune to come across.

Instead of being shanghaied on some hell-ship, it was my plight to be conscripted on a desperate, dirt voyage, with a cargo of thousands of recalcitrant cattle, facing God knew what odds; Indians, border raiders, and very likely, a mutinous crew, to say nothing of the shortage of supplies due to an angry sky.

Sacks of beans, flour, and coffee left behind in the mire of a vast expanse called Texas.

Texas—in my mind I tried to visualize a map of Texas, of where we might be now, and of where we were going—names and places I had heard the drovers mention—The Brazos, Illano Estacado, Panhandle, Staked Plains, Dry Tortuga; but they might as well have been talking Chinese, and we might as well have been in China.

Somewhere along the way there had to be at least an outpost of civilization. If not a city or village—a fort, or even a ranch.

Wolf Riker, himself, had acknowledged that I, unlike the others, had not signed on for the drive.

At any of those places he could not prevent me from abandoning the drive—and taking Flaxen with me if she survived.

And I would be more than happy to compensate Riker for his trouble. I had no money with me, thanks to that thief, Cookie. But I still had my bankbook to prove my financial worth—and would make it worth his while.

If there were such a place, an outpost, Wolf Riker would stop and purchase supplies.

And I would purchase my freedom—mine and Flaxen's. Somehow, the thought of all this set my mind somewhat at ease.

In the meanwhile, I would begin a new journal, of the characters and events chronicling at least one small chapter in the history of the West.

If I survived it might be published and read by

some of those countless thousands of pilgrims from all corners of the European continent who now reside in the Eastern region of this continent. The daring, restless souls who dream of adventure and fortune in the Western states and territories—the seekers who hark to what has been called the Manifest Destiny of this great nation.

The first entry into that journal is made up of the hundred or so lines written above—and the journal is entitled

THE RANGE WOLF
CATTLE DRIVE

CHAPTER XVII

The next morning at first light I was awakened by a cackle and a familiar voice struggling to read words that were familiar to me—familiar because they were words I had written the night before.

". . . seekers . . . who . . . hark to the . . . Man . . . Manifest . . . Dest . . . inee . . . hmmp . . . and the . . . journal . . . is . . . is . . . en-tite-led THE RANGE WOLF . . . heeh . . . heh—CATTLE . . ."

"Goddamn you!" I leaped up and grabbed the pages from Cookie's dirty hands.

"Here! Here!" He cawed. "Ain't you the twitchy one. I seen you scribblin' away last night. Just wonderin' what you was up to . . . just . . ."

"Just mind your own damn business . . ."

"Everythin' that goes on around here *is* my business. Get that straight, shorthorn, 'cause Eustice Munger, that's me, Eustice Munger, is the eyes and ears of this outfit who reports what he sees and hears directly to Mr. Wolf Riker."

"So you're the official informer, is that it?"

"That's one way of puttin' it."

"Well, you can inform Mr. Wolf Riker, or anybody else, of whatever you see and hear, but whatever I write on my own time is my private affair . . ."

"You ain't got any 'own time' or any 'private affairs,' not on this drive, not while you're workin' for me. Better get that straight, too, waddy. As for what you write from now on, I don't give a short bit. That'll be between you and Mr. Riker. Now get your stringy ass over to the oven and get to work, NOW!"

So much for my standing up for my rights and privileges on the drive.

I got my stringy ass over to the oven and went to work on what had to be done in preparation for the morning meal.

But I was not prepared for what ensued.

There had been some murmured remarks from some of the drovers in the breakfast line, but Simpson's remark was not murmured as he held out the tin cup.

"This doesn't taste much like coffee."

Cookie's retort was just as audible.

"That's 'cause I didn't use much coffee in the makin' of it—used grain that we got more of—

and the beans is gonna be damn sparse, too, come noon and suppertime—and the bread . . .'"

Wolf Riker pushed his way to the head of the line.

"Cookie, give me a cup of that coffee."

"Sure thing, Mr. Riker." Cookie nodded with his seldom smile. "Comin' right up."

"And fill it up," Riker added.

"Sure thing," Cookie repeated. "Right to the brim, Mr. Riker."

Wolf Riker lifted the cup to his mouth and drank. Drank it all.

"Anything more you want to say about the coffee on this drive, Simp?"

"The name is Simpson, Mr. Riker. Karl Simpson."

"The name is anything I say it is, Simp. And on second thought, I think I'll have another cup."

Cookie lifted the coffeepot, ready to pour, but Wolf Riker grabbed Karl Simpson's tin cup and drained all the contents.

"Now get out with the herd, Simp. And that goes for the rest of you. I said we're going to make up for lost time and that means starting now. And I don't want to hear any more bellyaching about coffee or beans or anything else."

Wolf Riker slammed the cup onto the serving table and paused momentarily in case of any retort that might come from what he had just said—none came. He moved away and walked toward Pepper, who stood near a wagon whittling on a mesquite branch with his Bowie knife.

The drovers, including Karl Simpson, dispersed to their respective tasks without further comment or hesitation. Some of them had not even finished their morning meal, but, as if given a battlefield command, they automatically reacted to an order from a superior officer.

In addition to what Wolf Riker had said just a few minutes ago, I remembered his words from the night before—'most of us have lost a war— or so they say. This is a different kind of war, and I promise you one thing—we're not going to lose this one.'

I had avoided any real danger in the Civil War, any real possibility of becoming a casualty; but here, years later and thousands of miles away, I had found myself in a different kind of war. A war for which I did not volunteer.

The Range Wolf's war.

Wolf Riker's cattle drive.

But that morning I was not the only irresolute member of the Wolf Riker cattle drive. I had plenty of company.

I recalled some of Simpson's defiant words, his admonition to me earlier on—"You're a man . . . stand up to him . . . the more they take advantage of you, the more they will . . . don't let him break you . . . fight 'em any way you can . . . never give up . . ." But that morning Simpson didn't give much evidence of defiance. Neither he, nor any of the others, did any "standing up" to the Range Wolf—not yet.

But it was a long way to Kansas.

CHAPTER XVIII

Wolf Riker kept his word about making up lost time.

That day, the herd, even though it wasn't yet what the drovers term "trail broke," covered just over fifteen miles through dust-chocked terrain.

Riker did not mount Bucephalus, but he wore out three other good horses from the remuda. He must have ridden three or four times those fifteen miles—back and forth, twisting and turning, riding from one side of the herd to the other, from point to drag and back again.

Wherever he rode, nothing quite pleased him, or else something quite displeased him, and he didn't hesitate to let the drovers know what they were doing wrong, and how they could do it better. Lead steers were moving too slow. Flankers and swing men were moving too wide. Here the herd was driving too loose; there the beasts were bunched too tight.

Wherever he rode, Riker barked commands, and those commands were carried out amid inaudible, dust swallowed curses from the drovers. Tempers rose with the arc of the sun, but not within sight and sound of Wolf Riker. Past noon with the sun just past its upmost arc and just beginning its long slow descent, we had set up the serving table and began our routine of dishing out beef and scrimpy beans and coffee to the dirty, sweat-streaked drovers.

"Just coffee," Riker ordered from Cookie.

"Me, too," Pepper stood directly behind him.

"Two coffees," Cookie nodded and served them up.

"Looks like Chandler's in one hell of a hurry," French Frank pointed to the approaching rider.

"Maybe he's just hungry," Dogbreath shrugged.

"Nobody's that hungry," French Frank countered.

The trail boss flew off his mount and knocked the dirt and dust from his flapping chaps.

"Mr. Riker."

"What is it, Chandler? Another stagecoach?"

"Nope. Tracks."

"What kind of tracks?" Riker took a swallow of his coffee.

"Pony. Unshod ponies."

"How many?"

"Hard to tell."

"Enough to make up a war party?"

"Hard to tell."

"Which way they headed?"

There was a pause.

"Yeah, I know," Riker said. "Hard to tell."

Chandler nodded.

Riker looked around.

"Smoke. You with the bloodhound eyes. You're part Indian, aren't you?"

"Some," Smoke took a step forward. "Lived with 'em a couple years."

"Read tracks?"

"Some."

"That'll have to do. Get mounted. Chandler, you, too, get a fresh animal. The two of you go ahead and see if you can figure how many and which direction. Don't either of you get killed. I need you both."

"Haven't 'et."

"What?"

"Haven't 'et," Chandler pointed to the serving table. "Can I eat first?"

"Sure you can. Take five minutes. Dogbreath, saddle him up a fresh mount."

"I told you he was hungry," Dogbreath said to French Frank, and moved away.

In spite of the interruption and the news that Chandler brought, we continued to make good time, and Wolf Riker continued to think it wasn't good enough.

But the drovers moved on, not knowing what they were moving on toward, but hoping it wasn't the mutilated bodies of Chandler and Smoke.

I did manage to bring a plate of food over to Dr. Picard.

"This outfit's in an all fired hurry today, isn't it?" he remarked.

"Riker's orders."

"The wolf man," Picard nodded.

"How is she? Better? Or worse?"

"Better . . . in spite of the wolf man."

"Good," I smiled and left.

Just before the sun slid beneath the western saw tooth peaks, Chandler and Smoke rode in, weary but not mutilated, and reported to Riker, while the rest of us listened.

"See anything?" Riker had asked Smoke.

"Tracks. Not enough for a war party. Led up to rocky hillside and disappeared. Coulda been a scouting party."

"You think they spotted us?"

"Hard to miss. All that dust. We could spot it miles away. They got eyes, too. Better eyes."

"Well, there's nothing we can do, but be ready for anything. Say, Smoke, any way of telling which tribe?"

Smoke shook his head negatively.

"Around here . . . maybe Comanch' . . . maybe Kiowa."

"Which tribe did you live with?"

"Kiowa."

"Well, if we run into any, let's hope they're some of your relatives."

"That won't cut much mustard," Smoke's expression never changed. "As you white eyes say."

CHAPTER XIX

That night, after serving supper and cleaning up the residuary, I assumed my day's work was done and began to make my daily entry into my journal.

I was mistaken in my first assumption and interrupted in my literary endeavor.

"You! Guth!" came Cookie's voice. "Get off your stringy ass and get back to work."

"Doing what?"

"What I say."

"And what *do* you say, Mr. Munger?"

"Mr. Munger says"—Cookie actually seemed pleased at my appellation—"get over to Wolf Riker's wagon with this pot of tea and these clean sheets. Change the sheets and bring back . . ."

"The soiled ones?"

"Soiled? That's right, the dirty ones."

"Very good, Cookie." I thought one "Mr. Munger" was enough for the day.

There was a blanket of uneasy silence in the encampment. No campfire singing or tall tales, or levity of any kind among the tired drovers.

Balancing the sheets and tea tray, I made my way to Wolf Riker's wagon and knocked on the door.

"He ain't in."

I turned toward the sound of Pepper's assertion.

"Where is he?"

"Out."

"Out where?"

"Out there," Pepper pointed toward the vast darkness.

"I see."

Actually I didn't see anything but vast darkness.

"I was ordered to bring tea and clean sheets to Mr. Riker." I held out both items.

"So I observed," Pepper nodded toward the tea and sheets.

"There's something that I observe, or rather, don't observe."

"What's that?"

"This is the first time around the camp that I don't see you within sight of him."

"There's a lot of firsts in life, I guess that's one of them."

"And I guess that'll have to serve as explanation."

"I guess . . . except for this. There are times

when Riker likes to take a walk at night out in the open . . . by himself . . . just to think about things . . . so that's what he's doin' out there . . . and that's why I'm over here."

"That's a very good explanation."

"Glad you like it . . . not that it much matters."

"May I ask you one more question?"

"Ask."

"Do you always respect his wishes?"

Pepper nodded.

"And vice versa."

"I must say that that is a rarity between two people."

"It happens to be the way it happens to be . . . between me and Riker."

"Very commendable, and"—I nodded toward the tea tray and clean sheets—"what do you suggest I do about these?"

Pepper took a step to the door of the wagon, twisted the knob, pushed open the door, pointed toward the interior, turned, and limped away.

I entered for the first time . . . and, as I turned up the lamp, marveled at what I saw. It seemed more like a paneled library in a minor mansion. An oak desk, leather chairs, carpet, an oversized bunk, on the wall what I presumed to be Wolf Riker's un-surrendered sword, and . . . racks of books.

Shakespeare, Tennyson, Poe, DeQuincy, scientific works . . . Tyndall, Proctor, Darwin, astronomy, physics. A copy of *The Dean's English*. The Cambridge edition of Browning. And on the desk an open book with a passage from Milton's *Paradise Lost* underlined in pencil:

> *Here we may reign secure; <u>and in my choice</u>*
> <u>*To reign is worth ambition though in hell:*</u>
> <u>*Better to reign in hell than serve in heav'n*</u>.

And as I read to myself I heard that unmistakable voice, turned to find Wolf Riker standing near the doorway.

"And in my choice to reign is worth ambition though in hell. Better to reign in hell than serve in heaven," Riker closed the door and moved closer with that powerful, yet graceful stride.

"One of the better lines," he said, "from one of the better poets."

"Milton was a great poet," I affirmed.

"Surprised at what you see here, Guth?"

"Yes, I am, Riker. Astounded."

"*Mister* Riker."

"Astounded, *Mister* Riker," I set the tea tray on the desk.

"Why?" he moved still closer. "Because I read . . . and have a command of books as well as . . . people?"

"It's just difficult to reconcile your conduct with . . ."

"Milton? Not at all. It's all the same. All a part of strength. The strong survive."

"So do the weak."

"Only at the whim of the strong."

"But not in a civilized society. That's what differentiates man from beast."

Wolf Riker took another step with what seemed a look of appraisal, and amusement.

"I'm informed you're keeping a diary."

"The eyes and ears of the drive."

"Who? You?"

"No, Cookie. That's what he terms himself, the eyes and ears of the drive, and I imagine it was he who informed you. Yes, a diary. Journal."

"What do you intend doing with it?"

"Writing a book."

"Have you written before? Books, I mean."

"Yes, I have. Articles. Reviews. Plays. And books."

"Published? You've earned money from them?"

"Yes, sir."

"So then you've stood on your own legs as well as dead man's."

"Mostly I write sitting down."

"Yes," he smiled. "When you're on your own time, but now you're on my time . . ."

"Twenty four hours, seven days a week?"

"As long as you're on this drive, but tell me, what are your books about?"

"Romance. Fiction."

"Ah, but this isn't fiction. This is life, Guth, reality and not romantic."

"There's a certain romance."

"With Miss Brewster?"

I paused for just a moment.

"Yes . . . and with the hopes and dreams of the men on the drive."

"A ragbag collection of riffraff. A company of idiots festering in ignorance. It doesn't matter whether they live or die . . ."

". . . It matters . . ."

". . . To whom . . . ?"

"Dr. Picard."

"A drunk."

"Not anymore."

"We'll see."

This time it was Wolf Riker who paused.

"Will you write about me?"

"Yes."

"Good. Hero or villain?"

"I'll have to decide . . . when I get to know you better."

"And so you will, Guth, so you will. And I'll get to know you better."

There was a momentary silence.

At first I thought it was just my imagination, but soon determined that the appraisal in Wolf Riker's eyes when he looked at me had indeed changed. Not changed completely, but somewhat. And somewhat in my favor.

I was no longer simply a fop, a coxcomb, who lived from, and enjoyed, the cream of a dead man's endeavors. A worthless dandy, an object of derision.

After what he had just heard, Wolf Riker couldn't help but be somewhat impressed.

In little more than a moment I broke the silence.

"Would you like me to pour your tea, Mr. Riker?"

"Never mind the tea, Guth. I have here something more . . . stimulating."

He moved to a cabinet, opened it, and reached for a bottle and a pair of glasses.

"Brandy. Napoleon brandy. We'll have a swallow or two. Sorry I can't provide snifters, too delicate for the drive. These glasses will have to suffice."

"They'll suffice just fine, Mr. Riker."

He proceeded to pour, handed me a glass, and raised his own.

"Confusion to the enemy."

"Yes," I smiled, "even though Napoleon did not succeed in confusing the enemy . . . at Waterloo."

"A pity. But we were talking not about history, but about you and me. Why did you come West? To marry Miss Flaxen Brewster?"

"That's part of it."

"What's the other part?"

"To write that book."

"Ah, yes. But you said you wrote fiction."

"Not always. Besides, someone once said all writing is autobiographical."

"So your book will include you?"

"Yes."

"And me."

"Yes. But as I said, when I get to know you better . . ."

As we spoke I noticed that, from time to time, Wolf Riker raised his hand to the scar on his temple as if to sooth the jagged mark.

". . . and I've already learned a great deal about you, Mr. Riker, from this visit to your . . . wagon."

"And I about you. But we'll see how you survive on this drive. I'll be interested in the change."

"In me?"

Wolf Riker took another sip of Napoleon brandy and nodded.

"Ah yes. There will be a change, there has to be. Even as there was a change between my brother and me, a man who might go to any length to see this drive fail. To kill me if it comes to that, just as I'll kill him if that time comes. But you know, Guth, I'm glad you're with us. There's nobody to talk to. Except Doc, when he's sober. And that's seldom."

"What about your friend, Pepper?"

"Yes, Pepper. But that's a different kind of talk. Not like the conversation we've had this evening."

I felt this was the opportunity to broach a subject I had been contemplating.

"There is something I wanted to talk to you about, Mr. Riker."

"Literature?"

"No, Mr. Riker. Theft. I've been robbed. All the money I had in my pocket. I've reason to believe it was our culinarian."

"Who?"

"My immediate superior. Cookie."

"Pickings," Wolf Riker shrugged and smiled. "Cookie's pickings. That's what I meant when I said you'll learn to take care of yourself and your money. I suppose up to now your lawyer's done it for you. Well, there is no lawyer out here."

"How can I get it back?"

"That's your lookout. Beat it out of him if you're able enough. If not, kill him."

"Do you seriously mean that? For three hundred dollars?"

"Three hundred . . . that much? But men have killed for less . . . even gentlemen."

I felt the conversation had become futile and moved toward the bunk with the clean sheets.

But I noticed another change. A more serious change in Wolf Riker. He seemed to stagger slightly in sudden pain. His thick fingers now rubbed at the scar on his forehead as if trying to squeeze out the pain. I did my best to ignore what was occurring.

"I'll make the bed, Mr. Riker."

"Never mind," he commanded. "Just leave the sheets. Think I'll lie down."

I placed the sheets at the foot of the bunk and started to leave.

"Guth."

"Yes, Mr. Riker."

"You'll learn."

"Yes, Mr. Riker."

"Or you'll die."

Riker extended both arms forward, faltered, and pitched toward the bunk.

So ended the first meeting between just the two of us.

I did learn . . . a great deal about Wolf Riker.

Maybe more than I wanted to know.

CHAPTER XX

It had been an engrossing day and night, but the night was not yet over.

Far from over.

So I discovered as I took just a few steps from Wolf Riker's wagon and was slapped full across the face by a wet, dirty towel. The force of the impact knocked me off balance and nearly off my feet.

Of course I knew the identity of the blow giver before seeing the sight, or hearing the sound of his shrill voice.

"Why you skylarkin' scum. What were you doin' in there all that time?"

As I wiped the slough off my face, I did what I could to gather some semblance of dignity.

"Well, you see, Cookie, I was . . ."

Before I could finish any sort of explanation, true or false, I felt the impact of the wet, dirty towel across my face again.

"Damn you, Cookie, you ever do that again and I'll . . ."

"You'll what? With what? A gun? I don't see any. A knife? You ain't got one. Them frail fists? I don't think so. Now what was you doin' in there for so long? Was you talkin' about me?"

"We had more important matters to discuss."

"Such as what?"

"Such as evolution, from monkey to . . ."

"Never mind that fancy talk, fancy pants . . . and what happened to them dirty sheets you was supposed to bring back?"

"They're still on Mr. Riker's bed and so is he. You want to go in and get them? There's the door, but I don't think he wants to be disturbed. Not tonight, so enter at your own risk."

"Well, then . . ."

"Well then, what?"

Now it was Cookie's turn to gather some semblance of dignity, although I doubt if he knew what the word meant.

"Bring 'em back tomorrow mornin'."

"Very well, *sirrah*. Any further instructions for the night?"

"You'll hear from me if there is."

Eustice Munger turned and walked away carrying the wet, dirty towel.

I stood there cursing the filthy bastard, silently,

of course . . . until a blade whined past my head and stuck into the wagon close by.

A figure with a limp appeared out of the darkness, moved past me and extracted the Bowie while I stood there stiff as a broomstick.

"The offer still stands," Pepper said as he replaced the knife into its sheath.

"What . . . offer?" I managed.

"To borrow the Bowie . . . or my .44, if you prefer.

"And do what?"

"Settle Cookie's hash."

I pointed toward Wolf Riker's wagon.

"Someone else suggested something like that just a few minutes ago."

"I'm not surprised."

"You and Mr. Riker seem to think alike."

"Mostly. 'Cause 'til you do . . ."

"Do what?"

"Settle his hash, you're gonna keep gettin' slapped around . . . or worse."

"You also suggest I kill him?"

"If it comes down to it, that's one solution."

"Maybe there's another."

"Maybe."

"If I did kill him . . . who'd do the cooking? Did you ever think of that?"

"Don't tell me that's what's stoppin' you," Pepper smiled. "'Cause if it is, there's a couple other fellas on the drive who've done some fryin'. Both Morales One and Two."

"Well, that does make a difference."

"Don't it, though."

I didn't know whether Pepper—or for that matter, Riker—was serious, or just prodding.

"And just remember one thing," Pepper added.

"What's that?"

"Like I said . . . the offer still stands." He patted the handle of the Bowie and limped away.

I glanced back at Riker's wagon. The pain he endured as we were talking must have been overwhelming to have affected a man as powerful as he, the way it did. He very nearly lurched into his bunk. It probably would have felled an ordinary man.

But Wolf Riker was no ordinary man.

CHAPTER XXI

As I moved across camp I could not help but reflect on the day's events—from early that morning when Cookie discovered my journal— to Simpson's complaint about Cookie's coffee and his silence in the face of Wolf Riker's confrontation—to Riker's wearing out three horses while spurring the drive and almost wearing out all the drovers in the bargain.

Then at noon, Donavan's report of unshod pony tracks—Smoke and Chandler unable to trace the tracks or the whereabouts of the red riders of those animals.

Dr. Picard's guarded optimism of Flaxen Brewster's condition.

Tea and clean sheets for the wolf man, and the revelation of Wolf Riker's literary bent and philosophy—"*better to reign in hell than serve in heaven*"—the fact that Eustice Munger more than likely did me a favor in informing Riker of my journal—Riker's fascination at my own literary endeavors—his assent, and even cooperation, in my writing about his life and times—and then, that sudden shudder and jolt, striking a numbing blow that sent him stumbling to his bunk.

If Cookie did do me a favor by telling Riker of my journal, then he retaliated with a pair of slams across the face from a wet, dirty towel, while I took the blows without any overt requital.

But there was still the standing offer of Pepper's arsenal.

Something to think about. But at that time I was thinking about something else.

Someone else.

I knocked on the door of the wagon.

"Come in. Come in."

I entered and closed the door behind me. The interior was dimly lit.

Dr. Picard sat at a table about to open an un-tapped bottle of whiskey. Flaxen Brewster lay in the bunk, delirious . . . muttering indistinctively.

"Yes. Do come in, Mr. Guthrie. I was just about to have my first drink since you joined the drive."

"But why?"

"To celebrate."

"Her recovery?"

Dr. Picard uncorked the whiskey bottle and smiled a confidential smile.

"No. But she *will* recover."

"Then what?"

"I was about to celebrate the fact that for once . . . Wolf Riker was wrong."

"About what?"

The doctor ceased smiling, lifted the bottle off the table, and pointed it toward Flaxen.

"Call her name."

I moved closer to her.

"Flaxen . . . Flaxen . . . it's Christopher . . . Christopher Guthrie. Can you hear me?"

Her maundering became less halting and more distinguishable.

"Mr. Guthrie . . . please, Mr. Guthrie . . . you won't testify against us . . . you have your wallet back . . . the police . . . It'll mean prison . . . please . . . my father and I . . ."

Dr. Picard poured a drink into a tumbler and set the bottle on the table.

"So, the omniscient Wolf Riker was wrong . . . about her being a lady. It is ironic, isn't it?"

"Dr. Picard . . ."

"What I saved is a thief."

His hand moved toward the tumbler; but I moved quicker and slid the glass away from him.

"The point is you saved her. Listen to me."

"I'm listening."

"Because of your skill a human life will go on living. Yes, Doctor, you saved her . . . and in a way I think she helped you."

"I see what you mean," Dr. Picard nodded. "Riker can't say that all my patients die."

"No. He can't."

"But . . . why the ring? The engagement ring on her finger. Why the fairy tale about her being your fiancée?"

"Riker called her a piece of fluff. What else might have followed if he, and the rest of them, knew the circumstances of our . . . meeting? I thought the ring and the 'fairy tale' as you call it, might put her in a more beneficent light. I . . ."

"But the ring? Where . . ."

"My mother's. A keepsake."

"Quite a gesture, Mr. Guthrie . . . a *beau geste.*"

"And you, Dr. Picard, since you've saved her life, will you do something else for her? As far as Wolf Riker, and everyone else is concerned, Flaxen Brewster is my fiancée."

"But when he finds out that she's not . . ."

"He doesn't have to find out anything. Neither does anyone else on this drive."

"They'll find out. There are no secrets . . ."

"No, they won't. Not from me . . . or you."

"But when she recovers she'll . . ."

"When she recovers, I'll talk to her, we both will. It'll be all right. Let's leave her some dignity."

"Dignity. I haven't heard . . . or even thought about that word in a long time. You know, Mr. Guthrie, there is something *sympathique* between us. Now I'd be pleased if you'd do me a favor."

"What's that?"

Dr. Picard pointed at the table.

"Pour the whiskey in that glass . . . back into that bottle."

"Do it yourself, doctor," I smiled. "Your hand is certainly steady enough."

"Yes." He grinned. "Thank you, Mr. Guthrie."

"Thank you, doctor."

CHAPTER XXII

It was the kind of morning writers write about. Livid. Limitless. The invitation to a perfect day. But I had had no time to make even a sentence entry into my journal.

It had been a short night.

And instead of a rooster's crowing, it was Cookie's cackling that proclaimed the coming dawn and the grind ahead.

I was at my usual station behind the serving table when I looked up and saw Wolf Riker's face directly in front of me and Pepper's whiskers directly behind him.

"Coffee and biscuit," Riker said.

"Good morning, Mr. Riker, and how are you this morning?"

"If you're asking how I feel, Guth, I feel splendid."

And he did, indeed, look splendid, with no aftereffect or even any hint of the seizure I had witnessed the night before. If anything, he seemed even more vital than usual this morning.

"By the way, Guth. I meant to ask you. Do you ride? Horses, I mean."

"I have ridden horses, Mr. Riker"—I handed him his coffee and biscuit—"but not western saddle."

"English? Is that it?"

"Yes, sir."

"How civilized . . . and impractical out here. Pepper, would you kindly pick a gelding out of the remuda for Guth?"

"Tobacco ought to fit the bill," Pepper said.

"And have somebody throw on a saddle, a western saddle."

"Sure, since that's all we got. He can use Donavan's."

"Good. Have Dogbreath see to it. And Guth, take a turn or two along the herd. Think you can manage that with a western saddle?"

"I think so."

"Just a minute, Mr. Riker."

"What is it, Cookie?"

"I heard what you said about him joy ridin' out there . . ."

"Did I say anything about joy riding?"

"That's what it sounds like, and I need him around here to do a full day's work with me."

"Well, you'll just have to do a full day's work

without him. I want every man on this drive to be able to ride hard and shoot straight."

Riker took a swallow of coffee and as he bit into the biscuit French Frank spoke up.

"Mr. Riker. There's something you ought to know."

"What's that?"

"That saddle that belonged to Donavan now belongs to me."

"How'd you come by it?"

"Gambled. Me and Latimer. I drew high card and won."

"What're you going to do with two saddles? You got two asses?"

"No, I ain't. But it's my saddle fair and square."

Riker took another swallow from the cup and looked at me.

"What do you say to that, Guth? Want to fight him for it?"

I did not want to fight French Frank, or anybody.

"No, sir. But I'll make a bet with you, French Frank."

"What kind of bet?"

"How much do you think that saddle's worth?"

"I'd say up to twenty dollars."

"Very well, I'll double that. Forty dollars if you win—against the saddle if I win. High card. You have a deck of cards with you?"

"Always."

"I'll even sweeten the deal. You can draw two cards against my one. My card has to be higher than both of yours combined. Face cards don't count. Aces count one apiece."

"I thought you wanted to get an early start this morning," Chandler, the trail boss, reminded Wolf Riker. "We're burning daylight."

"This won't take long," I said. "If French Frank wants to bet."

"Forty dollars," French Frank scratched his chin. "I get two cards to your one. Right?"

"Right. Shall we get on with it? As Mr. Chandler said, 'we're burning daylight.'"

French Frank produced a deck of well-worn cards from the pocket of his corduroy shirt.

"You're on. Who draws first?"

"You, of course. But . . ."

"But what?"

"May I shuffle?"

French Frank slapped the dank deck into my outstretched palm.

I proceeded to shuffle my Bureau of Military Justice shuffle and extended the deck.

French Frank drew a card and displayed a six of diamonds.

"Very good," I nodded. "Draw again."

He turned up a jack of clubs.

"Face card," I smiled. "Doesn't count. Draw again."

French Frank drew a three of hearts.

"Six and three," I said, "totals nine. My draw."

I picked my card and turned over the ten of spades.

"Well, it was close," I remarked and replaced the winning card.

French Frank's mouth twisted downward. He thrust the deck back into his shirt pocket.

"I want to think this over. I think maybe you pulled a fast one."

"Think it over later," Riker said, "and get to work now."

I thought something over, too.

Wolf Riker's attitude toward me—and the perceptible change that appeared to accompany it.

I wasn't quite sure why, but it definitely seemed like a change for the better.

However, as I had noted before, it was a long way to Kansas.

I stood by, watched and listened, as Dogbreath bridled, saddled, and cinched the paraphernalia onto the horse called Tobacco, which was indeed the color, or colors, of a bright leaf.

The procedure was simple enough for even a Harvard graduate to understand and execute.

Dogbreath's description of the horse was a trifle less intelligible, with such phrases as *bridle wise, clear footed, can carry the news to Mary, neck reiner, smooth mouthed, swimmer*—but I discerned that it all added up to a positive appraisal of the gelding called Tobacco.

I mounted and rode slowly past the kitchen wagon where Cookie and French Frank were carrying on a conversation, a conversation that most likely didn't concern the day's menu.

It did not take long to determine that, as Dr. Picard would say, Tobacco and I were *sympathique*. And almost the same could be said for the late Donavan's saddle. It was much more form fitting and comfortable than the pancake English version.

Within an hour Tobacco and I had ambled, trotted, and even galloped past many of the riders prodding the cattle: Smoke, Dogbreath, Reese, Latimer, Drago, Simpson, Morales One, Morales Two, and some of the rest, at first near, then farther away from the herd. At that point I reined up, patted Tobacco's neck, and even spoke a few flattering words to my newfound acquaintance and friend. That's when another acquaintance rode alongside and started an all too amiable conversation.

"How're you gettin' along, pard?" French Frank inquired. "You and ol' Tobac?"

"Ol' Tobac and I are getting along very compatibly, thank you."

"Uh-huh. And the saddle?" He pointed.

"Also compatible."

As he pointed, I noticed that he held a flexible,

woven leather whip with a short stock about a foot long and with a loop attached to his wrist. The whip carried a lash of three or four heavy, loose thongs. Later I was to learn that it was called a quirt—and soon I was to learn one of the purposes for which it could be used.

"O.K., pard. Let's see how you and ol' Tobac can really get along."

With that he thrashed Tobacco's rump, again and again, flogging the animal into a frenzy. Tobacco bolted ahead like a rifle shot, his hooves barely touching the ground.

French Frank roared with glee and laughter and chased after us for even more merriment. He managed to catch up to us, then, with all his might swung a backhanded blow with the quirt at Tobacco's head. I held the reins with one hand, reached out and took the blow on my wrist, wrapped my hand around the thongs, braced both feet into the stirrups and jerked back with every fiber of strength I could muster.

Once again French Frank flew off his mount, this time even more abruptly, and hit the ground even more violently than the time Wolf Riker backhanded him off the saddle.

Tobacco came to a halt and looked back, and I swear that if horses can laugh, Tobacco was laughing.

So was I.

French Frank was not laughing. He was sprawled

on the hard ground, belly down, his hat a few feet from his head, his gun flipped out of its holster, and the dank deck of cards scattered galley west.

He was spitting dirt out of his mouth, maybe a tooth or two, and cursing a dark blue streak with the loop of the quirt still attached to his wrist.

I neck-reined Tobacco, and as we moved past French Frank on his hands and knees, I inquired.

"How're ya getting along, pard?"

Ol' Tobac and I didn't wait for an answer.

CHAPTER XXIII

Since we had been a considerable distance from the herd, it was hard to tell the number of witnesses to our equestrian encounter, but there had to have been some, and those who did witness it were not reluctant to recount the event to those who did not.

French Frank failed to show up for the noon meal. I did not know if he was nursing his wounds, his pride, or collecting scattered kings and queens. And I did not care. I was too busy making up for lost time in doing my kitchen chores.

Cookie was even more dour than usual, and to my relief, more taciturn. He barely spoke a word, just slapped the three B's—beef, beans, and biscuits, on the plates and motioned for the drovers to move briskly through the line—and they did.

All except Wolf Riker and Pepper who moved at their own pace and stopped in front of me to serve them.

"I understand you had a pleasant ride, Guth."

"Yes, sir, I did."

"Got along well with Tobacco, did you?"

"Yes, sir, I did."

"Good. Take another turn or two this afternoon. And, Guth . . ."

"Yes, sir?"

"I said you'd change. And this is just the beginning. By the way, Tobacco is yours exclusively . . . for the rest of the drive. We'll talk later."

While I was saddling up, Pepper approached within talking distance and talked.

"Be cautious, sonny. That French Frank is a skunk. Him and Cookie make good company."

"Thanks for the advice, Mr. Pepper. Consider me Captain Caution. And why is he called French Frank? He doesn't seem in the least bit French."

"That's the name he give to himself. Claims his grandfather worked the guillotine back during the French Revolution. Beheaded somebody called Rose-pierre. Most likely just another one of his lies."

"Very colorful."

"Yeah. But he's still a skunk, so be on the lookout, front and back, and around the corners."

"I will, and thanks again."

I did take a turn or two on Tobacco that afternoon without incident. And without sight of French Frank.

Supper went smooth enough, and French Frank

did show up, without his quirt, but with bruises on his face and probably more under his shirt and pants.

No one said anything to him, but there was a noticeable difference in the way the drovers looked at him. Chandler, Smoke, Dogbreath, Reese, Latimer, Drago, Simpson, even Morales One and Morales Two. And I must admit there was a difference in the way those drovers looked at me.

I had finished my nightly chores and was about to make my nightly entry into my journal when I heard the voice of Alan Reese.

"Mr. Guthrie."

"Good evening."

"Mr. Guthrie, I was just passing by Dr. Picard's wagon. The door was open, and he asked me to tell you he'd like to see you as soon as possible."

"Thank you. I'll go right over."

Dr. Picard was at the door waiting.

"She's awake," he whispered, "fully conscious and beginning to ask questions. I thought it better if you'd be here and provide some of the answers. A friendly face, you know."

"Yes, it might. At least I'm a familiar face. We'll see how friendly."

I made my way to a chair next to the bunk where she lay.

In spite of the ordeal she had suffered, Flaxen Brewster looked more beautiful than I had ever seen her.

Her eyes were open and looking straight ahead until she heard the sound of my voice.

"Flaxen. Flaxen . . . it's Christopher Guthrie. Do . . . do you remember?"

First her eyes, then her face turned toward me.

"Yes. Of course I remember, Mr. Guthrie."

"Flaxen, this is Dr. Picard."

Picard took a step forward.

Flaxen nodded.

"The stagecoach," I went on, "overturned. You were seriously injured. Very seriously. Dr. Picard operated days ago. He saved your life."

She smiled but for only an instant. Then the smile faded.

"My father . . ."

"I'm sorry."

She breathed heavily.

"The others?"

"There were no other survivors. Only you and I."

"Miss Brewster," Dr. Picard moved closer. "There's something you ought to know. I did perform the operation, but it was Christopher Guthrie who saved your life. Without his insistence Wolf Riker would not have allowed me to operate. It was almost too late as it was."

"Who is . . ."

"Wolf Riker," Picard finished.

She nodded.

"He's the leader of this . . . expedition," I said.

"Where . . . where are we?"

"Some might say hell," I answered. "Others purgatory. But it's a cattle drive . . . from Texas to Kansas . . . and Wolf Riker is the 'driver.'"

"I'm not sure I . . ."

"You don't have to be sure of anything for now, Flaxen, except for one more thing."

"What?"

"There's a ring on your finger. A diamond ring. An engagement ring."

With some effort she raised her left hand high enough so that the ring became visible to her.

"But, why? How . . . ?"

"Flaxen, please. Save your strength. I'll explain as much as is necessary. Just listen. Will you do that?"

She acknowledged silently.

"Most of the men on this drive are . . . well, less than civil, even less than civilized. If they knew, that is if they . . ."

"Knew about our first meeting?"

"We thought it better that they believed you and I are . . . engaged and . . ."

"Miss Brewster," Dr. Picard interrupted, "it was Mr. Guthrie's idea, and a good one . . ."

"Mr. Guthrie told you . . . about . . ."

"No. It was you. You did a little talking while you were delirious."

"But the ring, how . . ."

"Don't ask a lot of questions. No one will find out," I said, touching her hand. "For now just rest and gain your strength. You'll know everything soon enough. Now, will you do that? Please."

"Yes," she murmured.

"I *am* sorry about your father, Flaxen. And this time, it seems, you did lose Louie."

Flaxen Brewster closed her eyes.

At the door, just before I left, Dr. Picard took my hand for a moment.

"Thank you, Mr. Guthrie. I don't know what I would have done without you."

"I can say the same for you, doctor, both Flaxen and I."

As I walked back toward the kitchen wagon the door to Wolf Riker's wagon opened and he stood at the entrance.

"Guth."

"Yes, sir."

"Are you in a hurry?"

"No, sir."

"Then come in. We'll have a nightcap."

I could not have been much more surprised if he had invited me to high tea. Still, I could not refuse a drink or much else Wolf Riker suggested.

He poured two glasses of Napoleon brandy.

"You paid a visit to your fiancée, did you?"

He knew very well I had, but I nevertheless nodded.

"And she's recovering?"

I nodded again.

"Then we can toast to her recovery."

"And confusion to the enemy."

"That, too," he smiled.

We drank.

"But you and I don't have to be enemies. You're not my enemy, are you, Guth?"

"No, sir. Just captive."

"A pinwheel of fate. And a Boswell. Have you written about me?"

"Haven't had much time."

"But you will, as time goes by, won't you?"

"I'll write about everything and everyone on this drive . . . if I have time."

"Then we must see that you will . . . have time. So long as it doesn't interfere with your duties."

"I'll do my best."

"I'll see that you will. In a way this is a historic drive. Part of the destiny of Texas."

"And Wolf Riker."

"That, too."

"Neither of us knows how it will end, but I don't even know how it began."

"We'll go over that some other time. But I'll tell you part of the beginning."

Wolf Riker took a swallow of his brandy and looked deep into the glass.

"It began between two wars. The war for Texas and the war for the Confederacy—and two brothers. Wolf Riker, the older—years of bone weary work on the docks and at sea to send Dirk, the younger, through school and college, and how the two of them rode west with five hundred dollars that Wolf had saved, to seek their future and fortune.

"And one night after they had crossed the Texas border and made camp, it appeared that they would have neither a fortune—nor a future . . ."

I leaned forward.

"Please go on."

Wolf Riker's eyes seemed somewhat out of focus. I thought it might be the onset of another spell that he was doing his best to fight off.

"I said I'd tell you part of the beginning. The rest will have to wait until another time."

"Yes, sir."

I finished my brandy and rose.

"Guth."

"Yes, sir?"

"French Frank. What you did today. You're gaining strength. Remember what I said . . . 'The strong take it from the weak.'"

"Yes, sir. And at times, the smart take it from the strong."

"Good night, Guth."

"Good night, Mr. Riker."

As I approached the kitchen wagon, Cookie and French Frank were engaged in another whispered conversation, and as I came nearer French Frank turned and walked away. I believe there was a patina of lard on his bruised face.

"You're a busy little bugger, ain't you?" Cookie sneered.

I did not respond.

"I said . . ."

"I heard what you said; but I didn't hear any orders from you so I went about my business."

"Spent time with your fancy fiancée, didn't you?"

"That's none of your business."

"And with Riker in his wagon. Gettin' kind o' chummy with him, ain't you?"

"I visit Mr. Riker only by invitation. Maybe sometime he'll even invite you."

"That's enough of your lip, pansy."

He picked up one of the longest galley knives.

"And don't you forget who's still the cock o' this walk."

Later, by moonlight, I made several entries into my journal, including the first part of Wolf and Dirk Riker's beginnings in Texas.

I found myself eager to hear more.

CHAPTER XXIV

The next day began calmly enough. The air warm and windless. The overall attitude of the drovers temperate enough.

Wolf Riker was determined to get, and keep, the cattle moving at a lively pace, and that's the way the drive began that day, right up to and through the noon meal.

But soon after, the air turned warmer and not as windless.

I had taken Tobacco out for a stretch when I saw some of the drovers, at first Chandler and Smoke, then others, slow, then stop their mounts, lift themselves out of their saddles by straightening their legs from the stirrups.

All looking in the same direction as did I.

There in the distance, just above the flat horizon, there appeared to be a fine, rusty cloud.

The drovers shook their heads, pulled their hats lower onto their brows and settled back into their saddles, some of them lifting kerchiefs from their throats onto their faces.

The cloud slowly sprawled wider and nearer, not gusting, barely spreading.

"Damn."

I heard Smoke mutter as he rode by.

Later I heard some of the rest express themselves more volatilely.

But I was to learn that this was not what the westerners sometimes call a twister—other times call a whirlwind—tempest—sirocco—squall—dust devil—sometimes, son of a bitch.

Those sons of bitches are propelled by wind, usually blinding, gusting, buffeting, swirling wind. But not this son of a bitch.

This was a fine, almost motionless, clinging fog—a fog composed of noxious soot-like dust.

But still it took its toll.

On the cattle, the horses, and on the men.

The cattle were in no mood to move at all, much less at the pace that had been set earlier in the drive.

The horses in the remuda and those being ridden did their best to turn their heads and blink away the particles of dust, but to little avail.

And the men on horseback did their dry-throated best to keep the cattle moving through the impervious blanket of powder.

They cursed and close rode their horses along the cattle, waving their circled lariats at the recalcitrant beeves, while Riker and Chandler exhorted the drovers, who were exhorting the cattle.

This went on for hours. There seemed no end to the rusty pall.

The setting sun was barely visible, a dim circle, fading into the indistinguishable skyline.

Supper was served among more coughs and curses, but general conversation was sparse. No one was in the mood to open his mouth except to eat and drink and rest his dust-caked body.

Leach, in particular, wheezed and coughed more than the rest. Young and strong though he was, he had been riding tail all through the day and swallowing more than his share of dust from both the sky and the wake of the cattle. He barely touched his food, and swayed, almost staggered, as he made his way near the campfire where he'd spread his blanket.

I did manage to take food and drink to Dr. Picard's wagon.

To my pleasant surprise Flaxen was sitting up, leaning against the headboard of her bunk, even though the air inside the wagon was spangled with particles of dust.

She had total recall of our conversation of last night and even smiled.

"Mr. Guthrie," she said, "I hope I didn't seem unappreciative last evening for what you've done. Dr. Picard filled me in with more of the details. I am most grateful, and . . ."

"And you needn't say any more, Miss Brewster."

"Oh, but I must. Something most important."

"Yes?"

"This ring," she held out her hand. "I promise to return it . . . just as soon as possible. You needn't worry."

"I'm not in the least worried. At least not about the ring. There are more important things . . ."

"Such as?"

"Such as the fact that you certainly seem to be improving. That's what's most important. So keep improving."

"I will, and let's hope, so will this dust storm."

"The Greeks have a saying."

"They have a lot of sayings. Which one?'

"*Veltio avrio.*"

"Which means?"

"A better tomorrow."

I walked past Wolf Riker's wagon and, after the day's setback, didn't think he'd be disposed for company, not even for Pepper's—who was leaning against the wagon.

"Good night, Pepper."

Rather than use up any words, Pepper just nodded.

I moved past the campfire, where most of the men were asleep, but a few were still coughing, most noticeably, Leach.

I went to sleep hoping for a better tomorrow.

But it didn't start out that way.

CHAPTER XXV

Unlike the afternoon yesterday, the sky was clear without any aftereffects from the dust.

Unfortunately, the same could not be said for some of the drovers.

As Riker, followed by Pepper, moved up to be served, Leach stood waiting with head bowed almost to his chest.

"Mr. Riker . . ." Leach cleared his throat.

"What is it?"

"Could I speak to you about something?"

"Go ahead and speak."

"No, I mean . . ."

"Alone?"

Leach nodded.

"We have no secrets here, Leach. Anything you have to say you can say in front of your compadres. Go ahead."

Leach muffled a cough with his hand. "Well, you know I been riding tail . . ."

"That's your assignment."

"Well, yesterday, that dust got to me, got to me bad . . ."

"A young, strong specimen like yourself?"

"And I was wondering . . . that is, I . . ."

"Go ahead, man, quit stammering and say what you have to say."

"Could I ride on the flank, or someplace else this morning? Just until . . ."

"Do you hear that, gentlemen?" Wolf Riker interrupted in a loud, clear voice. "Our prison graduate here has turned soft. Up to a short time ago he was chopping rocks, but now he can't abide a little dust, he . . ."

"Mr. Riker," Alan Reese stepped forward. "I'll ride tail this morning if it's agreeable with you."

Simpson moved up next to Reese.

"I'll take a turn at tail after that."

"No, you won't. Neither of you pair of bleeding hearts. Because it's *not* agreeable. You've all been given your assignments, including Leach, and I will brook no insubordination from anyone. Not today or ever, so long as I am in command of this drive . . ."

Leach started to lift his head in what might have been appeal, or defiance, but we were not to find out.

Faster than the eye could follow, Wolf Riker slapped Leach's face forward and backward knocking him to his knees as both Reese and

Simpson grabbed ahold, preventing him from falling to the ground.

"No. It is *not* agreeable," Riker repeated. "My orders stand. Chandler, where are you?"

"Right here, Mr. Riker," Chandler stepped nearer, brushing at his oversize mustache.

"See to it that every man is at his assigned station and stays there. No deviation. Do you understand?"

"I do."

"Good. And we've got to get cracking."

Riker turned toward the serving table.

"Cookie. Guth. Move this line along and keep it moving."

"It'll move," Cookie chortled. "Damn right it'll move."

Then Wolf Riker looked at me and spoke in a soft, matter of fact voice.

"Coffee and biscuit."

I must admit that my hand shook perceptibly as I handed Riker his breakfast, but if the Range Wolf took notice, and I'm certain he did, for little if anything escaped his notice, he ignored my tremor.

He took a bite of biscuit and walked away.

"I'll have the same," Pepper said, then added, "Where'd you say you went to school?"

"Harvard."

"Uh-huh. Well, there's different sorts of schools, son . . . and this is one of 'em."

Pepper, breakfast in hand, moved off toward Riker who stood some distance away.

As I continued serving I noticed that Reese and Simpson, with Leach still propped between them, stopped by Dr. Picard's wagon and knocked on the door. The doctor appeared and after a brief conversation left for less than a minute and returned with a small bottle of liquid which he handed to Reese who nodded, then along with Simpson, escorted Leach away from the wagon and toward the remuda.

Whatever balm was in the bottle might help Leach some, but it was no cure for the treatment Riker had administered.

And I knew that Wolf Riker had seen what had just taken place at the doctor's wagon.

Years ago I had completed my education at college, but on this trail drive my schooling had a long, long way to go.

CHAPTER XXVI

In the time that followed, the drive progressed at a pace that came close to pleasing even Wolf Riker.

One of the things that did not please him, or any of the rest of us, was the sight from time to time of riders in the distance, Indian riders on the rim of hills, silhouetted against the sky. Three, four, sometimes more. Far out of shooting distance, but close enough to keep track of what was going on below.

"Maybe they'll come down and ask for a few beeves," Chandler conjectured at the campfire, "then go away."

"And maybe not," Smoke said. "Maybe they're a scouting party waiting to tell the rest of 'em a good time to hit us."

"Like when?" Dogbreath asked, puffing on a corncob pipe.

"Like when we're crossing a river, or when

there's enough of 'em, or whenever they damn well feel like it," Smoke said.

"The ones that hit the stagecoach didn't have many guns," Latimer observed.

"Yeah," Smoke shrugged, "but maybe these ain't the same ones."

"Then let's change the talk," Dogbreath advised. "This is gettin' pretty damn distressin'." He took a puff from his corncob and did change the talk. "There was this one-eyed saloon gal I bought a drink for at the Bella Union up in Deadwood . . ."

I did not stay for the rest of the story. Neither did Alan Reese.

On the way back to the kitchen wagon I passed Leach and French Frank, who were away from the campfire and the other drovers. Both were sitting under a tree, leaning back against the trunk, smoking.

Both were conversing in subdued voices and nodding to each other, maybe comparing bruises and grievances—and both fell silent and grim at the sight of me coming out of the dark.

My disposition was quite different.

"Good night, gentlemen," I smiled.

"Go to hell," said French Frank.

"And flights of angels sing thee to thy rest," I replied and moved on.

Cookie was already asleep and snoring.

And after a while, as far as I know, so was I.

The pace of the cattle drive was not the only thing that quickened. So did the pace of Flaxen's recovery. Within days she was on her feet, walking inside the wagon, just a few steps at first, but more and more, as she gained strength and even became restless.

During one of my visits Dr. Picard looked at her and smiled.

"One of us is going to have to move out of this peripatetic abode, Miss Brewster, since I don't think we can be considered doctor and patient much longer."

Flaxen started to speak, but Picard continued.

"I think it'll do me good to sleep in the open . . ."

"Oh, no, doctor. I . . ."

"Say no more. I insist. And I will come by from time to time to look in on my former patient. Don't you think that that's a satisfactory arrangement, Mr. Guthrie?"

"I do. But we'd better check with Mr. Riker. He disapproves of any change without his prior permission."

"Why, certainly," Wolf Riker said when I went to his wagon. "I think that's a good idea and I'm happy your fiancée is recovering so rapidly. In fact this calls for a celebration. Miss Brewster, Doc, you, and I will have supper here tomorrow. You think she'll be up to that, Guth?"

"Yes, sir, I think so."

"Good. Cookie can serve and he can get someone to help him. And now sit down, Guth. Do you want me to tell you more about the beginning? For your book, I mean."

"Yes, I do."

It was hard to believe that this was the same brute who threw himself onto a crazed animal with nothing but his bare hands, who mercilessly drove the men past exhaustion, cursed and humiliated them and me, and slapped Leach senseless. The same man who now sat across from me, smiling, inquiring.

"Will you take notes?"

"No, sir. I'll remember."

"Very well. Where were we?"

"You and your brother came to Texas with five hundred dollars," I said and sat at a chair.

"*My* five hundred dollars."

"You had made camp."

"That's right, the two of us."

"And then?"

Wolf Riker lit a cigar, reflected a moment, and went on with his narrative.

"It was late. That day we had covered almost forty miles. We were bone tired, almost asleep on our feet.

"The journey from our native Virginia had

begun weeks before, but the real journey of the two brothers began years before, orphans of a plague, raised in an orphanage, if you could call it that, until I was old enough to run away at the age of thirteen and begin doing a man's work for a man's pay—the railroads—the docks—the sea—scraping and saving every penny, nickel, dime, and dollar to get Dirk out of that pesthole and into a proper boarding school, then university.

"As for my education, most of it came from a professional gambler named Duncan Ravenal. I went to his rescue when he was being beaten up by a couple of sailors who had accused him of cheating at a game of poker. I became his bodyguard–factotum, and in return he taught me the subtle art of shortening the odds at cards.

"Luckily for me, besides being physically strong for my age, I had an excellent memory and deft hands. By the time I was sixteen I could count the cards at blackjack and within a year under his tutelage, just before he died of drink, I could deal seconds and thirds at poker.

"But I made it a point never to win so much as to cast suspicion on a young innocent poker player. Just enough to get by and allow Dirk to finish his education.

"When that time came we traveled west by various modes of transportation and in Arkansas bought guns, holsters, and two beautiful mounts with attendant saddles, and crossed into Texas with my remaining five hundred dollars to seek our fortune.

"Sometime after that we were at the campfire I spoke of. Weary as we were, we fixed and ate supper, took off our gun belts, and started to lie on our blankets to sleep.

"Voices came out of the night, followed by two figures, with drawn guns, each pointing at each of us. Their faces, even though smiling, were no more hospitable than their guns.

"'Well, look here. A couple of jaspers gettin' ready to go to sleep.'

"'They're gonna go to sleep all right.'

"'Good lookin' horses, saddles . . . and guns.'

"He pointed to our gun belts on the ground.

"'And most likely with a bankroll tucked away somewheres.'

"'That'll be easy to find . . . later.'

"Two gunshots splintered the night. But not aimed at us. Both men hit the ground face first, with their guns unfired and with bullets in their backs.

"A man limped out of the shadows, made his way to the two bodies, probed each of them with the toe of his boot, nodded a satisfied nod, then holstered his gun.

"'Evenin', boys. Name's Pepper. What's yours?'

"'Wolf Riker.'

"'Dirk Riker.'

"'Brothers, huh? So were them two.'

"He took a folded poster from a pocket, unfolded it.

"'Sam and Seth Keeshaw—worthless, except for the four hundred dollar reward. Dead or alive.'

"'You didn't give them much chance to stay alive,' Dirk said.

"'They never gave anybody any chance. Not long ago, among other things, they hit the Olang ranch, raped and murdered the mother and daughter, staked the father on an anthill. There wasn't much left of him when I come along.'

"'You a lawman?' I asked.

"'Was. Texas Ranger. Hunter now. Bounty hunter. So was they, in a way. Woulda robbed you and left you dead. Not in that order. From back east, are ya'?'

"We both nodded.

"'If you want to stay alive out here, the first thing you gotta learn is, in the open you either sleep in turns, or with your guns at the ready, not on the ground.'

"'We've learned the hard way,' Dirk said.

"'Not as hard as it might've been.'

"'Thanks to you,' I said.

"'Think nothin' of it,' Pepper smiled. 'I didn't do it for you . . . altogether. Been trackin' 'em for this.'

"He waved the poster, folded it, and put it back in his pocket. 'You fellas thinkin' of settlin' around here?'

"'Might be,' I said. 'If we find a good deal.'

"'Got a poke?'

"'Five hundred.' I patted my pocket.

"'That's a start. Might try Gilead up the trail apiece. There's some prospects around there. The Olang ranch for one.'

"'Say, Mr. . . . Pepper, is it?' I said.

"'Just plain Pepper.'

"'Are you going to take those bodies back for the reward?'

"'Not altogether. Got a sack on my saddle horn.' Pepper pulled a thick, long knife out of a sheath on his belt. 'Just enough from the neck up to identify 'em.'

"And that, Guth," Wolf Riker said, "is how it began. At least with Pepper."

Riker took a puff from his cigar and blew a perfect smoke ring.

"You think that that's enough for tonight, Guth?"

"Yes. I think that's quite enough, Mr. Riker."

CHAPTER XXVII

The next day the good omen was that the Indian riders on the rims of the hills were gone.

The bad omen was that the Indian riders on the rims of the hills were gone.

Among the drovers there were all sorts of conjectures and counterconjectures. But as Pepper put it, all the guesses in the camp weren't worth a spit in the river . . . "Injun figures to do one thing, most likely he'll do 'tuther."

When I saw Pepper that morning I couldn't help looking at the Bowie knife on his hip and thinking of what tales it could tell if that blade could talk. But Pepper did talk, about something else.

"You're gonna have supper with the boss tonight, you and the lady and Doc."

It wasn't a question, but a statement. But he did follow with a question.

"Know who's gonna take your place with Cookie for the time?"

"No, I don't."

"Morales One . . . and Morales Two."

"Why do they call them that? What are the rest of their names?"

"They both stumbled into the ranch some while back, both of 'em bedraggled, on foot, hungry, and with hardly any American to speak of at the time, lookin' for work, any kind of work for any kind of pay—or none at all, just food and lodge."

"'Can you ride?' Riker asks 'em. '*Vaquero?*'

"'*Sí. Vaqueros,*' the older one nods.

"'What else?' Riker inquires. '*Què mas?*'

"'*Cocinero. En la cocina.*'

"'We already got a cook. Don't need anymore,' Riker gets across to 'em, 'that makes you riders— *vaqueros.* What's your names? *Nombres?*'

"'Morales,' one points to himself.

"'And him?' Riker points to the younger one.

"'Morales.'

"'Where from?' Wolf asks the older one. '*Donde?*'

"'Durango.'

"'And you? *Usted?*' To the younger.

"'Durango, Durango.'

"'Oh, so you're both from a place called Durango . . .'

"'No-no.' Says the older one. 'From Durango, Durango.'

"You see, Mr. Guthrie," Pepper explained, "Durango is the name of the village in the state of

Durango in Mexico. So Morales One and Morales Two are from Durango, Durango." Well, Pepper scratched his whiskers and explained further. "We didn't know, or care, whether they was father and son, or uncle and nephew, or cousins or what. So we started callin' the older one Morales One and the younger Morales Two. And it stuck ever since, even though now they do speak some American, not as good as me."

"Thanks, Pepper," I said. "I do appreciate the information, on both counts."

But Cookie didn't appreciate the fact that I was getting the invitation to dine with the boss even though he was getting two helpers instead of one—at least for that night.

The drive made good mileage that day and that made Wolf Riker a more pleasant host that evening.

I had brought Flaxen's suitcase from the utility wagon. She had selected and changed into a more appropriate dress and looked as if she were the "*soigné*" of a society celebration. And she was beautiful and fresh as a spring garden.

In spite of the circumstance of our first meeting, I almost believed that Flaxen Brewster was what she appeared to be. Maybe because I wanted to believe it.

Dr. Picard and I spruced up as best we could, and we three made our way toward Wolf Riker's wagon.

As we passed the campfire, it was not hard to

notice the reaction of the drovers, who stopped talking and smoking as they turned their attention to the three of us. But their attention was not focused on either Dr. Picard or me.

It was as if they had never seen anything like the vision that Flaxen Brewster manifested. And they probably hadn't.

Wolf Riker greeted us pleasantly and played the role of amiable host as if he were on a theatre stage, even to his wardrobe, which was now not all black. Gray was the prevailing color, with a white shirt, and a pearl gray string tie. He did indeed look like the leading men of several plays I had reviewed.

He offered us a before-supper drink, which we all accepted, all except Dr. Picard.

"Still abstemious, eh, doctor? I never thought I'd live to see the day," Riker smiled.

"I hope you live to see many days," Picard returned the smile.

"I'll drink to that," Riker countered.

We sat at the table as Cookie, Morales One, and Morales Two served the best meal I had had since leaving Baton Rouge.

"May I say, Miss Brewster, that you are quite a dazzling enhancement to our . . . expedition. Mr. Guthrie is indeed fortunate."

"Thank you, Mr. Riker. I'd say that Christopher and I are mutually fortunate."

"Yes. And that diamond ring is also quite dazzling. How long have you been engaged?"

There was a momentary hesitation. Dr. Picard glanced at both Flaxen and me.

"A few months," I said. "We were on our way to San Francisco to be married; but now, after what happened to . . . Mr. Brewster, we may postpone . . ."

"Ah, yes. Miss Brewster is in mourning. However, I wouldn't advise waiting too long. Anything can happen."

"Thank you for your advice, Mr. Riker," Flaxen said flatly.

"Pity this isn't a sailing ship," Riker lit a cigar. "Do you mind if I enjoy a cigar, Miss Brewster?"

"Please do."

"The captain could perform a marriage ceremony," Riker inhaled.

"And they could spend their honeymoon on the trail," Dr. Picard added. "Among these blissful surroundings."

"Are you married, Mr. Riker?" Flaxen asked.

This time it was Riker who hesitated momentarily as if stiffened by the unexpected question.

"No."

But he quickly recovered and even smiled.

"But then, I've not been as fortunate as Mr. Guthrie . . . in some ways."

The rest of the evening's conversation amounted

to chitchat and, at times, forced pleasantries, until we rose from the table.

"Do you mind, Miss Brewster, if I offer just a little more advice?"

"Please do."

"I would advise that you find some, shall we say, 'duds' more fitting for the trail. These . . . men, aren't used to viewing such . . . feminine finery."

"I only dressed for this special occasion."

"Very good. And I suppose, like Mr. Guthrie, you are used to having things done for you. Well, I think doing a few things for yourself will hardly dislocate any joints. It seems to have done Mr. Guthrie some good."

"I have done things for myself and will continue to do so, and try not to make myself a . . . burden, until we leave your . . . hospitality."

"And I suggest you keep your door locked when you are alone, Miss Brewster, as a precautionary measure. Mr. Guthrie will accompany you whenever necessary."

"Yes, I'll do that, Mr. Riker," I nodded, "and try not to have it interfere with my duties."

Just a few jottings, by lantern light, in my journal later that night.

I had been unprepared and pleasantly surprised by Wolf Riker's appearance and mostly gracious attitude at supper. He received us more like a southern gentleman of Virginia than a truc-ulent brute, relentlessly driving men and beasts through unforgiving terrain with a contentious crew. He was for the most part civil, and even courteous. Not once did he refer to me as Guth.

Dr. Picard was anything but the trembling, in-ebriated wreck I first met on the drive. Now, he was the picture of sobriety with a ready riposte to Riker's occasional innuendo.

And Flaxen, Flaxen Brewster. I could not have been prouder of her, of her mien and manner, if she actually had been my fiancée.

But Wolf Riker was right about one thing. She had to be heedful about her appearance from here on.

I did not appreciate the way that Cookie eyed her more often than not during the course of the evening. He could barely constrain the lascivious look in his wanton eyes.

At the doorstep of her wagon I could not resist a concluding comment.

"Flaxen, you were magnificent this evening."

"Why, thank you, Mr. Guthrie."

"Don't you think, since we are engaged *pro forma*, we should call each other by our first names?"

"Of course I do," she smiled, "when other people are around."

"You never can tell," I whispered, "when other people are listening—or watching."

"In that case," she also whispered, "a good night kiss, Christopher."

She leaned forward, close, but not quite close enough. From a distance, and in the dark, it did seem like a kiss.

But not to me.

CHAPTER XXVIII

The next morning Cookie's demeanor was even more belligerent toward all the drovers, and even more so toward me. Complaints were followed by curses, then by threats, all mumbled and scrambled so there was nothing specific to reply to. But I gathered it all had something to do with a man of his rank reduced to serving a drunk, a fizzy female, and a stringy ass lackey, who didn't know dishwater from duck soup.

He kept slamming food into plates and shoving the plates across the serving table, almost defying each drover to fetter the plate before it flew onto the ground.

After the drovers were fed I was preparing to take a tray to Flaxen when, unlike last night, Wolf Riker once more became the Range Wolf.

In the distance, Smoke, with something in his hand, extended it to Bucephalus' mouth, and with his other hand patted the horse on its forehead. Buchephalus' head pumped twice up and down, and shuddered; he nickered, and his massive body bolted a step backward.

From out of nowhere Wolf Riker appeared and with whirlwind speed spun Smoke around and smashed his fist into the black man's face with an impact that would have felled and ox.

Smoke did not fall. He staggered, and dropped to one knee.

For an instant it seemed that Wolf Riker would strike the stunned man again. Instead, he stood legs apart and pointed his doubled fist toward Smoke, then motioned and pointed toward Bucephalus.

"Don't you ever touch that animal again, much less try to feed him. No one does that but me. Understand?"

"I understand. And I was wrong, Mr. Riker."

Riker started to turn away but stopped as Smoke's voice went on.

"But don't you ever lay a hand on me again, or I swear to God in heaven . . ."

When Riker did turn, Karl Simpson was standing in front of Smoke with his hands on Smoke's shoulders, silently restraining the black man from doing, or even saying, anything more.

Riker stood another moment, like a human Colossus, then turned not fast, not slow, and walked away past Pepper, who had an insouciant look on his bewhiskered face.

Alan Reese came to Simpson's side, and the two of them led Smoke in the opposite direction.

I thought to myself that if any of the other men, with the possible exception of Karl Simpson, were hit that hard, he would be unconscious for a long, long time, if he survived at all.

I also promised myself that under no circumstance would I go anywhere near a horse called Bucephalus.

And I was grateful that Flaxen Brewster had been spared the sight of such brutality.

But as I had noted before, it was a long way to Kansas, and it seemed inevitable that something similar or, more than likely, even worse, would occur, unless she and I could somehow bow out of Wolf Riker's so-called expedition. And I also noted that for some time I had begun to think in terms of "we," rather than "me." But I said to myself, "we" only until the two of us were out of, and away from, the present circumstance. That's what I said to myself, however, not altogether convincingly.

And in accordance with Wolf Riker's suggestion, Flaxen did find from her suitcase more appropriate "duds" for the trail. To my surprise, Dr. Picard took the reins of his wagon, and Flaxen, from time to time, sat next to him and vacated the narrower confines inside the conveyance.

As often as possible I vacated the seat next to the odiferous Eustice Munger and saddled Tobacco whose fragrance was much more pleasing.

I did my best to ride alongside Dr. Picard and Flaxen as much as possible, but it was not nearly as much as I would have liked.

At one point Riker, straddling Bucephalus, rode up next to the three of us, tipped his black hat with the hint of a smile.

"It's good to see you up and around enjoying the good clean Texas air, Miss Brewster, and those duds are as becoming, or even more so, than your gown."

"Thank you, Mr. Riker," she replied with more than a hint of a smile.

"I hope, Mr. Guthrie, later tonight you'll find some time for us to continue with a certain part of your journal."

"I certainly will, Mr. Riker."

"Good, I . . . goddamn it, Latimer!" he hollered. "Don't ride that animal so close to those horns. I don't want to lose a good horse because you're asleep in the saddle."

And he galloped off toward Latimer and the herd.

Wolf Riker was still the Range Wolf, and not for one minute would he forget his mission, or neglect his obsession in driving the cattle north through Texas, the Indian Territory, the Oklahoma Strip, and into Kansas. After baiting Latimer, I saw him ride toward the rear to admonish Leach because the drag was falling back too far.

It caught up fast.

And during the noon meal I overheard Leach, Latimer, French Frank, and a couple of others grumbling over their beef and beans and what passed for coffee.

But for once Cookie was not grumbling. Quite the opposite. He was grinning as he poked a dirty finger in my face.

"You and your kind ain't the only ones to get invited by Riker," Cookie piped. "He's asked me to come over after supper tonight. What do ya' think of that, Mr. Pansy Pants?"

"I think that's very egalitarian, Mr. Munger."

"Damn right," Cookie smirked.

CHAPTER XXIX

That evening the two of us, Flaxen and I, supped out in the open, but apart from the others. And after, we sat under a star studded sky, silent, but not for long.

She looked at the diamond ring on her finger as it sparkled in the moonlight.

"Do you believe in fate?"

"Call it fate, destiny, chance, kismet." I looked upward. "The stars. Divinity. The Bard put it his way, 'There is a divinity that shapes our ends, rough-hew them how we will.' It's hard to look up there and not believe in something. What makes you ask?"

"The way we met. Being on the same stagecoach. Just the two of us surviving. Dr. Picard. This ring. It all must add up to something."

"Survival. If we're not devoured by wolves. One wolf in particular."

"Would you say that he is evil?"

"I'd say that his scale tips in that direction. His favorite quote is 'better to reign in hell, than serve in heaven.'"

"And you? Do you have a favorite quote?"

"Right now I'd have to say, '*Les choses ne sont pas toujours ce qu'elles paraissent.*'"

"Translation please."

"'Things aren't always what they seem.'"

"Who wrote it?"

"That great French poet Christopher Le Guthrie."

As we both laughed we saw Cookie walk out of Wolf Riker's wagon, rather unsteadily, and move toward the kitchen carriage.

"What do you think of our chances?" she asked.

"Better than the cattle."

Cookie weaved his way back toward Riker's wagon with a fistful of money, money that I knew damn well was mine.

"Probably"—I nodded toward Mr. Munger—"even better than his, tonight."

"What do you mean?"

"I mean, let's not talk about him."

"All right, then tell me about yourself."

"Why?"

"Because I'd like to know. How is it that you were on your way west? Were you in the war?"

"I'd have to answer your second question first. But then will you tell me more about yourself?"

"Yes. Later. But please, go ahead."

"All right."

Without benefit of too much embellishment I capsulized my background with my father, Harvard, the law firm of Guthrie, Talbot and Flexner, my enlistment and service with the War Department's Bureau of Military Justice, my father's death and my mother's diamond ring, my literary achievements, and critical contributions to Horace Greeley's *New York Tribune.*

"Christopher Guthrie," she nodded, "you know, now that you've refreshed my memory, I have heard of you. I believe I even read one of your novels . . . *The Conquering* . . . something or other."

"*The Conquering Coward*, but don't hold that against me."

"But why did you leave Greeley's newspaper and New York?"

At this point I smiled and went into a little more detail.

"Well, you see Flaxen, it was like this: Horace Greeley, as you may or may not know, is one hell of a newspaperman, self-made, self-educated son of a poor New Hampshire family, who set out for New York and new horizons, which he found at the bottom of the newspaper game and from which he worked himself up to publisher of one of the two most powerful papers in the city. Greeley looks like a scarecrow, with a circular face and circular spectacles, giving him an owl-like countenance; but he is politically wiser than any wise old owl. The night before, I had written a review of a play that starred an actress named Ann Treadwell, and the next morning I was summoned into the office of lord and master Horace Greeley. I knew what to expect so I went prepared.

"'Good morning, Mr. Greeley.'

"'Mr. Guthrie,' Greeley did not rise from his desk or offer his hand. 'This is Mr. Jamison Damask.'

"Mr. Damask also failed to rise from his chair or offer his hand, but did nod toward the beautiful lady sitting next to him.

"'This is my fiancée, Miss Treadwell.'

"'Ah, yes,' I responded. 'The actress.'

"'Not according to your review,' Miss Treadwell pronounced in her studied stage voice, which was much too studied.

"'*Most* of the reviews,' I noted.

"'But yours,' Damask replied, 'was particularly scathing.'

"'Incisive,' I corrected.

"'Invective,' Damask retorted.

"'And,' Miss Treadwell added, 'how would you like to have that smirk slapped off your face?'

"'It's been tried.'

"'Only by women?' Damask rose to his full height.'

"'Guthrie,' Greeley growled, 'I think . . .'

"'*I* think Mr. Damask was about to challenge me to a duel.'

"'Would you accept?' Damask somehow grew even taller.

"'No.'

"'Why not? I think a duel between you and I would be . . . interesting.'

"'May I choose the weapon?'

"'Of course.'

"'Then I choose grammar . . . and between you and *me*, Mr. Damask, you've already lost.'

"Jameson Damask took a step toward me.

"'Just a moment, sir,' I smiled.

"'Will you write an apology?' he said.

"'Better than that. Mr. Greeley can write it, if he chooses.' I removed a folded paper from my pocket. 'My resignation from the Tribune, gentlemen . . . and Miss Treadwell. I do hope that is satisfactory to all.' And I placed the paper on Greeley's desk.

"'Well, in that case,' Damask grunted, 'I believe that concludes our business here. Come, my dear.'

"They both left with Miss Treadwell making a center door fancy stage exit.

"Then Greeley rose and picked up the resignation paper.

"'Chris, this wasn't necessary, you can . . .'

"'No, I can't, Horace. I know Jameson Damask is a big business man who buys a lot of advertising space in your paper. I also know that you're going to run for president against U.S. Grant and Damask is a big party boss whose endorsement can get you the nomination.'

"'Well . . .'

"There's no well to it. Besides, I'm going to take your advice.'

"'What advice?'

"'You've been saying it for months—'go west, young man.'

"'Oh, that,' he smiled.

"'Yes, that. But I'm also going to write a book, about the glorious prospects the west has to offer: adventure, opportunity, riches, romance. When I've finished you can serialize it in the Tribune. Mr. Damask should have cooled off by then.'

"'Not a bad idea,' Greeley grinned, and this time he did offer his hand.

"We shook, and I walked to the door but turned back.

"'One more thing you ought to know, Horace.'

"'What's that?' he asked.

"'I'm going to vote for Ulysses Simpson Grant.'

"And that, my dear Flaxen, is how I happened to come west and meet a certain young lady."

"And you, my dear Christopher Guthrie," she smiled, "are quite a raconteur."

"Now tell me your story."

"I said 'later' and it's getting quite late."

"You're right. And I have a date."

"With whom?"

"Wolf Riker. He asked me to stop by and listen to his story. But first I'll walk you 'home.'"

I did.

And this time she did lean forward, quite close enough, so it more than seemed like a kiss.

CHAPTER XXX

On my way from what was now Flaxen's wagon, under which Dr. Picard now slept, walking toward Wolf Riker's wagon I heard voices whispering through the night, voices emanating from silhouettes sitting in a semi-circle smoking pipes and cigarettes.

The voices, as best as I could determine, belonged to Leach, French Frank, Smoke, Dogbreath, and probably Latimer.

"He's gone crazy or skin close to it."

"Coulda killed Smoke, the way he hit him."

"I'm sick of eatin' drag dust."

"We'll soon be deep into Indian country."

"Maybe we already are."

"For what? A payday we'll never live to see."

"Drinkin' swill that passes for coffee."

"There's gotta be border raiders ahead."

"Once we cross the Texas border we'll never get back."

"I say we make a break and head home."

"What home?"

"Anything's better than this."

"Gettysburg wasn't."

"The war's over."

"This one ain't."

"I say we grab what supplies we can and . . ."

I cleared my throat louder than necessary, much louder.

"Good evening gentlemen," I remarked.

"How long you been standin' there?" French Frank bristled.

"Not standing. Just passing by."

"Where to?" Dogbreath sucked on his corncob.

"As a matter of fact, to Wolf Riker's wagon."

"To tell him what you heard?" French Frank stood up.

"What I heard, if anything, nobody else will hear. I give you my word."

"That ain't good enough for me," French Frank doubled a fist.

"I'm afraid it'll have to be. As a matter of fact I'd like to throw my lot in with you if it weren't for . . ."

"For what?" French Frank said.

"For Flaxen Brewster, my fiancée."

"He's right," Leach nodded, then turned to me. "Maybe sometime you can be of help to us."

"Maybe I can," I said and walked toward Riker's wagon.

"Come," Wolf Riker called out in response to my knocking. I entered and stood inside the threshold without closing the door.

"Yes, do come in Guth."

"Sorry to interrupt, Mr. Riker, but you did ask me to come by and . . ."

"Of course I did. Close the door. Cookie and I are drinking a gentleman's drink and playing a gentleman's game."

From what was left in the bottle of Napoleon brandy, he poured some of the contents into two tumblers in front of Cookie and himself. There were cards and a pile of money on the table between them.

Cookie's wet, pale eyes were swimming like lazy summer seas, and he was mumbling something about being the son of a gentleman born on the wrong side of the blanket as he downed a deep gulp of brandy. It was evident that he had already downed many deep gulps.

Riker also drank with no apparent effect and picked up the cards.

"You know how to play NAP, Guth?"

"No, sir. That's a game I never learned."

"Well, Cookie does. You care to play some more, Cookie?"

"No, no, I don't," Cookie slurred as he finished

the brandy left in the tumbler and rose unsteadily. "Not now."

"Well, there seems to be more than three hundred dollars here," Riker collected the money and stacked it into a neat pile.

"You know that's my money, Mr. Riker," I said.

"That's a lie!" Cookie screeched. "A dirty goddamn lie!" He swung wildly with his fist at my face.

I stepped back and he missed and would have fallen if I hadn't grabbed him and held him upright, but not any longer than I had to.

"A dirty goddamn lie," he continued to mumble, but managed to weave to the door, open it, step through, and slam it shut behind him.

Suddenly, Wolf Riker emitted a spate of laughter, and just as suddenly his face turned serious.

"Why did you take that, Guth? Let him swing at you and even held him up when he was going to fall? He's drunk; you could have taken the advantage."

"And done what?"

"Whipped him. That's what! He's your inferior and still you suffer his abuse. You're still soft. You should have smashed him."

I looked at the money in Riker's hand, then back at him.

"You have my money now. Shall I try and smash you?"

"Ah, but that's different."

"How different. Because you're my superior?"

"On this drive, yes. Besides, might makes right. It's the law of nature."

"Does that justify your stealing my money?"

"Be careful, Guth."

"Yes, I will be that."

"Don't you ever play cards, Guth?"

"Not NAP, but I'm a pretty fair hand at poker."

"So am I. We should play a few hands sometime."

"No, thanks."

"Why not?"

"Because . . . either way, I'd lose. And now shall we say good night, Mr. Riker?"

"No. Not at all. I feel like talking if you feel like listening to the next part of the story."

"Yes, I do."

"Well, then, get yourself a clean glass and sit down."

I did both.

"All right," Wolf Riker said. "Where were we?"

CHAPTER XXXI

"Where were we?"

Riker had asked. I knew that he knew damn well where we were the last time he left off with his story, and that he was just testing me and my memory.

I took a sip of brandy.

"Pepper had just saved you and your brother's lives by backshooting two wanted killer-bandits and was about to utilize his Bowie in decapitating the bodies and carrying back their heads in a sack as identification to collect a four hundred dollar dead or alive reward. He also mentioned that there might be some good ranching prospects around a place called Gilead where you could invest your five hundred dollar poke."

"Very comprehensive summary," Riker nodded. "You *were* paying attention."

"I still am. What happened after that?"

"We took Pepper's advice and sometime later we were in Gilead at a saloon called The Prairie Port. It looked pretty nearly like any other Texas saloon except it had a painting of a schooner over the bar and was owned by an erstwhile sailor, with a peg-leg, named Captain Jack, and who was, often as not, upstairs with one of the saloon doxies.

"The Prairie Port featured whiskey, women, and poker. Neither Dirk nor I was much interested in whiskey or women at the time, but the poker game was another matter. We tarried over three or four drinks while I studied the game and the gamblers.

"There were six players and more money on the table than there is in some banks. The most colorful character called himself Reginald Truscutt-Jones, wore a fancy hat and everything that went with it including a pearl handle pistol more fit for a woman.

"He also had more money in front of him than any of the other gentlemen, and they all were gentlemen; ranchers, a lumberman, a steamship owner, and I didn't catch, or much care, about the rest.

"Truscutt-Jones spoke with a haughty English accent, had a straight, narrow nose, hawk eyes, and a pencil mustache over his pink upper lip.

Mr. Truscutt-Jones, from time to time, removed his hat, wiped with an embroidered handkerchief at his brow and the hatband, then went back to winning.

"Standing at a distance, leaning against the wall, was an interested spectator who could have been, and probably was, until recently, a prizefighter. He wore a semi-squashed derby and a semi-squashed nose.

"As I nodded to Dirk after analyzing the situation, we both saw a familiar figure limping down the stairs accompanied by another figure, female, very female, who didn't need all that war paint to go with her orange hair.

"'Greetings, fellas,' Pepper grinned a satisfied grin, and bowed toward the orange-haired lady. 'Velma, these here are the Riker brothers, acquaintances of mine, and I'm gonna buy the four of us a round or so of drinks and spend some more of that four hundred reward money you boys helped me collect.'

"Pepper ordered, and we drank while Velma scrutinized both Dirk and me, while I continued to scrutinize the poker game.

"After a while one of the gentlemen who was devoid of money, rose from the table and went out of the door minus a couple of thousand.

"I nodded at Dirk and he nodded back in favor.

"'Excuse me,' I said and took a step toward the game.

"'Just a minute, son,' Pepper said, 'you ain't thinkin' what I think your thinkin', are you?'

"'I wouldn't, mister,' Velma added. 'Those boys don't play for marbles and chalk.'

"'Listen, boy,' Pepper shook his head. 'I been watchin' that game some and . . .'

"'I've been watching it, too, Pepper, and I thank both of you,' I said and started to move away.

"'That poor cooked calf,' I heard Pepper say. 'Your brother's walkin' himself straight into poverty.'

"'My brother'—Dirk swallowed his drink—'can walk on fire or water . . . he thinks.'

"'Is that chair open, gentlemen?' I smiled as I inquired.

"'By invitation only,' one of the players answered, 'and it takes cash to get invited.'

"'Five hundred cash for openers,' I said and withdrew a roll of bills from a pocket.

"'Welcome, stranger,' the Englishman nodded. 'There's your chair. We play five card draw, jacks or better to open.'

"Without bothering with introductions the game proceeded.

"After about half an hour I had at least doubled

my poke. Truscutt-Jones' pile also increased, and the rest of them were luckless.

"I seldom went directly up against the Englishman and his fancy hat.

"In due time the other players went broke and Truscutt-Jones and I each had over five thousand stacked in front of us.

"'Well, stranger,' the Englishman said, 'it seems that you and I are the two survivors.'

"'So it seems.'

"'You have won a great deal of money.'

"'So have you.'

"'I'm used to winning.'

"'I'd like to get used to it, myself.'

"'To keep winning, you have to keep playing.'

"'Sounds logical—up to a point.'

"'The point is we can call it a day, each with a healthy profit or . . .'

"Or what?'

"'Keep playing until there is one winner with a huge profit. What do you think, stranger?'

"'It's your game. I'm just sitting in. What do *you* think, Mr. Jones?'

"'Truscutt-Jones.'

"'Ah, yes. Truscutt-Jones. Your call.'

"'One hand for the entire pot.'

"He put the deck on the table.

"'High card deals.'

"I nodded and cut. Drew a jack.

"He drew a king, shuffled, and started to deal. Nobody in The Prairie Port drew a breath as each of us read our hand.

"'Cards?'

"'Two.'

"'Dealer takes one.'

"He dealt himself a card, removed his hat, put it on the table, drew a handkerchief from his pocket, wiped his brow, then the inside of his hat, put it back on, and looked at his cards.

"'Well, stranger,' he smiled, 'what do you have?'

"'Just a minute,' I said. 'You have two choices, Mr. Truscutt-Jones.'

"'What are you saying?'

"'I'm saying you can fold without showing your hand or . . .'

"'Or what?'

"'Or play the hand that's in your hatband, because that's the hand I'm calling. Take your choice.'

"Truscutt-Jones looked up at the man with the semi-squashed nose who took a step forward, then stopped.

"'In that case . . .'

"Truscutt-Jones started to draw his pearl handle pistol but he was already looking into the barrel of my .44.

"'Mine's bigger,' I said.

"'Then I have no choice.'

"He rose, holstered his pistol, and started to move away.

"'Come, Stoker.' He nodded to the man with the derby who began to follow him, but suddenly turned toward me.

"However, Dirk had leaped across the room and threw a left into Stoker's kidney, followed by a right into his oblong jaw, felling him like a shot buffalo.

"Both Truscutt-Jones and I were aiming at each other when a shot rang out and the Englishman fell gripping his right shoulder.

"Pepper limped toward us with his gun ready for anything more.

"But there wasn't anything more. At least not to speak of."

Wolf Riker finished the brandy in his glass and smiled.

"Well, that's the end of that part of the story. That enough for tonight?"

"No," I said. "What about the Double R? How did that come about?"

"You want to hear that part, too?"

"Yes."

"Well, that'll call for another drink."

He opened a fresh bottle of Napoleon and poured.

"A few days later we were back at The Prairie Port and so was Pepper—he was *still* there."

"'Have you two fellas made up your minds how you're gonna spend all that money?'

"'We already spent most of it. Bought a ranch,' I said. 'We were just going to have a drink and ride out there.'

"'Mind if I ride along? I've pertiner spent that four hundred and not on no ranch,' he grinned.

"'There it is,' Dirk pointed in the distance. 'Ten thousand dollars worth of adobe, sticks, bricks, and thousands of acres of land.'

"'We bought it from the widow of Don Carlos Acosta, Consuela, who wanted to go back to her birthplace in Mexico,' I said. 'She signed the Spanish land grant over to us, and I've got it right here in my pocket.'

"'Looks like you got somethin' else,' Pepper said, 'company.'

"Three swarthy figures stood on the porch of the otherwise deserted main building of the ranch. Pistols on their hips and one of them held a rifle.

"I introduced my brother and me as the new owners.

"'Who's the other gringo?' The rifleman pointed with the rifle.

"'A friend,' I said.'

"'You haven't brought enough friends,' the leader said.

"'What does that mean?'

"'It means we are Don Carlos' brothers, and we want our share.'

"'The ranch belonged to his wife, and we bought it from her.'

"'We don't think so.'

"'This deed in my pocket thinks so.'

"'A thousand pesos apiece will close the deal.'

"'Got no pesos—or dollars—for you.'

"'Gold? Silver?'

"'Just lead,' Dirk said.

"'Lead won't buy anything—but death.'

"'Ride away, Pepper,' I said.

"'I intend to.' Pepper turned his horse.

"Two of the swarthies went for their guns. The other one started to raise his rifle. He never brought it up.

"Pepper shot him in the chest. Then killed another one as Dirk and I drew and fired again and again, some shots alternately missing and hitting, until all three were on the ground twitching and dying.

"Pepper appeared more amused than otherwise affected by the incident. He stepped off his horse, glanced at the trio of bodies, and began to reload his gun.

"'Glad you came along,' Dirk said.

"'Had nothin' better to do. Still don't.'

"'What about the Texas Rangers or bounty hunting?' I asked.

"'Leg's gettin' a mite stiff for either; 'sides, I'm gettin' a little tired of travelin'. I ain't no gypsy.'

"Dirk and I looked at each other and smiled.

"'You know, Pepper,' I said, 'three times now we've been beholden to you.'

"'Right,' Dirk nodded. 'If it weren't for you we wouldn't be here—have this ranch.'

"'Why don't you stay here with us?' I suggested. 'Be foreman, or whatever you want to call yourself.'

"'Call myself Pepper. What're you gonna call this ranch?'

"'The Double R,' we both said, since we had already talked it over.

"'Double R. That's a good brand. But like I mentioned before, if you two fellas want to stay alive . . .'

"'We do,' both of us said.

"'Then there's a few things'—he pointed to our holsters—'I gotta teach you about guns.'

"And that"—Wolf Riker started to lift his glass—"is how the Double R . . ."

But suddenly he put the glass down on the table, closed both eyes, and rubbed his forehead.

"That'll be all for tonight, Guth. You can go now."

"Do you want me to . . ."

"I don't want you to do anything but go." He slammed a fist on the table.

I rose and moved toward the door.

"Good night, Mr. Riker."

CHAPTER XXXII

I had just closed the wagon door and taken a step or two when I saw a figure leaning on the side of the wagon with a cigarette glowing in the dark.

"Hello, Pepper."

"Hello yourself."

"Just had an interesting session with Mr. Riker."

"That so?"

"Told me about a certain card game, then a visit with his brother and you to what became the Double R ranch."

I waited momentarily for some reply from the figure but none was forthcoming. Only smoke from the darkness.

"Did you ever teach the two of them more about the use of guns?"

This time there was a reply.

"There's them that found out the hard way."

"Dead?"

"That's the hard way."

"Uh-huh. May I ask you one question?"

"You can ask."

"What caused the animosity between him and his brother?"

"It's more than . . . animosity."

"You didn't answer the question."

"I'm not goin' to."

"Why not?"

"'Cause that's up to him to tell you that . . . when, and if, the time comes."

"I see. Maybe you'd better go inside. He doesn't seem to be feeling so well."

"He'll let me know if he wants me."

"How?"

"I'll know."

"I'm not sure I understand."

"No. You wouldn't. But you might say we're close as Siamese sisters. Good night, Mr. Guthrie."

"Good night . . . Mr. Pepper."

As I moved on I heard another voice identifiable as George Leach.

"Just answer the question, Reese. Are you with us?"

"I'll answer, and don't ask me again. I signed on to finish the drive and I'll stay on until it's finished one way or another."

"Well, we've got the other. French Frank, Dogbreath, Smoke, and some of the rest of us."

"Don't tell me about it. I don't want to know."

"He's crazy and before long you'll change your mind and be with us."

"'For they have sown the wind, and they shall reap the whirlwind.'"

"What's all that about?"

"It's about the Bible."

Alan Reese turned and walked away. So did I. In another direction. This time I thought it best not to be heard or seen.

Crazy or not, I had found myself, while listening to Wolf Riker, completely fascinated, and even carried away from the situation we now faced. I wanted to hear more about the ranch, the two brothers' struggle for its success . . . and why they became such bitter enemies. Even now I thought about how he was suffering in the wagon and did not want me, or anyone else, ever to witness him in such a weakened and vulnerable state.

But my thoughts were interrupted once again. This time by the sight of Dr. Picard sitting and leaning against a rock near his and Flaxen's wagon, while smoking a curved ivory pipe.

"Seems like everyone's up late tonight, doctor."

"When I drank I didn't smoke, but now . . . well, everyone has to have some vice."

"And some have more than one," I smiled.

"You've been visiting our leader again, have you, Mr. Guthrie?"

"Doctor, were you ever with him when he has those . . . headaches?"

"Yes. But he won't let me stay, or try to help him."

"I think he goes nearly blind. Do you know what causes them?"

"I'd like to think it's some sort of divine retribution. Of course that's not a medical opinion."

Picard took a moment to relight his pipe.

"Mr. Guthrie, I've heard different versions— also that an operation might cure the condition. But, of course, he refuses to discuss the situation. However, there are other issues to contemplate."

"Such as?"

"Such as . . . we have the better part of a thousand miles to go on treacherous terrain with dwindling supplies, the makings of a mutinous crew, Indians on the horizon, a maniac in command, who has a brother who might do anything to stop him and us. Just to mention a few."

"That's quite enough, thank you."

"You're welcome. Pleasant dreams, Mr. Guthrie."

CHAPTER XXXIII

Of all that had happened the day and night before—Wolf Riker's confrontation with Smoke over Bucephalus—his verbal blistering of Latimer and Leach—driving the drovers at a headlong pace—supper with Flaxen and telling her of Horace Greeley—bidding her good night—overhearing half a dozen drovers conspiring to pull out, or worse—Riker winning my money from a drunken Cookie—listening to Riker's tale of winning another card game with an assist from Pepper—the three of them, Wolf, Dirk, and Pepper, disposing of three interlopers—the birth of the Double R brand and ranch—Riker struck by another seizure—Alan Reese's refusal to join the other conspirators—and Dr. Miles Picard's appraisal of our prospects and odds of ever finishing the drive to Kansas—the last thing that came to

my mind before falling asleep was a kiss from
Flaxen Brewster.

For a good part of the next day the drive moved
at what now was our customary pace.

Ridges. *Rincones.* Barrancas. Cathedral moun-
tains in the distance. Dry. Desolate. Land that had
been conquered time and again.

Yet remained unconquered.

Tobacco and I were riding near point not far
from Wolf Riker, astride Bucephalus.

Chandler and Smoke, who had been scouting
ahead, came riding back as if their hair was on
fire. They reined in close to Riker and pointed
back to the direction they had come from. I rode
up within hearing distance. So did half a dozen of
the drovers.

"Eagle Pass ahead," Chandler said swallowing his breath. "Can't go around. Got to go
through . . ."

"So?" Riker said.

"Indians."

"How many?"

"Maybe a dozen at the pass. Maybe more elsewhere."

"Comanch', I think," Smoke added.

"Armed?"

"Most of 'em," Chandler nodded. "Seems like
they want to talk . . . for starters."

"Then we'll talk . . . for starters. Guth, go back.

Bring up a bunch with guns. Leave enough to guard the herd. Smoke, you talk Comanch'?"

"Some."

"Stay close to me. Well, Guth, get moving."

I did.

Within minutes word had spread along the drive.

I rode up to the wagon with Dr. Picard at the reins and Flaxen next to him.

"Indians," I said. "Flaxen, you get inside and stay there."

"No, I . . ."

"Don't argue. It's best they don't see you."

"He's right," Picard nodded.

Pepper pulled his wagon alongside.

"Guthrie." He reached down under the seat, brought up a gun belt and holstered revolver, and held it out toward me. "Strap this on. At least you'll look dangerous."

I complied, then started to ride and catch up with Riker and the others.

Pepper produced a rifle and followed in his wagon.

At Eagle Pass there was a line of about a dozen mounted red men and a line of more than a dozen drovers with Riker in front, along with Chandler and Smoke next to him.

Riker moved his horse ahead a short distance and motioned to the Indian who carried the coup stick of a chief. A coup stick that was at least as old as the chief.

Without saying a word Wolf Riker took a cigar out of his shirt pocket, struck a match, lit the cigar, and inhaled. He motioned for Smoke to come forward and pointed to the Indian leader.

"Ya-ta-hey," Smoke said.

"I talk white man's language," the old Indian replied.

"Good," Riker nodded. "You talk good. Where did you learn, white man's school?"

"White man's prison."

"I see. My name's Wolf. Yours?"

"Moondog, chief Blue Snake lodge."

"Congratulations," Riker removed another cigar from his pocket and extended it. "You smoke, Moondog?"

"Later. Maybe."

"Good. What do we do now?" He put the unlit cigar back into his pocket.

"You have many cows."

"And many guns. So what do we do now?"

"You want to take cows through," Moondog pointed at the pass.

"We're *going to* take them through."

"Maybe."

Moondog spoke in his language to a young buck near him who then held up a rifle.

"One shot," Moondog said to Riker, "your cows stampede, scatter."

"He fires one shot, Moondog"—Riker nodded, and pointed to Pepper and his rifle—"and the second shot will be in your heart, which is not made of stone."

There was an uneasy silence while Moondog thought it over.

From what I could determine, the venerable chief and most of his followers did not appear to be in first-class fighting condition, or anywhere near it. Most were undernourished. But there was still the matter of how many more might be skulking and what condition they might be in.

"We take cows to lodge," Moondog said.

"Maybe. How many?"

"Ten cows . . . and . . ."

"And what?"

"Five horses."

"Two cows . . . and no horses."

"One horse . . . yours."

"About the time you grow whiskers."

"What is whiskers?"

"Beard," Riker scratched his chin and pointed to Pepper. "Besides, this is too much horse for you, Moondog."

Without any apparent signal Bucephalus reared high and chopped both his forelegs in the air.

"You can take four cows, and"—Riker and Bucephalus moved closer to the chief, then Riker reached into his pocket again, removed another cigar, extended both the lit and unlit cigars—"two smokes."

Moondog looked at Riker's face, down to the two cigars, over to Pepper with the rifle, then back to Riker's face. The Indian's expression never changed. Neither did Riker's.

Then Moondog spoke.

"Four fat cows. Two smokes," he nodded. "You go through." He took the cigars, put the lit one in his mouth and puffed, then pointed the coup stick at Bucephalus. "You got good horse."

"And you, chief, got good sense."

I thought to myself, Wolf Riker, you are not only a dictator, you are a diplomat . . . at times.

We spent the rest of the day getting the steers, the wagons, and the remuda through the pass and into the vast Texas plain that lay ahead.

CHAPTER XXXIV

Later that evening I made sure I had occasion to talk to Pepper alone.

"Thanks, Pepper."

"What for?"

"The opportunity to appear dangerous." I started to unstrap the gun belt he had loaned me.

"You'd best keep it, Mr. Guthrie, chances are you'll have more such opportunities. It's a good rig, belonged to a good man. Me."

"Thanks. I know you don't like to answer questions about Wolf Riker . . ."

"Depends on the question and who's askin'. Go ahead."

"Well, I was curious about him and his horse, how . . ."

"That's somethin' I don't mind you askin', or me talkin' about."

Pepper pulled out the makings and started to roll a cigarette.

With mathematical precision, but without seeming to think about it at all, he began construction—with the tissue thin paper in one hand and pouch in the other, he poured the precise amount of tobacco across the rounded frame, rolled it with thumb and forefinger into a perfect cylinder, while exposing the outer edge which he passed along his tongue, pulled the pouch closed by its string in his teeth, replaced the pouch in his pocket, produced a match, stroked it against the seat of his canvas pants, lit the pale white tube, inhaled its effect, and spoke.

"In the few years that passed since the Double R brand was burned into the first hide, them two fellas became first-class cowboys. They could both of 'em rope and ride and handle guns and rifles, and I do admit to doin' a little tutorin' along the way.

"The Double R prospered and more than tripled in area. That Dirk, he was a shrewd businessman, got us a contract to sell beef to the U.S. Army, although Wolf weren't particularly partial to the Union. He come to be a staunch Texan.

"We raised a lot of beeves, hired a lot of hands, and needed a lot of horses for the roundups.

"That's where a fella named Julius Kokernut come in. Horse breeder and trader. As fair and square a fella as ever you'd want to cross the river

with. Prior to the spring roundup he brings in a
string of forty or so: roans, buckskins, overos,
strawberries, sorrels, and palominos—stallions,
mares, colts, and among 'em a yearling, bigger
and blacker than the rest, a wild fractious bastard;
but Wolf couldn't take his eyes offen' him. He was
a horse and a half. Nervous. Wouldn't stand still.
Eyes burned and flashed. Nostrils flared and he
kept showin' a lot of teeth.

"'How much for that one?' Wolf asked Kokernut.

"'Same as the rest. Forty dollars, but I want to
keep doing business with you boys so I got to warn
you, nobody's been able to ride him, or even get
a saddle on him, just a bridle as you can see. Even
tried throwin' a cape over his head to saddle him,
but he just backs away, swirls, circles, and kicks
out. Don't like to be blinded. He's crazy, tried to
stomp me, came near shooting the son of a bitch.
He'll do for breeding; but don't try to ride him.'

"'I'll ride him. Forty dollars, right?'

"'Done deal,' Kokernut nodded.

"Wolf started to walk toward his new horse.
Dirk put an arm on his brother's shoulder.

"'Wouldn't want to see you crippled.'

"'Neither would I, and I won't be.'

"'Wolf,' I pointed, 'that hellbender might have
a different opinion.'

"He was stompin' his forelegs and kickin' up
behind him.

"'Pepper,' Wolf smiled, 'you ever hear of Alexander the Great?'

"'Nope . . . and neither has that horse.'

"Wolf paid no mind to what anybody said. He just glided toward that horse with the bridle reins danglin', shyin' away from his own shadow, and joltin' his bull-broad head up and down, while Wolf's whisperin' to him like a Dutch uncle. Slow and easy, Wolf takes hold of the reins, and gentle-like leads him into the sun, away from his own shadow so the shadow is behind him, sweet talkin' all the time, 'til the horse drops his muzzle toward the grass, then does Wolf swing up onto his bare back with just a little pressure of the reins on the bit, soft strokin' and calmin' that animal who settles down to just quiverin' some. Wolf loosens the reins even more, applies a dollop of pressure with his knees, and turns him loose Comanche style. By then Wolf's made a friend who just wants to gallop free, and gallop he does like a black spirit of the wind almost as far as the eye can see and back, until Wolf reins him down to a cantor and brings him to a stop right near where they started with the sun straight ahead.

"From then on it was him and the horse—and the horse and him. Named him Bucephalus, just like that Alexander fella's horse."

Pepper took the last drag of his cigarette, the last that it was possible to take without burning his whiskers.

"That horse went with him to war, through many a campaign with J.E.B. Stuart, clear across the country. Truth is, never thought either one of 'em would ever come back, but they did, man and horse, both with the scars to show for it."

"What about his brother, Dirk?"

"What about him?"

"Did he go to war?"

"He did. But that's another story for another time. It's a long way to Kansas."

"What if we don't make it to Kansas?"

"Then maybe you won't hear the story."

"Just one more thing . . ."

"Make it short, I'm not about to build another smoke."

"You mentioned you did a little cowboy tutoring to the two of them."

Pepper nodded.

"Including guns?" I asked.

Pepper nodded again.

I pointed to the handle of the gun and holster he had given me.

"Would you tutor me?"

"It'ud have to be away from the herd, so they couldn't hear the shots."

"You mean I'd actually have to shoot bullets?"

"What do you think you kill people with, marchmellas?"

"Well, would you?"

"Maybe," he said, looked at me and almost smiled.

Then we both said it together.

"It's a long way to Kansas."

Pepper turned and limped way.

'It's a long way to Kansas.'

That phrase had been repeated several times recently and probably would be repeated several more.

But distance isn't always measured geographically. It was much farther in mileage from New York to Baton Rouge and the Texas border, but I had traveled that distance in relative comfort and safety, by steamboat and rail—and even stagecoach—until we crossed into Texas. The food was mostly palatable, the beds usually comfortable. But once fate flung us—Flaxen and me—into the world of Wolf Riker and his compulsive cattle drive, distance was no longer measured by mileage—but by obstacles and odds.

Comfort and safety were things of the past. Each day and night, each mile was gauged by hindrance and hazard.

I had intended to write about the glorious prospects the west had to offer, opportunity and riches of Horace Greeley's west—and now I wondered if, instead, I were writing my own epitaph, an epitaph that no one would have the opportunity to read.

But such thoughts were interrupted by someone

I had least expected to see until I immediately remembered something Pepper had once said: "There are times when Riker likes to take a walk at night out in the open . . . by himself . . . just to think about things."

And evidently, that's what Wolf Riker had been doing.

"Hello, Guth," he said with a black cigar still in his mouth.

"Good evening, Mr. Riker. Out for a little constitutional?"

"You might call it that."

"What would you call it?"

"Contemplation . . . quiescence."

"Conscience?"

"I left that behind sometime ago, otherwise I wouldn't be this far."

"How far do you intend to go, Mr. Riker. Kansas?"

"And back to Texas, and the Double R as it once was, and far beyond."

"An empire?"

"You might say that."

"No matter what it takes?"

"What do you think it took to get me where I am? To educate myself? To dig it all out? To read those books you see in my wagon and a hundred more. To fight the odds with every fiber of my being . . ."

"To kill?"

"That, too. The earth is full of brutality, even as life is full of motion . . ."

"You've read Darwin . . ."

"Yes, and it all comes down to might is right and weakness is wrong."

". . . and misunderstood him."

"Not at all."

"But to take a life . . . lives."

"Life is the cheapest thing in the world, Guth. There's only so much water, earth, and air. But life demanding to be born is limitless, nature spills it out with a lavish hand."

"What gives you the right to take it?"

"Strength. Ambition. And infinite loneliness."

"Out there . . . by yourself?"

"That's part of it."

"But today I saw another part of you . . . with that Indian chief."

"There's a time to fight and a time to negotiate . . . so you can fight later. That, too, is a part of this place called Texas."

"I've learned one thing about Texas."

"What's that?"

"There's a hell of a lot of it."

"Not enough for my brother *and* me."

Wolf Riker dropped the dead cigar, turned, and walked away.

I started to move in the opposite direction near the campfire where the drovers were asleep.

But Leach, Dogbreath, French Frank, Smoke, and a couple of the others were not asleep.

I didn't know how much they had seen and heard of Riker's walk alone, or of our conversation—but I knew it was too much—and did not bode well.

CHAPTER XXXV

Cookie at one time had described himself to me as "the eyes and ears of the drive," as part of the connection between him and Wolf Riker. But as the drive progressed, if that's what you could call it, and after Riker relieved him of the money Cookie had stolen from me, that connection seemed to become somewhat tenuous. Even more so since Riker and I spent more time in each other's company.

Eustice Munger's antagonism toward me became increasingly overt, except when Riker was present. Cookie was quick to find fault. I didn't move fast enough to suit him, didn't clean the pots thoroughly enough, served too much, or not enough, food on the drovers' plates—a dozen other misdeeds, including spending too much time on Tobacco, and far too much time on my journal.

One night, he broached the subject even when

I hadn't begun to write. We were still cleaning up after supper.

"And what is Mr. Daffodil goin' to write about tonight?"

"What I do and write about on my own time is my own business, Mr. Munger."

"Is it about you and Riker? Or I'll wager it's about you and that fancy fiancée . . . describin' her 'charms' . . . haha . . . she's a chesty piece of work for one so delicate—I seen you kissin' her and feelin' her up and down . . ."

"Shut your filthy mouth about her, or . . ."

Before I finished, Cookie picked up his dirty towel from the table and swung it hard across my face, then lifted his knife and held it close to my throat.

"You'll listen to me talk and take it, Guth. That's what you'll do. You might've put on some muscle since comin' on this drive, but you're still no match for ol' Eustice Munger and his little friend."

He laughed, sheathed the knife, and started to turn away.

I grabbed hold of a meat cleaver and twisted him back around. I clutched Cookie by the throat and thrust the sharp edge of the cleaver against his nostrils forcing his head upward.

"You shut up about her, you insufferable bastard . . ."

My voice trembled and so did my hand. Anger. Even madness.

". . . You lay a hand on me again and by heaven, I'll split your head. You son of a bitch."

"Guth . . . hold on . . . I . . ."

"I'll clean the pots and peel the potatoes . . . do my work, but if you ever so much as say anything about her . . . or touch me again, you'll have to kill me or I'll kill you."

I shoved him away and swung the cleaver down, driving the blade into the table.

I'm not sure who was more surprised, Cookie or I. But it was Cookie who moved away. Who retreated. And it was I who stood my ground, at least for the present time—my ground—and hoped that it was not apparent that my hand still trembled as I realized that I was not alone.

The incident had been witnessed by half a dozen or so drovers who were still standing nearby, among them Leach, French Frank, Dogbreath, Smoke, Alan Reese, Karl Simpson, Dr. Picard, and in the background Wolf Riker and Pepper. To my great relief, Flaxen Brewster was nowhere in sight.

As Riker moved toward me, followed by Pepper, the other men receded, slowly at first, and then at a more lively pace, amid murmurs of astonishment.

"Well, Guth," Riker almost smiled, "it appears you're beginning to get your sea legs, even though we're not at sea. You might even get to be one of us, if you survive. That meat cleaver came in handy. But you can't carry it around in your holster." He pointed to the gun. "That's not just an ornament, you know. Better be prepared to use it when the time comes."

I said nothing because I didn't know what to say.

"In the meanwhile"—Riker took one of his black cigars from his pocket and extended it toward me—"enjoy one of these. There's an old saying, 'smoking serves to steady nerves.'"

He started to move away, but turned back. This time he was smiling.

"You look like you could use a little steadying."

The truth was I did need more than a little steadying, and I knew it. So did Pepper.

For just a moment, he touched my shoulder with his left hand.

"You did good, son. Damn good. But Riker's right about that gun, and he's about as good with one as anybody I ever seen, him and his brother both. But there was a time when they wasn't. You said you wanted to hear about my 'tutorin'' 'em. Still do?"

I nodded.

"Well, it's early yet. Let's find a spot to sit where you can light up that stogie and relax."

We did just that.

Wolf Riker's black cigar was not nearly as potent as it appeared, and after a while I did find myself relaxing as Pepper talked.

"Well, durin' that little set-to between them

Meskins and us at the ranch, I found myself havin' to do more'n my share of killin' in order to settle the situation. Them two boys did more shootin' and missin' than the situation called for.

"So once we got sort of settled, I took both of 'em out to a place where they weren't likely to shoot any bystanders 'cause there weren't none . . . and started tutorin'.

"Had 'em stand side by side and me nearby offerin' gun lore.

"'Now, first off, there's them that keep the hammer on an empty chamber. I'm not one of 'em, might need that extra chamber. Now, the most important thing is this: Never, never squeeze the trigger unless you're willin' to kill. Understand?'

"They both nodded.

"'Because if you're not willin' to kill without hesitation, you could be killed, because the other fella probably won't hesitate. And that's the difference 'tween the quick and the dead—that one split second of hesitation—understand?'

"They both nodded again.

"'And don't do anythin' stupid like aimin' to wound. That lets 'em get off another shot and maybe kill you. Got that?'

"'Got it,' they said.

"'Good. Now, don't go aimin' for the head.'

"'Why not?' Dirk asked.

"'Too small a target and moves quicker than

the rest of the body. The chest, boys, that's the place, broader and slower and where the heart is. A vital organ.'

"'Now speakin' of that, don't give 'em a good target by standin' square on. The less they have to shoot at, the better chance of comin' out alive.'

"'And forget that crap about watchin' their eyes. Nobody shoots with his eyes. He shoots with his thumb and trigger finger. When he starts to move you move—unless you figure he's faster and you decide to move first.'

"'That's not exactly fair,' Dirk noted.

"'Sometimes it's exactly necessary. Don't worry about bein' fair . . . worry about bein' alive. Don't squeeze unless you got a damn good reason to kill . . . Like us with them Meskins . . . otherwise they'll probably hang you. Ever see anybody hang?'

"Both boys shook their heads.

"'It ain't pretty. Now, let's give it a try.' I pointed to the guns in their holsters. 'Hook. Draw. Fire.'

"'See them two branches hangin' down on that tree over there?'

"They nodded again.

"'Them two branches is the hearts of two bastards who want to kill you. When I say 'now' their hands are commencin' to move. You boys move, too.' Dirk's on the left. Wolf's on the right. 'Hook.

Draw. Fire. Fast but not too damn fast or the barrel won't be level. You ready?'

"Again, they nodded.

"'So're they. Now!'

"Hook, draw, fire is what they done.

"Both missed. But not by much.

"After dozens of times and dozens of branches, bottles, and cans, and I don't know how many cartridges . . . they didn't miss anymore.

"They was both first-class pistoleros and not a hair's breadth of difference between the two of 'em."

Pepper shrugged as if to say that that was as much of the story as I was going to hear tonight. But I wanted to hear more. I took a puff and persisted.

"I've heard both you and Wolf Riker talk about his brother, but I've no idea who he really was, or is. Or even what he looks like. Do they look alike? Same size? Same eyes, blue? Cold blue?"

"Well, I don't go around lookin' at eyes, men's eyes. But yes, I guess they're both changeable blue. And you could sure tell the two of 'em apart. As for size, Dirk's a mite taller, but Wolf's broader. Dirk's smoother and more educated, but Wolf's got what I call a 'native cunnin' and unpredictability. You never know which way he's gonna spring."

"I've noticed that."

I took another puff of Wolf Riker's cigar.

"If it came to a . . . well, a . . ."

"Showdown?"

"Uh-huh, let's call it that, a showdown . . ."

"They had one of them, just before the war . . ."

"And?"

"They're both still around, but next time one of 'em won't be."

"Which one?"

"Well, like I said, 'there's not a hair's breadth of difference between 'em.'"

This time there was a note of finality in Pepper's voice.

I still wanted to hear more. But this time I thought it better not to persist.

On my way back to my sleeping quarters, still smoking what was left of Wolf Riker's cigar, I got as far as Dr. Picard's wagon and stopped. The reason I stopped was because of Flaxen. She was standing just outside.

"You shouldn't be out here," I said.

"I just stepped out when I saw you coming. Actually, I was looking and waiting, hoping you would. I see you've taken up cigars," she smiled.

I let the cigar drop to the ground.

"Cigar, singular. Don't think I'll make them a habit out here."

"You never can tell. I also saw part of what

happened between you and Cookie. Are you all right?"

"Yes. But I didn't see you."

"I didn't want you to see me."

"In case I . . . lost?"

"But you didn't lose. What was it about?"

"Don't remember," I lied.

"Did it have anything to do with me? Because I don't want you to have to defend . . ."

"I was defending myself . . . and here I thought you were waiting to . . . say good night."

"Maybe I was. But from now on, I think we'd better just . . . 'say' it."

"Are you breaking our engagement?" I smiled. She lifted her left hand.

"I'm still wearing the ring."

"Keep wearing it."

"I will . . . while we're on this drive."

"That'll do for now, but remember . . ."

"Remember, what?"

"It's along way to Kansas."

"Good night, Christopher."

"Good night, Flaxen."

CHAPTER XXXVI

How close we were getting to the Red River and the Texas border, I did not know, and none of the drovers was sure. There were no maps available; but we were all sure of one thing. With every passing day we were getting that much closer. And with every passing day Riker was that much more and more demanding of the drovers. Consequently the men seemed to feel less like men and more like galley slaves.

Outwardly, they couldn't, or wouldn't, be too obdurate toward Wolf Riker, so, more and more they gave vent to their antipathy by taking it out on each other. The least little action or word was taken as an affront. They had never been King Harry's few, the happy few, the band of brothers, but now they became for the most part a regiment of resentment and discontent.

I recall part of the conversation I overheard early one Sabbath morning at breakfast between

Dogbreath and Alan Reese as Dogbreath let loose with a litany of complaints.

". . . but, Dogbreath, look around, behold the wonders about you, examples of God's plenty . . ."

"Yeah, plenty of what we don't need—rocks, dirt, sand, shit, and Indians . . ."

"Dogbreath," Reese smiled, "the trouble with you is you are an inveterate pessimist."

"And the trouble with you, tongue-wagger, is you're a born sugar eater."

Each workday began earlier, sometimes even before first light, and lasted longer, sometimes until the men and animals were but moving silhouettes blending into the darkness.

Some of the men, though far from content, bore the situation in sullen silence, and went about their tasks. But others were not so silent and gathered in small groups with thundercloud expressions on stark faces, harsh voices, and sidelong glances in the direction of Wolf Riker.

These more overt dissenters included Leach, French Frank, Dogbreath, Smoke, and Latimer.

Rumors of defection became rampant, but Wolf Riker continued pressing without seeming to take notice—until one morning at breakfast when he began addressing the drovers, almost casually—at first.

But not so casually as he went on.

"What I'm about to say isn't due to all of you, but it's meant for every man jack of you who saddled up back where we started. So all of you listen. Listen, and remember."

A sheet of silence fell over the camp. There was no more rattling of plates or slurping from cups. No one ate or drank as Riker continued.

"You all knew what we were up against before you signed on. I told you plain enough. But sign on you did.

"And I promise, I swear—you're going to stick to that agreement. Most of you didn't have two plug nickels to rub together—and your only possible payday was, and still is, in Kansas.

"Look around you. Everything you see belongs to me.

"The cattle is mine.

"The remuda is mine.

"And for most, the horses and saddles you ride are mine.

"The food you eat, and the coffee you drink, such as it is, are mine.

"And I know the kind of talk that's been going on between the would-be quitters among you.

"Quitters and thieves who'd take horses and food that belong to me, and desert.

"For those of you who harbor the notion of deserting, know this, I'll do what the army does to deserters.

"I'll shoot you.

"If any of you think you can outdraw me—try it now.

"Any one—or more than one."

Wolf Riker paused—and waited.

Nobody said a word—or moved an inch.

Except Riker.

"Then that's all. Now finish your breakfast and get to work."

Riker turned and walked away as he had at other times—toward Pepper, who canted slightly to one side, with that imperturbable look on his face.

Just a few hours later, a seemingly different Wolf Riker rode up beside me.

Tobacco and I were out for a sprint some distance from the drive when I heard hoofbeats from behind, then turned and saw the horse and rider next to me—Riker and Bucephalus.

But this was not the grim visage of the man who had confronted the dissentient drovers earlier that morning. There was an almost pleasant aspect, even a touch of humor, in his disposition.

"Out rather far from the drive, aren't you Guth? Thinking of defecting, by any chance?"

"No, sir, just daydreaming. Didn't realize I'd ranged this far. Besides, after that lacing you gave everybody this morning, I wouldn't think of chancing it."

"Or of leaving your betrothed behind."

"That's an even better reason."

"That lacing, as you call it, wasn't for everybody—just a few turn-tails in the ranks."

"You can't have that."

"I can't and won't. By the by, does your fiancée ride?"

"What?"

"Ride. Horseback. Your fiancée, does she ride?"

"Uh, why . . . yes."

"When she's up to it, I'll have Pepper pick a horse and saddle for her so the two of you can ride together sometime. It'll be a change from that bone-bruising wagon."

"Speaking of Pepper . . ."

"Were we? Oh yes, about the horse and saddle you mean?"

"Not that."

"What then?"

"The knife. The Bowie knife. How it came into his possession."

"I told you—Jim Bowie gave it to him."

"But under what circumstances?"

"He probably won't tell you the truth, so I will. Pepper and Bowie were rangers together. They, and a dozen more, were sent after a band of Comanche raiders. When they ambushed the Comanche camp there was a hell of a remembered fight. Hand to hand. Bowie was wounded. Shot in the right arm. Dropped the knife and fell to the ground. As a Comanche buck raised his lance to make the kill, Pepper picked up Bowie's knife and split the buck's head in two.

"Later, when Houston needed time to build a force against General Santa Anna's advancing Mexican Army, he sent Bowie to command the Alamo along with Colonel Travis. Pepper wanted to go, too. But Houston wanted Pepper to stay with him.

"Before Bowie left, he told Pepper that he had had three of these knives made. He had given one to his brother, Rezin, and since Pepper had saved his life with Bowie's own knife, the second Bowie knife would go to Pepper—the third to the Alamo with Bowie. Nobody knows what happened to the Alamo knife, since there were no survivors . . . but ol' Pepper still has his."

As we rode I was mesmerized by his tale of Pepper and the casual way Wolf Riker told it.

"That is an amazing story and certainly worthy of being written about."

"Go ahead and write it—if you get the chance. But that's not quite the end of the episode."

"Then please—go on."

"Well, you know about the Alamo. After thirteen bloody days came the final assault by four thousand Mexican troops. All one hundred eighty-three Texans were killed, but so were over fifteen hundred of Santa Anna's soldiers. Santa Anna ordered the bodies of the Texans to be burned, but out of those flames came a battle cry, 'Remember

the Alamo' and Houston got the time he needed.
A little more than a month later, Sam Houston
with Pepper at his side, led eight hundred Texans
in a surprise attack at San Jacinto on Santa Anna's
army of more than twelve hundred and fifty,
killing over six hundred and capturing the rest,
including Santa Anna.

"But in the battle Pepper was wounded in the
leg. And that's why he still limps."

I turned to look at Riker and make a comment,
but Wolf Riker was looking at something else.

In the distance three mounted Indians had cut
out a half dozen steers and were doing their best
to herd the abducted beeves as far away as they
could get.

Riker and Bucephalus bolted ahead as if
primed from a cannon.

I don't know why, but I followed. Maybe it was
because I instinctively reasoned that two riders
would be twice as discouraging to the Indians as
only one. Maybe it was because I didn't think at
all. But follow I did, although at not nearly the
same pace. Or nearly with the same effect.

Truthfully, I had no effect at all, nor did Wolf
Riker expect, or need, any.

Without slackening his pace Riker started to
pull his Henry out of its boot, but halfway, changed
his mind. He decided to go with his handgun.

One of the fleeing Indians with a rifle fired
his single shot Spencer. It was the last shot he'd

ever fire. The Indian missed. Riker's Remington handgun didn't.

The Indian tumbled to the ground and Riker and Bucephalus trampled over him and kept shooting and riding through the scattered beeves and after the two remaining red men who did their best to fire their ancient weapons and escape.

Their best wasn't good enough.

Riker's fourth shot shattered the lagging Indian's spine, his fifth and sixth shots brought down number three. All three dead.

We had been too far away from the main herd to be stampeded by the exchange of gunfire, which must have sounded like little more than "pop-pops" in the distance, but close enough to be heard by the drovers riding point.

By the time Riker reined in, patting Bucephalus, and I rode up next to him, Chandler, Smoke, and Reese were galloping toward us with their guns drawn. Since all three Indians were on the ground deceased, it was obvious that the drovers might as well holster their firearms. And they did.

Riker didn't waste any words in his instructions.

"Get some more help. Gather up the steers and bury the red bastards. Smoke . . ."

"Yes, sir."

"Comanche?"

"Comanch'."

"Poor artillery . . . and poor shots."

Then Riker turned to me.

"Come on, Guth; let's get back."

He started to ride and I followed.

After we'd gone a ways, I felt it suitable to make an observation.

"You didn't handle these Indians like you did Moondog, Mr. Riker."

"I told you there was a time to negotiate. This was not such a time. In the first place, these Indians weren't inclined to talk things over. They started shooting."

"And in the second place?"

"I don't need a second place."

CHAPTER XXXVII

During the rest of the day and into dark, during supper, the conversation mostly centered around what happened between Riker and the three expired Indians.

Chandler, the trail boss, was particularly vocal and descriptive of Riker's mettle and marksmanship, even though he hadn't witnessed the actual encounter. The results spoke for themselves. Particularly when the drive passed the site of the three fresh mounds of earth and rock that marked the outcome.

While some of the "turncoats," as Riker had referred to them, undoubtedly still harbored thoughts of defying or defecting, the prospect of going up against Wolf Riker must have been somewhat dampened—at least temporarily.

As for Riker himself, it was as if nothing out of the ordinary had occurred. His only overt reaction to the incident was the fact that he was seen emptying the shells and re-loading his Remington handgun. Otherwise, it was just another day on the drive to Kansas.

I did see him paying a little more attention to his mount, patting, currying, feeding, and whispering to Bucephalus.

There was one other thing.

Pepper made it his business to come up to me when I was alone.

"The boss says you showed some grit when you was with him earlier today."

"I don't call it grit, just watching him dispatch those three red rustlers—not by any stretch."

"The point is—you didn't ride in the other direction," Pepper said, and limped away.

It was sometime later that night that Riker did bring up the subject.

Alan Reese, Dr. Picard, and I were near the campfire when Riker walked up with his cigar. He spoke to Reese, but so all of us could hear. There was more than a touch of irony in his voice and attitude.

"Mr. Reese, I understand that after burying those Comanches, you took the time to say a prayer over their graves."

"If you're concerned about the time it took, I'll make it up to you, Mr. Riker."

"No, that's not it at all."

"Then, what, sir?"

"You think those savages believe in an afterlife?"

"I've heard that they do."

"The happy hunting ground?"

"Something like that."

"Where they can steal cattle, horses, and wives?"

"Maybe where they don't have to."

"I see. Well, so long as it's not my cattle . . . you think your prayers can help them get there?"

"I don't know, but . . . it's possible."

"However, you and they don't believe in the same God."

"Maybe there's only one God . . . with many faces."

"I don't remember reading that in that Bible you have from the man they killed sometime back."

"There are many interpretations of that Bible, Mr. Riker."

"There are also many fools who interpret it. Good night, gentlemen."

When Riker had walked too far to hear, Dr. Picard looked after him, shook his head, and sighed.

"It was easier to listen to that man when I was drinking. But drunk or sober, I can't fathom what the hell obsesses him. At times he seems to be Lucifer incarnate."

"That," I said, "may not be so far from wrong,

and in accordance with his favorite quotation—
'better to reign in hell, than serve in heaven.'"

"Yes," Reese added, "but at one time Lucifer
was an angel. Milton's quotation goes on. 'Hurled
into hell, he was unbeaten. He led a lost cause
and was not afraid of God's thunderbolts. A third
of God's angels he took with him.'"

"Well, here's one angel," Picard said, "he's not
going to take with him. Not after this drive, no
matter what happens. I think he's crazy, don't
you, Mr. Reese?"

"There's another quotation from another
book, 'Judge not, that ye be not judged.'"

"What is this? Some kind of Bible session?"

George Leach smirked and took a step closer.

"I heard what the three of you and Riker were
talking about."

"I imagine you did," Picard smiled. "You're
quite adept at that sort of thing, Mr. Leach."

"And other things, too."

"The sort of things that land you in prison."

"There's no law against listening."

"Or eavesdropping?"

"Not if it means staying alive, and that's what I
intend to do—and so do some of the rest of us."

"There are three dead Indians buried back
there who had the misfortune of coming up
against Wolf Riker," I said.

"Maybe so," Leach grunted. "But I ain't no Indian."

"Nor a grammarian," I noted.

"How's that?"

"Not important, Mr. Leach."

With that, Mr. Leach smirked again, and left the three of us.

On the way to my quarters I saw something I didn't like. Flaxen and Cookie near the chuck wagon. And I particularly didn't like the look on Cookie's dirty face, and by the tone of my voice, had no qualms about expressing my point of view.

"What are you doing out here, Flaxen?"

"Why . . . just returning the supper plate and . . ."

"Oh, hello Guth," Cookie grinned, "the Missy and me was just visitin' and talkin' about . . ."

"Whatever it was, the conversation and the visit are finished. Come along, Flaxen."

I took hold of her arm more firmly than necessary and led her away.

"Well, well," Cookie cackled, "if that don't beat all."

He went on cackling and mumbling but by then we were far enough away that we didn't have to listen.

"Christopher," Flaxen said, "do you expect me to stay in that wagon all the day and night?"

"No, I don't, but stay away from that skunk. He's rotten to the bone and . . . well, just stay away from him. Will you promise me that?"

"Any other instructions, master?" She smiled.

I knew that she was being coquettish, but I didn't mind a bit . . . so long as she kept her distance from that unsavory son of a bitch. And the truth was, the less distance between her and me the better I liked it.

Whether it was her hand that first reached out, or mine, I wasn't quite sure, but by then we were walking hand in hand. And I do believe that, for both of us, it felt quite normative.

"By the way, speaking of your getting out, earlier today Wolf Riker said he'd ask Pepper to pick out a horse for you to ride, that is, if you can ride. Of course, I told him you could. You can? Can't you?"

"You'd be surprised." She went on in her coquettish fashion.

"Miss Brewster, nothing you can do would surprise me."

"That could be taken several ways."

"It was meant to be taken several ways."

"I don't know whether to be flattered, or flustered."

"I think you do," I smiled my most cavalier smile.

"Flattered it is then . . . and Christopher . . ."

"Yes?"

"Seriously, I do appreciate all you've done for me, I . . ."

"Say no more, fair maiden. 'Tis no more than

any gallant knight would do for a beautiful damsel in distress."

"I *was* in distress, Christopher, in more ways than one. Sometime I'll have to tell you about it, about my father and . . ."

"Don't tell me a damn thing. There's nothing more intriguing than a mysterious woman, besides, as for being in distress—right now, I'd say that describes both of us."

"You're not," she smiled, "going to say 'it's a long way to Kansas,' are you?"

"You've already said it. And since we've arrived at your boudoir, I'll just say, in parting, good night."

"None of that 'sweet sorrow' stuff?"

"Not tonight, Juliet."

"Then good night, Señor Montague."

She let go of my hand, but her face leaned forward, then slightly upward.

There was only one thing to do—and I did it.

CHAPTER XXXVIII

Pepper picked out an eight-year-old mare and brought it to Flaxen while I was there.

"I'm mighty particular about who rides her, and from now on it'll be nobody but you, that is if the two of you take to each other. Call her Bluebell on account of her color. She is smooth as velvet and can go the distance. Saddled and ready to set out . . . if you are."

"I am." Flaxen nodded.

"Here, give her this lump of sugar and some sweet talk, then step up."

A short time later we were galloping side-by-side, Flaxen and Bluebell, Tobacco and I, and it wasn't that easy for the male contingent to keep up with the female set. But it was easy to see that the two of them had "taken to each other."

On the way back to the drive when we were no longer galloping, I had the opportunity to inquire.

"Where did you learn to ride like that?"

"You ought to see me bareback."

"I'd like to," I smiled, "but you haven't answered the question."

"A fellow I know once said 'there's nothing more intriguing than a mysterious woman.'"

"About some things, not horses."

"This is no ordinary horse, this is Bluebell."

"And you, Miss Flaxen Brewster, are no ordinary woman."

"You know, Christopher, riding out here, just the two of us, it's hard to believe what's happening to us is real."

"It won't be hard to believe when we get back to a wolf named Riker, who's taking seven thousand beeves to slaughter—and maybe us with them."

And it wasn't long after we did get back that reality once again became amply evident.

"Guth, did you use, or take, or see one of my Messermeister blades? The six-incher?"

The pride of Cookie's collection of cutlery was a set of six kitchen knives imported from Germany, with blades of four, six, eight, ten, and twelve inches.

I answered that I had not.

This prompted an outburst of the loudest,

foulest, most vile curses I had ever heard, so filthy that even the hardened drovers looked at each other in disgust.

And with each string of epithets, Cookie's inflection became louder and more repugnant as the veins in his filthy throat seemed about to burst.

Until all of us, including Cookie, heard the sound of Wolf Riker's voice.

"Shut up, Cookie! Right now, shut your damn mouth!"

Silence.

But Cookie was still shaking as Riker broke the silence.

"What the hell is going on? What happened?"

"I'll tell you what happened. One of these bastards stole my six-inch Messermeister blade. Sharp enough to cut through stone, and when I find out him who done it, I'll . . ."

"You'll do nothing. I do the doing around here. And if that blade isn't returned, all of you'll be the sorrier for it."

Riker suddenly backhanded Latimer and knocked him to the ground in a quivering heap.

The poor man was still shaking as he managed to stutter and speak.

"I . . . did . . . didn't take it . . . I . . . swear . . ."

"I didn't say you did. But that's just a sample if

I find out who did take it before it's returned. You just happened to be standing closest."

Once again a shroud of silence fell over all those present.

And at first nobody moved.

Chandler, Leach, Smoke, Simpson, French Frank, Dogbreath, Reese, Drago, Morales One, Morales Two, Dr. Picard, and all the rest. Then Reese and Simpson stepped out, bent over Latimer and lifted him to his feet. Latimer, still in a daze, instinctively rubbed at his tufted face as the two men helped him move away.

"All of you," Riker commanded, "finish up here and get back to the herd."

Then it was Wolf Riker, whose hand went to his own face, stroked at the scar on his temple and turned, walking in the opposite direction where, once again Pepper was waiting.

As we collected plates and cups Cookie continued mumbling curses until both Reese and Simpson came back.

"Mr. Guthrie," Reese asked, "would you give me a cup of coffee for Mr. Latimer?"

"Yes, of course."

"I don't know who took that knife," Karl Simpson said. "But if he wants to cut stone, he might try it out on Riker's heart."

Reese glanced at Cookie, then put a restraining

hand on Simpson's arm as if to warn him against further comment.

It was an expedient gesture on Reese's part. I was certain that Eustice Munger still considered himself the "eyes and ears" of the drive and in order to curry Riker's favor would eagerly report and exaggerate any insubordinate remark made by anybody on the drive.

After Reese and Simpson left, Cookie squinted and started to reach out to tap my arm, but I managed to move just far enough to avoid his touch.

"Guth," he said, "you got any suspicion?"

"About what?"

"Not what. Who."

"Who what?" I gibed.

"You know—who lifted my blade."

"No, I don't, Mr. Munger, but if I were you I'd keep a close watch on the rest of those blades."

"What do you mean?"

"Nothing much, except he, or they, might want to add to the collection."

"You all think you're pretty smart 'cause you're educated, don't you? You and Picard and that Missy . . ."

"I also wouldn't say another word, particularly about Miss Brewster."

"I seen you and her ridin' off to some place where you . . ."

"Cookie." It was Pepper's voice. "Fix up a plate I can take to the boss."

"Right away," Cookie nodded and began to 'fix up a plate.'

"How is Mr. Riker?" I asked Pepper.

"'Livin' lightin','" he answered.

But that was the first time I'd ever heard Pepper volunteer to take anything to Wolf Riker.

CHAPTER XXXIX

Part of what happened next, happened while I wasn't there.

I have a feeling that that will be more and more the case before this journal is finished—if it ever is finished.

From time to time I would recall Wolf Riker's prediction concerning me—*'I'll be interested in the change . . . There will be a change, there has to be . . .'*

And up to that time I had changed some. I had begun to carry a weapon. I had become more and more protective of Flaxen. And I had tolerated less and less abuse from that misanthrope called Cookie.

But before the end of that particular day there was an even more evident and enduring change.

From first light the sky had hung heavy and humid, barely shielding the curling clouds that threatened to explode with the wet fury of a Texas downpour.

But the storm didn't come—at least not that storm.

We were, all of us, soaked with the sweat of our own clothes. Perspiration dripping into our eyes and lips as the drive pressed north toward the Red River. And we were getting closer, as evidenced by the narrow forks of its confluent streams, streams that were no more than knee deep, unlike the Red River, itself, which in rainfall could flood its banks and submerge the shoulders of a tall man on horseback.

Luckily for the drovers, Riker chose to camp near one of the streams, and the men took the opportunity to plunge belly down into the rivulet, some with, and others without, the clothes they had worn during the drive—but, of course, without their guns, gun belts, and cartridges.

Even I, stripped to my underwear, sank into the refreshing runlet—as did all of us, all except Wolf Riker, Pepper, Dr. Picard, Flaxen, and, of course Eustice Munger, who seemed averse to anything liquid except for whiskey, which he had been consuming more than usual through the entire day and evening.

It was late, and everyone was asleep, except for the outriders guarding the herd—or so I thought. I was awakened by some sort of sound. I was unsure of what that sound was, since my mind was still somewhat clouded by the effects of a restive sleep.

I stirred, leaned against both elbows and noticed that the area where Cookie normally slept was vacant.

I rose and looked around through the darkness, but there was no sign of Cookie or anybody else except the sleeping drovers surrounding the glittering campfire. I quickly made my way to Flaxen's wagon. To my relief the door was closed, but the relief was short lived as I instinctively turned the knob and the door opened. The wagon was dimly lit by a lamp; but the bed and wagon were empty. I turned and made, for no particular reason, toward the stream where I saw just what I did not want to see.

Two familiar figures—struggling.

And then heard a harsh, hushed voice—as I stood momentarily frozen.

"Shut up you little wildcat, or I'll choke the life out of you . . . I'll have my way, and you'll tell nobody!"

One hand was at her throat, the other under her nightclothes at her breast, while pressing his rude lips against her face. She tried to scream, but he then covered her mouth with one hand while the other searched and moved up and down the front of her body.

It was only for a scant couple of seconds, but it

seemed an eternity before I lunged like a mad man at the two figures by the side of the stream.

I crashed into Cookie, who let free of Flaxen as I grabbed him by his shirt and smashed my fist into his sweaty face. But with a fury he fought back in a whirlwind of kicks and blows, gaining the advantage with a knee into my groin.

He slid, then made it to his feet scrambling away, but with me in pursuit.

Dizzy from drink and the effect of my blows, he weaved toward the campfire as I rammed into his back and sent both of us onto the ground again.

The camp came alive with drovers aroused from their sleep.

I twisted him toward me, held him against the ground and beat my fist into his body and face as he did his best to unsheathe his knife.

They had appeared from everywhere, Leach, Dogbreath, Smoke, Simpson, Reese, French Frank, Morales One, Morales Two, and the rest including Dr. Picard, Pepper, then Flaxen and Wolf Riker.

Cookie's knife was in his hand, slashing toward me, ripping across my forearm, drawing blood from a palpable gash. I managed to grasp his knife hand and pound it against a stone near the campfire.

The knife dropped and I hit him—relentlessly—again and again, all my civilized instincts gone as

Cookie begged me to stop—but I didn't—until I saw:

Wolf Riker grinning.

I let loose of the battered, bleeding wreck, who dropped in an unconscious heap. I picked up Cookie's knife, paused . . . then tucked it into my own belt, breathing the deepest breaths I had ever drawn.

Most of the drovers seemed amused by this nocturnal diversion, but not Dr. Picard who appeared incredulous. As I rose unsteadily, Picard, Reese, and Simpson moved to Cookie's inert form.

Flaxen's eyes turned toward me until she heard the sound of Wolf Riker's voice.

"What were you doing out here, Miss Brewster?"

"The stream. I thought everyone was asleep, I . . ."

"You'll know better from now on. Now it's best you get back to your wagon."

She turned again toward me.

"Christopher, are you . . ."

"I'm all right."

"Sure you are." Riker smiled, "Mr. Guthrie, you come with me."

Holding my torn and bleeding forearm, I followed Wolf Riker's command.

CHAPTER XL

Of all the entries in my journal of the Range Wolf Cattle Drive, this, I believe, is the most revealing concerning Wolf Riker, and me—the most revelatory so far.

A few minutes after beating the nelly-hell out of that lecherous bastard, Eustice "Cookie" Munger, I stood in Wolf Riker's wagon, my left forearm still bleeding as I held it, and my mind still reeling from what had occurred.

Riker opened a medical kit and pointed to a chair near a table.

"Sit over there."

"It can wait. Dr. Picard will . . ."

"Dr. Picard will be busy with Cookie for some ime. Besides, I want to. When Doc was soused I used to do a lot of this. Sit down."

I did.

Riker started to clean the wound from a basin on the table.

"These hands can kill or cure, depending on . . ."

"Your whim?"

"I told you, you wouldn't take much more. I knew it!"

"It wasn't because of what he did to me . . ."

I reflexively pulled back my arm.

"Here, hold that steady. Ah, yes, it was."

Riker continued his ministering as he spoke in an almost triumphant tone.

"You can tell yourself it was because of the lady, but when you were striking him, that was your own revenge. And it made you feel alive and strong. I told you you'd change. But you were going to kill him. What made you stop?"

"You."

"How?"

"When I saw you laughing, I realized . . ."

"What?"

"That I was becoming like you."

Riker shrugged and laughed.

"Suppose you had killed him? You believe in resurrection. Eternity. Immortality. You would have just boosted Cookie's imprisoned spirit to a better place."

"I've said it before, Mr. Riker, no man has the right to decide who lives or dies."

"Nonsense. It's done all the time. Well, *Mister* Guthrie, you're the king of the kitchen now . . ."

"I don't want to be . . ."

"Cookie'll wash the greasy pots, peel the potatoes . . . that's your reward because you beat him . . . but since you *didn't* kill him, be careful, there are other knives in the kitchen."

By then Riker had finished bandaging my arm. As well, I might add, as any doctor could have done.

"There you are."

"Thank you, sir."

"That must have been quite a love scene by the stream."

Riker closed the medical kit.

"Beauty and the beast, wouldn't you say?"

I paused for a moment before I answered.

"There are many things I wouldn't say . . . to you, Mr. Riker."

"Things about . . . love, for instance?"

I did not answer.

"Since you're writing about me, suppose I told you something I've never told anyone before?"

"About love?"

"That, too. And *maybe* I will tell you . . . sometime."

"Why not now?"

"Are you serious?"

"Never more serious."

"But after what happened you must be exhausted."

"Not too exhausted to listen."

"Very well, then. Listen, while we have a drink or two of brandy . . . and smoke a cigar."

Within a minute or two, we were doing just that, while we sat and he spoke.

"In those days, before the war, the Double R brand stood for Riker and Riker. That war divided a nation, state against state, father against son, brother against brother. Somehow my brother and I might not have been divided—at least not unalterably—by the war, but something, someone, else also came between us.

"Dirk's loyalty was to the Union, and against slavery. Mine was to my native Virginia and then Texas—and I didn't give a damn about slavery. I never owned a slave and never wanted to. All I cared about was the empire we were building and that empire was in Texas—and so was my loyalty.

"We both, Dirk and I, tried to avoid talking about it, but after we heard the news of Lincoln's election and after the gunfire at Harper's Ferry, gunfire we didn't hear, but gunfire that sooner or later had to affect us, because the smoke of that gunfire spelled out across the nation and territories, one word:

"*Secession.*

"On December 20, 1860, South Carolina seceded from the Union, followed by Florida, Georgia, then Virginia. Texas would not be far behind.

"And it was then that Pepper told us his niece, a schoolteacher from Baltimore, would be arriving on the next stage.

"He asked if it would be all right if she stayed at the ranch temporarily, until she began teaching in Gilead. Without hesitation we both said yes.

"Then he asked if we'd like to go into town with him and meet the stage and her. Without hesitation we both said no.

"It was almost impossible to look at Pepper and not imagine what his schoolteacher niece must look like. We glanced at each other and conjured up a vision of a skinny spinster who might even have a trace of whiskers and a limp.

"But a different vision stepped off the buckboard as Pepper introduced us to his niece, Elizabeth.

"Byron wrote of another lady:

> *She walks in beauty like the night*
> *Of cloudless climes and starry skies.*

"But Elizabeth walked in beauty night and day. And that beauty came with an inward glow that affected both Dirk and me as we had never been affected by anyone or anything before.

"Her eyes, midnight blue. Her hair black as a raven's wing.

"And even her traveling clothes could not disguise the flowing form beneath.

"'On the way here from the stage, Uncle Pepper has told me so much about you both.'

"Her voice had the slight lilt of a cultured Southern belle, completely honest and unaffected.

"But that damn Uncle Pepper had not told us what to expect. And even then he just looked at us with that self-satisfied grin that silently lorded over the both of us.

"Not only were the both of us more than pleased that we had consented to her staying at the ranch, but each of us was already . . . well, shall I say, thinking about considerably more than that.

"In spite of the fact that we had help in the house, she was the first to rise and have breakfast ready for Pepper, Dirk, and me.

"For the noon meal we were usually out on the range, but supper was ready when we were, a supper fit for royalty, a supper which we consumed while barely able to take our eyes off her every movement—and while Pepper looked at the two of us with unconcealed amusement.

"But soon that amusement turned to concern, as each of us vied for her attention—and favor.

"She did her best to show no favoritism and to divide her attention as equally between us as possible. She led neither of us on, even suggesting that she move into town until her term at the school began.

"But we wouldn't hear of it.

"On alternate Sundays she would ride with either Dirk or me. She also suggested that the three of us ride out and spend the afternoons together.

"But neither Dirk nor I agreed to that. Each of us wanted to be alone with her.

"I don't know where the two of them went, but the two of us had a serene spot where we would dismount and talk. After a time more than talk.

"When I put my arms around her, there was a quality about her that made me want to protect as well as possess her.

"It was during one of those times that she told me of a novel she had read, *Wuthering Heights*, by an English lady named Emily Bronte.

"Heathcliff and Cathy were doomed to be separated by Cathy's early death. A story I didn't want to listen to.

"And as the effects of the war affected Texas—and the nearness of Elizabeth affected Dirk and me—he and I found more to disagree about—until it was inevitable that those disagreements would erupt in violence—and even death.

"One afternoon in the presence of Elizabeth, Pepper, and others came the climax. It began about the merits of the Union and Confederate causes but our eyes were on Elizabeth.

"Choices had to be made.

"Elizabeth's eyes widened in apprehension.

"Pepper did his best to arbitrate and intervene.

"'Boys, this is crazy. You've worked together for years. The two of you own one of the biggest spreads in Texas.'

"'It's not big enough,' I said.

"'Not for the two of us,' Dirk added.

"'One flip of the coin,' I demanded. 'Winner take all.'

"'All?'

"He looked toward Elizabeth.

"'That's up to her.'

"'If you go through with this,' she said, 'I'll never see either of you again as long as I live.'

"'I'll take that chance,' I said and drew a coin from my pocket.

"'So will I,' Dirk said.

"I flipped the coin in the air. 'Call it.'

"'Tails.'

"The coin hit the ground. I looked at it, then at him.

"'You're standing on my land. Get out now.'

"I started to turn toward Elizabeth and I heard his voice.

"'I'll leave this with you.'

"He twisted me hard and hit me with all the strength he could muster. Hard enough to knock me to the ground where my head smashed into a jagged rock. In a haze I hollered out.

"'Draw you son of a bitch!'

"We both drew and fired. My shot hit his

shoulder. His shot hit Elizabeth, who had stepped forward to intervene.

"She clutched her heart and was probably dead before she fell."

I sat in silence, transfixed as he related those events, smoking his cigar and sipping his brandy—while I neither smoked, nor drank—just looked into his eyes and recalled that line from the Bard of Avon.

'*There is no art to find the mind's construction in the face.*'

What a piece of work was this man. What a contradiction. A fallen angel. The devil incarnate. A human pendulum sweeping between passion and brutality. And here he sat speaking of a lost love and forfeited brother as if it had all happened to someone else.

And in a way maybe it had. Maybe he was no longer the man he had spoken of. Maybe he had become someone else—something else.

But still he carried that scar on his temple, and who knew what scar was buried deep in his heart.

After a momentary silence, the mask that was his face broke into a slight smile.

"You think you can remember all of that, Mr. Guthrie?"

"How could I forget?"

"We'll see."

"About Elizabeth . . ."

He shook his head.

"No more about Elizabeth . . . except . . . like Cathy Earnshaw, she died an early death, but is not buried on the English moors. She rests on the ground that I'll never give up—in Texas."

Another moment of silence, then he pointed to the glass on the table.

"You haven't finished your drink, or cigar."

I rose and lifted the glass.

"I'll drink the brandy . . . and take the cigar with me. Thank you, Mr. Riker."

I swallowed the contents of the glass and started toward the door.

"One more thing," he added.

I paused.

"Suppose," he said, "I was at that stream with Miss Brewster. Would you have attacked me?"

I did not answer.

"Good night, Mr. Guthrie." He smiled.

CHAPTER XLI

The next couple of days were neither carefree, nor contentious. The weather neither too hot, nor too cold. The overall attitude of the drovers neither too defiant, nor too agreeable.

And for two days Cookie was in no condition to carry out his culinary duties. Morales One and Morales Two came to the fore and the quality and digestion of the meals noticeably improved.

It was hoped among the drovers that this arrangement would continue, but Riker would have none of it. He needed Morales One and Morales Two with the herd full-time. Particularly since we were getting closer to crossing the Red River.

Soon enough Riker informed Dr. Picard that his patient, regardless of his condition, had to resume his activities the next day.

In the meanwhile, I did everything I could to help the situation in the kitchen, and even Flaxen added her services to our endeavors. To her credit, the encounter with Eustice Munger seemed to have had no lasting effect on her psyche.

And when Munger did come back to work there was a very noticeable transformation in his demeanor.

He was no longer the audible, arrogant, insolent son of a bitch we had come to expect and disdain.

He treated the rest of us with almost the same regard and tractability he had previously reserved for Wolf Riker. Gone were the slam-bang harangues, the curses, the scowls and screeches. Instead, he smiled and addressed the drovers by name instead of epithets.

He referred to Flaxen as Miss Brewster instead of Missy and spoke to me almost in a civil manner, as if I had not beaten the unholy hell out of him. All the more reason I did not trust the dirty bastard and thought he was just biding his time until the opportune time to retaliate.

George Leach continued his steady diet of dust, dirt, and grime, along with what was served up at mealtimes. There were two or three other drovers who were assigned to drag, but they all alternated to other posts on the drive, not Leach. In accordance with Wolf Riker's orders, Leach saw only the asses and swaying tails of the ambling beeves, as he did his best to keep them ambling. His eyes were red and swollen almost shut and his voice harsh and raspy when he spoke. And I did notice that he had not been one of those who went to assist Cookie after the unpleasantness which had started at the stream and continued to the camp.

It was Dr. Picard and Reese who carried Cookie away.

And it seemed to me that the rest of the drovers took a certain satisfaction in Cookie's comeuppance.

Pepper made it his business to repeat Riker's warning to me regarding Cookie's cunning and artifice. His warning was unnecessary, but appreciated. Pepper also made mention of something else that somewhat surprised me.

"The boss said that the two of you had another interestin' session together."

I nodded.

"Quite interesting . . . and I'm sorry, truly sorry, about what happened to your niece, Elizabeth."

It was his turn to nod.

And I did not allow the opportunity to pass without inquiring.

"If things had turned out differently, and she had to choose, what do you think she would have chosen to do? Stay with Wolf? Leave with Dirk? Or leave with neither of them?"

I knew it was presumptive of me to ask, and for a moment I thought it a mistake, but Pepper did not take umbrage.

"I don't know. And with her last breath, I don't think . . . she knew either."

"But you decided to stay with Wolf Riker. May I ask why?"

"Maybe . . . I'm not sure of the answer to that either, but maybe because, in spite of his winning the toss of the coin, he needed me more than his brother did. Beside that scar on his head, the hurt went deeper . . . and then, too, Elizabeth was buried on that ranch."

"But they both left the Double R during the war."

"One went with the North, the other with the South."

"And you stayed with the Double R."

"Somebody had to."

"So that somebody just turned out to be you."

"Bad hoof and all," he shrugged.

With that, Pepper turned and walked away . . . bad hoof and all.

"Mr. Guthrie."

There was a blue pattern of smoke traveling from Dr. Picard's pipe as he approached.

"I've been meaning to talk to you."

"Now's as good a time as any. About what?"

"Cookie's knife and your arm. I know that *Doctor* Wolf Riker worked on it. How's it doing?"

"The knife or the arm?" I smiled.

"Both."

"The knife is safely tucked away . . ."

"And the arm? Would you like me to change the bandage?"

"Threw the bandage away this morning after changing my shirt, which suffered the real damage."

"Then let me see you hands."

"My what?"

"Your hands. Let's have a look at both of them."

I put forth both my hands, palms up.

"Turn them over."

I did.

"Uh-huh."

"Uh-huh, what?"

He rubbed the knuckles of both hands.

"Bruised, but not broken. That's more than I can say about Cookie's nose . . . and his jaw's not in too good a shape. It'll hurt to eat for a few more days."

"Pity."

"Yes, isn't it. It seems I've had a steady stream of patients on this drive."

"I'd say you've done very well so far, Doctor, but . . ."

"But what?"

"It's a long way to Kansas."

"Thanks for reminding me." He chuckled and walked away.

"What's so amusing?"

Flaxen had seen if not heard the conversation between Picard and me.

"Kansas," I said. "If we ever get there."

"I don't quite understand, but if I ever do get to Kansas it'll be thanks to you."

"Then save your thanks until we get there . . . and, then and there, I'll collect . . . the 'thanks,' I mean."

"There's something else you have to collect."

"There is?"

She held out her hand.

"The ring," she said.

"We'll cross that bridge when we get to it."

"Christopher," she smiled, "how can you cross a bridge *before* you get to it?"

"Come to think of it, you're right."

"But there is one bridge we've already crossed that you asked me about . . . my father . . ."

"Please. You owe me no explanation."

"I owe you everything. You and Dr. Picard. He was a character out of Dumas, my father, I mean. Strange, persuasive, debonair. He used to say that he was half Robin Hood—that is, he stole only from the rich. Of course, that was no excuse . . . for him . . . or me."

"Flaxen . . ."

"No. Let me finish. Reginald Brewster was once a professional magician. With soft, delicate hands. At first I didn't realized that he was using me as well as those hands to pick other people's pockets."

"You were quite a diversion."

"And then I was always afraid he'd be caught if I weren't around. He had a serious heart condition. The doctors didn't give him much longer to live and he wanted to leave me with . . ."

"Flaxen. I'll listen to no more. Not now or ever. Nothing about the past. We met on this drive. Forget about the past."

"I'll try, but will you answer just one question?"

I nodded.

"If you didn't have to leave Baton Rouge the next day, would you have testified against us?"

"You're asking a different man. I can't be held accountable for the values of Christopher Guthrie at that time. But I can speak now as the man on this drive . . . and the answer is no."

I took her in my arms.

CHAPTER XLII

But after those couple of days when things on the drive were neither too good, nor too bad—mostly middling—as we approached the Red River, dark clouds appeared in more ways than one—and things changed.

Bleak nebulae hung heavy close above, and the sky rumbled with warnings of what was to come.

Rain.

And rain meant a swollen river and a more hazardous, if not impossible, crossing—at least until the waters receded, which could take days. Days when anything could happen. Days that Wolf Riker had no intention of waiting.

Chandler rode back from beyond point with Smoke by his side, but it was Chandler who hollered within hollering distance.

"Red River! Red River ahead!"

It was the same Red River that Flaxen and I had crossed by stagecoach—but *not* the same. That was many miles to the south, from Louisiana into Texas, where the Red flows from north to south. Out here the Red moved west to east before turning south.

But it was the same Red River that the Austins had crossed, Moses and his son Stephen, and then so many others who were not born in Texas, but who gave birth to what would become the twenty-eighth state of the United States of America.

The others, men like Sam Houston, Jim Bowie, Davy Crockett, William Travis, Sam Maverick, Henry Kinney, Gail Borden, Robert Hancock Hunter, Ben McCulloch, David Burnet—pioneers, soldiers, newspapermen, physicians, speculators, statesmen—were all born somewhere else, but all died Texans.

For Texas.

But there were also Wolf and Dirk Riker, brothers who had been divided between their loyalty to Texas and to the United States of America.

Both brothers still alive, and whose fate had yet to be determined.

In many ways the Red River was their Rubicon.

It was sometime after the noon meal when Chandler and Smoke rode back after sighting the Red. Close to what the drovers thought would be supper and a good night's rest before starting the crossing the next morning.

But Wolf Riker had other plans and he made the announcement in no uncertain terms.

An announcement that nearly fired off an open revolt.

"We're crossing today."

The men looked at each other in stunned disbelief.

Leach, Smoke, Reese, Dogbreath, Latimer, Simpson, French Frank, Drago, Cookie, Morales One, Morales Two, Dr. Picard, Chandler, all the rest. All except Pepper whose stolid expression never changed.

"That'll take all night," one of the drovers hollered.

"It might," Riker answered. "But it might not if we drive 'em hard enough."

"Why not wait?!" somebody else questioned. "Fresh start in the morning."

"Because"—Riker pointed to the ominous sky—"*it* might not wait. If that river floods we're stuck . . . and I'm not going to get stuck."

"There's quicksand out there," came another voice, "and at night . . ."

"We could lose hundreds of head!" another piped.

"I don't care if we lose a thousand. It's better than losing the whole herd in a storm."

"We could lose our lives, too!" Another protest.

"I'm not going to argue, and I'll shoot any son of a bitch who moves in another direction. We're going to start crossing *now*!"

CHAPTER XLIII

It could not have been much time.

Not at all.

But that kind of time can't be measured. Time when life and death are in the balance.

When one move, or even one word, is the primer to an explosion.

They looked from Wolf Riker to each other, each expecting, or at least hoping, that someone would make that move, or say that word.

They had all been victims of Wolf Riker's abuse and brutality, of his relentless, unreasonable demands on the drive. Some had even felt the eruptive effects of his physical battering. Leach. French Frank. Smoke. They had suffered heavy blows dealt by the man who stood before them now and commanded, demanded, they risk limb and life unnecessarily.

Who, or how many, would challenge Wolf

Riker—and face a blue barrel of eternity from his .44?

As I stood there in that instant—in the moment that seemed to stand still forever—a member of that pack, yet not a part of it—I weighed what the outcome would be. Would one or more of them dare challenge the fury of this man-wolf?

Or would they instead back down and challenge the flowing red threat of crossing the wide torrent of the river into the dark night long after the day's work should have been done?

Draw against Wolf Riker and die now?

Or take a chance against the river?

Silence.

Then a barely discernable murmur.

Then the decision.

The Red River.

Preparations hastily made.

Each hour, each minute, each movement—precious.

Misting rain.

A raft. Big logs tied together with rope.

More logs fastened to help buoy the wagons across.

And at the point, tired beeves being driven ever closer to the spilling banks of the river.

Something came to mind afterward, something I paid little attention to at the time, because I had little else on my mind at the time—except survival—primarily my own and Flaxen's.

The drover known only as Drago, who had not uttered more than a fistful of words to me, or I believe, to anybody else on the drive, reigned up close by, looked at the river just ahead, then at me and smiled for the first time.

"I hope this pony can swim, 'cause I can't."

Flaxen, at Pepper's suggestion, had switched from Dr. Picard's wagon to Wolf Riker's, driven by Pepper. Riker's wagon was of better construction and Pepper, a better teamster than the medical man.

She sat next to Pepper and held on to the seat for dear life—and life was dear, and danger imminent, to all of us doing Wolf Riker's bidding.

And everywhere there was Wolf Riker on his mammoth black mount, Bucephalus, shouting commands.

Confusion. Seeming chaos. But out of the moving madness, the first ranks of the horned herd plunged into the mud-clogged banks of swirling cold water, pressed ahead by tons of moving beef, horns, and hoofs.

The battle was joined.

There was no turning back, the herd, the horses, the riders. It was either make the opposite bank or drown.

And I, aboard Tobacco, was in the thick of it.

Nobody is ever made into a cowboy in one day, or by one event, but this was as close as I, or anybody else, could come—and survive.

The broiling sky was torn by bolts of crooked lightning, followed by drumming thunder, as the leaders of the herd plunged into the sweeping current—ten, twenty, thirty, with drenched cowboys swinging their lariats, yelling, swearing, driving the wide-eyed beeves, their struggling hooves, digging across the muddy bottom, then farther into the water where there seemed to be no bottom—swimming steers, and horses with noses jutting out of the stream.

Voices.

Desperate.

Cursing.

Commanding.

"Keep 'em movin'!"

"Quicksand! Mark it!"

"Big log floatin'—watch it!"

"Mud knee deep—keep away!"

"Horse and rider stuck—need help!"

"Keep that line movin'!"

"More quicksand here! Mark it!"

Cattle bogged in the soggy mounds past midstream—some pulled out by riders, some drowned.

Chandler had never before been a trail boss, but that day, he was all cowboy. The first to reach the far bank with the lead steers—and the first to plunge back to do more of the same. The first, that is, after Riker and Bucephalus.

Damned fool that I turned out to be, in the midst of the maelstrom, trying to keep the outer flank of beeves from drifting downstream in the whipping waters—with Drago ahead and Dog-breath behind, doing the same.

And then it happened.

Not ten feet ahead, Drago's horse stumbled, buckled, and twisted into the rushing current. I had never seen a man drown, but had heard that he would go under, then rise to the surface before going down again.

That's not the way it happened. In a blinding flash, horse and rider disappeared. Almost immediately the horse's head and mane appeared, swimming riderless toward the bank.

But not Drago.

Only his hat on the surface drifted downstream and then vanished in the distance.

The rest of the crossing was a nightmare—and a sizeable part of it was all through the night.

The sun, what there was of it, came down—and the moon, what there was of it, came up—a scimitar floating across a deep, dark sea of sky.

It seemed that every animal ever born had been collected for this crossing—steers, cows, horses, mules, oxen, an endless mass of pitching, milling, unbridled creatures, buttheaded, and drenched—all clashing, as ignorant armies clash by night.

After what happened to Drago, it all seemed unreal—weary-laden flashes:

Riker changing mounts, from Bucephalus to a younger, but less formidable stallion—the wagons making it across—calves upside down with hooves flailing above the surging stream, then sinking from sight. The river rising with the night-falling rain.

We were sailors on horseback—in a churning sea—without rudder—without sail—sudden comrades—separate—but together—faces grotesque as I had never seen them before—lashed by rain—lit by rods of lightning; Chandler, Smoke, Reese, Dogbreath, French Frank, Morales One, Morales Two, and all the rest—even Leach, who could not now complain about the dust—there was no dust—instead, rain and mud and the river.

But in his own way Riker was right. If we had waited until the next day for a fresh start—the next day and fresh start would not have come for a long, long time.

The endless night finally ended, and the endless herd finally was across the Red River.

CHAPTER XLIV

The morning broke clean, damp, but not wet.
The rain had ceased to fall.

Breakfast on the other side after a sleepless night.

Cookie, Morales One, Morales Two, Flaxen, and I all pitched in.

Hot beef, hot biscuits, and pale coffee.

The drovers, barely awake but hungry, devoured breakfast and what should have been last night's supper, while the herd grazed not far away.

Wolf Riker made another announcement. A brief one.

"Finish eating and get a couple hours sleep—then we're moving on."

No thanks for a job well done, no word of commendation. No mention of Drago. Wolf Riker turned to walk away.

"Mr. Riker."

"What is it, Reese?"

"After we eat and sleep . . . before we leave . . . do you mind if we have a service for Drago?"

"You mean a prayer service?"

"Yes, sir."

"There's no body to bury."

"We can still say a prayer here, near the river where he drowned."

Wolf Riker shrugged.

"Make it a short one."

Then he walked away.

After moving north across the Red River, we were no longer in Texas—or any other state in the United States of America.

This was known simply as Indian Territory. A vast unsettled expanse that had to be crossed before re-entering the United States in Kansas . . . during the war called "bleeding Kansas."

From the rumors rampant, this was the most dangerous part of the drive, and the drovers had made it known that they'd already had their bellies full of danger.

Here, the drovers said, "there was no law and no God."

But on this drive there was Wolf Riker. And on this drive he was both.

After Riker made his latest announcement there was the look of disgust, of defiance, in the eyes of all trail men who had listened. But they were all too tired to convert that look into anything more.

At least for the time being.

I did get a chance to spend a few moments with my "fiancée."

"Did you have a pleasant journey?" I smiled.

"First-class transportation." She returned the smile. "And you?"

"Steerage," I retorted.

"I saw some of what you did, Christopher. You were magnificent."

"Scared stiff."

"That's what made it so magnificent."

"Flaxen, if we get out of this . . ."

"Not if . . . when."

"You've become an optimist . . . all right, *when* . . . there's something I want to talk to you about. '*Veltio Avrio.*'"

"A better tomorrow?"

"That's it." I nodded. "Good night. See you in a couple of hours."

I had been to funerals before.

But none like this.

There was no casket. No remains. No family. No clergyman. No chapel.

A hillock. By the side of a river.

All the members of the drive. All but Wolf Riker.

Alan Reese stood a short distance from the rest of us near the banks of the Red River.

In his hands, a Bible.

Unopened.

He spoke the words.

"The Lord is my shepherd; I shall not want. He maketh me to lie down in green pastures: He leadeth me beside the still waters."

All the heads were bowed.

"He restoreth my soul: He leadeth me in the paths of righteousness for His name's sake."

Reese looked toward the river and continued.

"Yea, though I walk through the valley of the shadow of death, I will fear no evil, for Thou art with me; Thy rod and Thy staff they comfort me. Thou preparest a table before me in the presence of my enemies."

Wolf Riker appeared and stood nearby. Some of the drovers were aware of his presence, others were not.

"Thou annointest my head with oils: my cup runneth over."

I took hold of Flaxen's hand.

"Surely goodness and mercy shall follow me all the days of my life: and I will dwell in the house of the Lord forever."

Reese turned toward the mourners.

"None of us knew much about him except that

he was called Drago and was a cowboy doing his job—"

"Murdered by a madman," Simpson's voice cut through the service.

"—a cowboy and one of God's flock doing his best and who is now at peace, looking down—"

"Cursing his killer," Simpson again.

"—at those of us who worked with him and who must someday join him—"

"Put an 'amen' to it," Wolf Riker said.

"—until that certain day of resurrection. Amen."

Wolf Riker walked closer and stood near Karl Simpson.

"I heard what you said, Simp."

"And so did God," Simpson said.

"But I'm right here in front of you."

"And so is God."

"We'll see about that, Simp. You had a few things to say just a minute ago. Do you have anything to say now, or are you afraid to?"

"I fear no man, Mr. Riker."

"We'll see about that, too, Simp."

"Mr. Riker, please . . ." Alan Reese took a step closer.

"Shut up, Reese. Well, go ahead, Simp. Maybe this'll help."

Riker's hand moved like a snake back and forth

across Simpson's face slapping him again and again.

Blood flowed from Simpson's mouth. He swung at Riker, but Riker was too quick and smashed Simpson with powerful blows, an avalanche of fury, to the face and body until the man buckled and started to fall. But Riker held him with one hand and with the other, pummeled him without mercy. Simpson tried to strike back . . . in vain.

A final, seemingly fatal, blow, then Riker let him fall.

Flaxen turned and ran away.

Riker stood over the crumpled form.

"I can't abide betrayal."

CHAPTER XLV

In that moment after Wolf Riker uttered those words and stood there without missing a beat or breath, I thought that it might be the end of the drive and of Wolf Riker.

Individually, the drovers were no match against Riker. No one of them could pull a gun faster, or fire with more accuracy. No one could match his speed and strength. When it came to strength, Smoke was the only one who had a chance. But after what Riker had done to Simpson, even that black giant could not be considered a formidable opponent.

No. There was nobody among them—among us—who had the potential.

But all of us together. That would be a different matter. A different contest.

If a score of men drew their guns simultaneously, springing hammer and trigger, with barrels exploding at the same human target—some would die—but so would Wolf Riker.

Or, if all leaped upon him with fists striking the face and body of one man, even a superior man that was Wolf Riker, he could not withstand the onslaught. Not even if Pepper rushed to his side.

Wolf Riker would be subdued.

His reign would be done.

And so would the drive.

But that moment came and went.

And nobody moved.

Not Leach. Not Smoke, or French Frank, Dog-breath, Latimer, or any of the others.

Nobody.

Except Wolf Riker.

He reached into his pocket, retrieved a cigar, put it into his mouth, lit the cigar, and moved away.

Then did Dr. Picard and Alan Reese go to the side of Karl Simpson.

And then the drive continued into the Indian Territory.

That night supper was served, but it was sub-dued, almost silent. The drovers were still stunned by the events of the crossing and what followed between Simpson and Riker.

Cookie kept a keen eye on his carving knives

and on anybody who seemed to come too close to them.

There were whispers and furtive glances between the drovers and toward Riker's wagon. Would he come out among them that night?

He wouldn't.

But Pepper did.

He had a late supper while standing, holding a plate and looking at no one in particular.

But from time to time they looked at him, knowing that in order to get to Riker they would have to go through him—or do it when Pepper wasn't around—which was seldom—or never.

I did have the feeling that if there was going to be an attempt against Riker, it would not be during the bright daylight, but under the cover of darkness—at night.

But not that night.

The men were still too shaken, too impotent.

They would wait and conceive some sort of plan when they could take Wolf Riker unaware— and also see whether Karl Simpson would survive.

At least that's what I thought.

I went to the wagon where Simpson lay, tended by Dr. Picard and Flaxen.

Simpson's face was swollen; he was still alive, breathing irregularly and even muttering.

"Doctor, how is he?"

Picard pointed.

"Ask him."

I approached and leaned close, although it was appalling to look at him.

"Mr. Simpson . . . it's Guthrie, Christopher Guthrie . . . can you hear me?"

He nodded, barely.

"You're going to make it . . . you're going to be all right."

His voice was just above a guttural whisper.

"I'm going to kill him . . . I'm going to kill Riker."

I had seen and heard enough.

Outside the wagon, Alan Reese was waiting.

"Mr. Guthrie. I saw you go in. Is he alive?"

"He's alive."

"Thank God."

"Yes, he's alive, Mr. Reese, and is swearing."

"Swearing?"

"Swearing to kill Riker, and speaking of God, Mr. Reese. I've seen many actors on the stage pretending to be someone else, a banker, doctor, lawyer, even a clergyman. But this morning I had the feeling . . . watching and listening to you, that I was not seeing someone pretending."

"Mr. Guthrie . . ."

"It was you who kept Mr. Yirbee's Bible . . . who suggested the service, who held that Bible in his hand, and who quoted words from that Bible without opening it . . . words that came from the heart and soul, words you had spoken before. Many times before. There were other things, signs that set you apart from the rest. You are not like the other men on this drive. Mr. Reese, are you a clergyman?"

Silence.

"Sir," I said, "you are not obliged to answer."

"I will answer. But only to you. Yes, I am a clergyman."

"I thought so." I smiled.

"I'm an unfrocked priest."

CHAPTER XLVI

There are all kinds of islands.

When someone says the word *island*, any one of a dozen visions might come to mind . . . a tropical island, a coral island, a volcanic island, a desert island, a polar island . . . an island composed of sand, or ice, or lava . . . any size; small enough to see all the way across, or a continent within itself—within sight of other land or isolated, thousands of miles from anything but water.

But we were on a different kind of island.

"Indian Territory," it was called.

And, unlike other islands, it consisted of land surrounded, not by water, but by other land. Land, that included some states—and some territories—Texas, Missouri, Kansas, Arkansas, and Oklahoma.

The Indian Territory was set aside by the Federal Government primarily for the so-called Five Civilized Tribes: Cherokee, Seminole, Creek, Choctaw, and Chickasaw. But during the Civil War the Five Civilized Tribes gambled on the side of the Confederacy and since then the vast region had become a cauldron of chaos.

Tribes, justifiably not called civilized—Cheyenne, Arapaho, Comanche, Kiowa, and Apache—charged in and considered everything they could kill, rob, rape, and exploit to be fair game.

Much of the land was rich and fertile, suitable for farming. But much of the trouble was that the Indians were not farmers. Not like white people, not like settlers who built houses and barns, raised cattle and crops; individuals who staked a claim to a section of the land, stayed and raised a family in one place.

The Indians were hunters—individuals who owned no land—who owned all the land—hunters who moved with their prey and their possessions, in tribes large and small, and felt no compunction in taking from other tribes, by strength or stealth, whatever they needed or wanted—horses, women, weapons, whatever suited their needs or desires— to ride, to copulate, or to hunt buffalo. They lived by percepts the whites did not grasp—nor did the Indians grasp the ways of the whites.

But one thing the Indians did grasp—that this territory belonged to them, by divine right, and by right of treaty with the white government— and whoever crossed into their territory could rightfully be considered invaders.

But beside the Indians—Comanche, Kiowa, Cheyenne, Arapaho, and Apache—there was another breed.

Comancheros. Dirty men in a dirty trade.

They were called Comancheros because they did business with the Comanches and other tribes—providing guns, ammunition, whiskey, assorted provisions, and prisoners, often women—stolen and kidnapped—often from wagon trains moving west—or cattle drives moving north.

Comancheros. Scalawags, highbinders, back-shooters, outlaws from both sides of the Civil War and below the border.

Into and across this terrain lay the destination of the Range Wolf Cattle Drive.

And it was on that night, after we had crossed the Red River, prayed for the immortal soul of one called Drago, after Riker had beaten Simpson nearly to death, after Simpson had sworn to kill Riker, and after Alan Reese had confided to me that he had formerly worn the round white collar, Pepper moved close to me and spoke just above a whisper.

"Mr. Guthrie, the boss wants to talk to you."

CHAPTER XLVII

"Hero or villain? Well, Guth, what am I so far in your appraisal? In your journal?"

Brandy and cigars.

We had settled, Wolf Riker more comfortably than I, on chairs across from each other in his wagon when he smiled and asked the question.

I had to weigh my answer. Weigh it carefully.

While I was no Boswell and he certainly was no Dr. Johnson, there was an advantage for me in these meetings and discussions, although Wolf Riker did most of the discussing.

And it was to my advantage to continue the meetings—from a professional point of view if I was going to write a book about this western adventure—and from a personal point of view in cultivating a relationship, if not friendship, with the mercurial creature who sat in front of me.

Besides, I was curious about the events that shaped this complicated network of paradoxes.

I did not want to be salient.

I wanted neither to flatter, nor to offend.

And so I sipped the brandy and inhaled the cigar as I weighed my answer—carefully.

Maybe too carefully. Riker seemed more than a trifle impatient.

"Well, Guth, what's your answer?"

"My answer is . . . how can I answer that question when your question includes two words?"

"What two words?"

"'So far.' It's like trying to solve a riddle knowing only half the anagram."

"By heaven!" He nodded. "You're right, and that's why you're here, to listen to the rest. All right, where were we?"

"Your shot hit your brother's shoulder, his shot hit Elizabeth. Like Cathy Earnshaw, she died early, but is not buried on the English moors. She rests on the ground that you'll never give up—the Double R. What happened to you after that?"

"Yes . . . well, I can't tell you about that without telling you about what happened to . . . my brother."

I was relieved he said that. It spared me having to ask.

"Please go ahead, Mr. Riker."

"By then the war was raging and both North

and South were breeding their hero generals. Most of them on both sides had been cadets at West Point, many of them at the same time. And many of them had fought under the same flag on the same side during the Mexican War; but just over a dozen years later, they were fighting under different flags, on different sides and trying to kill each other.

"For the Union: William Tecumseh Sherman, Philip E. Sheridan, John C. Fremont, George Armstrong Custer, Ambrose E. Burnside, Joseph Hooker, David G. Farragut, and a seemingly endless blue line of officers, under the command of Ulysses Simpson Grant.

"For the Confederacy: J.E.B. Stuart, P.G.T. Beauregard, T.J. Jackson, Joseph E. Johnston, Jubal Early, Albert Sidney Johnston, symbols of the South under the greatest symbol and soldier, Robert E. Lee.

"For reasons of his own, my brother chose to fight for the Union, even though Texas had seceded from that Union. He rose to the rank of Major in William Tecumseh Sherman's Army of Tennessee.

"My reason was simple. The Double R. No bunch of Yankee bastards was going to take it away from me . . . and that included my brother.

"In the first few months the Confederate Army seemed invincible, winning victories in battle after battle: Fort Sumter, Lexington, Belmont, Shiloh, Fort Royal, Bull Run.

"But as the war progressed—or regressed— matters grew worse for the South . . . and Texas. The seaports were blockaded by Northern gunships, and the Yankee armies had cut off passage by road and rail.

"The time had come for me to leave Texas in order to help save Texas.

"I had mortgaged the Double R for twenty thousand dollars to pay off my ranch hands, some who were enlisting, and some too old to enlist, and left enough money for Pepper to run the ranch, until I could come back and pay off the mortgage . . . in legal tender.

"I joined the general who, in the thick of battle led his Black Horse Raiders, better known as the Invincibles, like bolts of lightning into the Northern Brigades. He won more decisive Southern victories than any officer, including Bull Run, Antietam and Fredricksburg—J.E.B. Stuart— General James Ewell Brown Stuart—the boldest, most beloved cavalry commander in the ranks of the Confederacy. Bucephalus and I were a part of those ranks in time to charge at his side at Chancellorsville, where he took command when Stonewall Jackson fell, and we rode with him at Gettysburg, and the Wilderness.

"To me J.E.B. Stuart was more than my comrade

and commander. He was a legend. It would have been an honor to lay down my life in his stead.

"But it didn't work out that way.

"The South was fighting insuperable odds. There were over eighteen million people in the North, and nine million in the South, a third of them slaves. The North had nine-tenths of the nation's manufacturing capacity, two-thirds of the railroads, and most of the country's iron, coal, and copper. It controlled the sea. Attrition— Grant, Sherman, and Sheridan took their toll.

"Sherman made no secret of his strategy. 'War is hell,' he proclaimed, then added, 'At best it's barbarous and I intend to be just that—to break bridges, tear up railroads, smash mills, burn and destroy all supplies from here to the Atlantic salt water.'

"He did that and more, cutting a swath of death and demolition all the way—with my brother by his side—on the march that led to the destruction of the South.

"I presume that you were a part of all that, weren't you, Mr. Guthrie?"

I shrugged, then answered.

"Not a very active part, Mr. Riker."

"Well, I must say, my brother was—with two battlefield commissions—the second as Major, given by Sherman himself at Chattanooga. And Dirk marched through Georgia with Sherman and was with him when Sherman sent Lincoln a telegraph.

"'*Mr. President, I give you Atlanta.*'

"But Dirk, along with other Yankee officers, was given something else—spoils for their war chests. The Northern Army could burn the Confederacy's supplies and houses, but many of the Southerners were in a hurry to escape with their lives and left behind other valuables including coins and jewelry.

"Besides slaves and camp followers, there was another band that traveled with the Union Army, that band was composed of Yankee traders—money men, movable brokers—who would purchase the loot from the officers' war chests, or whatever the enlisted men could steal from the South, in return for Yankee dollars.

"This was the band that Major Dirk Riker did business with. He had no use for silverware, or necklaces, rings or loot of any kind—except for Yankee dollars that someday would buy him anything in Texas that he wanted. If he lived.

"And Major Dirk Riker did live.

"But General J.E.B. Stuart did not live.

"Not past the age of thirty-one. He led us on a path of glory. But it was too short a path. We would have followed him into hell, knowing that many of us would not come back. But as the poet said, 'the paths of glory lead but to the grave.'

"At the Battle of Yellow Tavern, General

George Armstrong Custer's forces charged against J.E.B. Stuart's Invincibles, and I was near my commander when he fell, mortally wounded.

"It was said that during the war, after J.E.B. Stuart died, the South never smiled again.

"Neither did I."

I looked into the eyes of the man whose thoughts still seemed to be at Yellow Tavern, and assumed that that would be the end of this session, but not so.

The next moment Wolf Riker appeared ready, even anxious to continue.

"Shall I go on, Guth?"

"Please do."

He sipped and smoked and settled back into his chair.

"After Yellow Tavern I knew the only possible way I could save the Double R for myself and against any Yankee bastards, including my brother, was to leave the Confederate Army and make my way across the Red River again. I knew the South had lost, but I hadn't lost the Double R and I didn't intend to. Bucephalus and I rode west."

"You deserted?"

"Some might call it that. But I volunteered in—and I volunteered out."

"With what rank?"

"Major."

"Like your brother."

"In rank only. He stayed in until . . ."

"Appomattox?"

"Appomattox. When I got back, Texas, including the Double R, was in bad shape. Pepper had done the best he could, but during those years there was no money for improvements or even maintenance. The only things that had grown and multiplied at the Double R and Texas were cattle and wild horses—and there was that mortgage that had to be paid off—$20,000—in coin of the realm, not Confederate money.

"There was only one way. It took a couple of months, with every drover that would take the chance, but the roundup began.

"And then one afternoon, after Pepper and I came out of the bank getting an extension on the loan, we came face to face with my brother.

"If we had met a few months earlier on the battlefield I would have killed him without a second thought, or the other way around. I still might have, but Pepper stepped between us.

"My brother wore clothes that closely resembled a Union uniform, obviously tailored, all deep blue and polished black boots. He had the look and bearing of royalty, except for the outline of the Colt under his coat.

"'Good to see you, Pepper.'

"'Heard you was back, Dirk, also heard you bought a spread near the Double R.'

"'Contiguous.'

"'With Yankee dollars?'"

"'That's the only kind that'll spend.'

"He turned and looked square at me.

"'How are things at the Double R?'

"'There's a No Trespassing sign on the ranch. That means everybody, specially Yankees.'

"He only smiled.

"'I understand you're making a roundup—beeves.'

"'Seven thousand, more or less.'

"'Just about worth branding. Might even bring a dollar a head.'

"'In Texas. Elsewhere, twenty dollars a head, more or less.'

"'Where's elsewhere?'

"'Kansas. Abilene.'

"'That's over a thousand miles. Hard miles. I'd say impossible.'

"'I wouldn't. Not for a hundred forty thousand, more or less.'

"He smiled again.

"'I'm making a drive myself, not that far.'

"'Beeves?'

"'Horses. Got an exclusive contract with a friend of mine. William Tecumseh Sherman. Army out west needs horses. Rounding up over a thousand head at twenty-five dollars a head.'

"'That's a good price,' Pepper said.

"'They're good horses. When do you start?'

"Pepper looked at me then answered.

"'Three weeks.'

"'I'll be leaving in about a month . . . with the best drovers . . .'

"'From the North?' I remarked.

"'Most of them. Now settling in Texas.'

"'Carpetbaggers.'

"'Cowboys. We probably won't be far behind you. Horses travel faster than cattle.'

"'You ready for some advice . . . brother?'

"'Why not?'

"'Don't get too close. Not to the Double R . . . or my drive . . . You try to stop me and I'll kill you.'

"'I won't have to. The odds—high, low, Jack, and the dame—are too strong against you. You'll never make it.'

"'I'll make it—even if it's over your dead body.'

"Before he could say anything I walked away. Pepper followed."

Riker's cigar had gone out. He knocked off the ash and relit. While he was doing that, I was at a loss for words after the events he had related. I didn't know whether it was wise to pursue the subject of his brother, so I remarked about someone else, someone he obviously admired.

"Of course I've heard of J.E.B. Stuart, Mr. Riker, but I was not aware of some of his exploits that you mentioned.

"There's one other *exploit* that might be worth mentioning. Luckily, I wasn't riding Bucephalus when we charged across the swamp at Brandy

Station with J.E.B., in the lead as usual—into a fusillade of bullets out of the brush. My horse was hit and toppled into the murky water and so did I. Stuart swirled back, reached out and down from his saddle, grabbed and lifted me so I could swing on behind him, and continued the charge. Otherwise I would've been dead in the water instead of telling you about the *exploit*—and there'd be no Double R and no cattle drive to save it, and I promise you, Mr. Guthrie, it will be saved. Do you believe that?"

"After what you've told me, Mr. Riker, and in spite of the odds . . ."

"Yes?"

"I wouldn't bet against it."

"Well," he said, "I believe my brother is betting against it."

That gave me the opening and the opportunity.

"What happens if . . . if you meet again?"

He paused, then lifted his brandy.

"I told you that if we had met on the battlefield I would have killed him without a second thought, or the other way around. Mr. Guthrie, there are different kinds of battlefields."

He swallowed the rest of the brandy.

I knew the session was over.

CHAPTER XLVIII

The drive pushed on into Indian Territory, but at a slower pace. The terrain was wet and muddy with patches of quicksand where rivulets fed into the Red—terrain where the beeves and horses were uncertain and reluctant to travel.

And so were the drovers.

More and more, when Riker was not in sight, I caught glimpses of two, or three, sometimes more, at supper, or around the campfire, or even in the saddle, leaning closer to each other, whispering. Most of the time Leach, French Frank, Dogbreath, sometimes Smoke.

I felt that if they were going to make a move—to desert, or do something even more desperate, it would be soon.

I stayed as close to Flaxen as I could while doing what I had to do, but thought it best not to alarm her. I certainly didn't tell her that Wolf Riker's brother might not be far behind.

Chandler and Smoke scouted ahead and reported that there were no visible signs of Indians, but also noted that Indians often provided no visible signs.

Cookie performed his duties, but I had the feeling he was waiting to see which way the winds for his advantage were blowing.

Reese was his solitary self.

And Dr. Picard was still sober. A couple of times he even mentioned San Francisco and the possible resumption of his practice in the city by the bay. But at this time his practice consisted mostly of tending to Karl Simpson, an amazing specimen. Few other men would have survived the beating he absorbed. Broken ribs, broken cheekbone, and heaven only knows broken what else, but not broken spirit. I believe that part of his hastened recovery was his vow to kill Riker. He was on his feet, but not yet able to ride horseback. He could, however, sit up next to the teamster of one of the wagons during the day.

Pepper was stolid as ever and never too far from Riker except when he knew that Riker wanted no company, as when he took his unaccompanied walks in the night.

I kept waiting for any indication of one of Riker's seizures, but if one did occur, it was when he was alone in his wagon.

And then something else occurred.

When everyone was sleeping—or seemed to be.

It was late and I was writing in my journal by dim lamplight. I saw the silhouette of Wolf Riker leave his wagon and disappear into the darkness. I went back to my journal and didn't know how much time had passed.

I was wondering and writing about what Wolf Riker's thoughts were, walking alone—resolute and confident—or in fear and dread—but determined; determined that his strength and will were indomitable. Or were his thoughts of Elizabeth, a lost love—Yellow Tavern, J.E.B. Stuart, a lost war—the Double R, and a twenty thousand dollar debt—the drive, and what was yet to come, Indians, Comancheros, the dissident drovers, more and more ready to rebel—his brother, who must not be far behind—and Wolf Riker's own words, 'there are different kinds of battlefields.'

I heard a sound, muffled sounds—and then the flames of the campfire went out. I had a feeling of foreboding—more than a feeling. I picked up the lamp, rose and made my way toward the direction that Riker had gone—but as far away from the banked campfire as possible—as fast as possible.

However, it was not possible to move very fast. The night was a dark, impenetrable veil, the ground uneven, strewn with rocks imbedded in the soft earth. I stumbled on, holding the lamp straight out ahead of me. In the distance, the night call of a coyote, or perhaps a wolf—an echo, or maybe the call of a mate responding. Then other sounds, not a coyote, not a wolf—not a four legged wolf—a human voice cursing—a familiar voice.

"Mr. Riker!" I cried out. "Wolf Riker!"

"Here!" came an answer. "Over here! Guth! Is that you?"

"Yes!"

"I can see you—the lamp! Move straight ahead—but careful! Quicksand! I'm up to my waist in quicksand . . ."

"I can see you now . . . I'm coming . . . don't struggle . . . just reach out, reach out . . ."

I caught sight of him, his massive figure sinking slowly into the mire. At the same time I saw a knotted length of wood by the edge of the area of quicksand. I set down the lamp, picked up the cudgel, and thrust it toward Riker as I fell to my knees.

"Grab hold!" I hollered.

"Can't . . . can't reach it . . . get closer!"

"I'm trying!"

And I was, crawling as close as possible without being swallowed by the sucking bog. But I could feel the muddy girdle tightening, tightening around my body.

"Can't get any closer, Wolf, you've got to reach out!"

I heard a great gasp as he must have called on his last store of strength . . . then I felt pressure from the cudgel. He had managed a grip onto the other end, first with one hand, then the other. Rather than try to pull him out, I felt it wiser to just hold as tight as I could and let him use his superior strength while I struggled to maintain my position and my grip . . . my fingers slipping, but, somehow, managing to hold on in spite of the slime seeping through them . . . my face half submerged into the sludge . . . throat and nostrils clogged with what seemed like tar . . . barely able to breathe.

I was on the verge of exhaustion and ready to let loose when I saw he was slowly, ever so gradually, emerging.

"Hold on, Guth!" he growled. "Hold on!"

I held.

And then, by the eerie glow of the lamp I saw the form inching closer, soaked in mud, the unmistakable face and eyes of Wolf Riker, his brow bloodied from a blow to the head, his Herculean shoulders and chest rising, his arms pulling him toward me and free from the muck.

I almost passed out, or maybe I did for a moment or two. The next thing I remembered was Wolf Riker lying beside me, still holding onto the length of wood that had saved his life.

"Those bastards! This is what they hit me with."

I did my best to spit out whatever was stuck in my mouth and throat.

"Who . . . who did it?"

"Couldn't make out . . . after the blow, three or four of them laid into me."

Wolf Riker looked like a ghost, and I must have looked about the same. Both of us dripping mud and filth, but he was also dripping blood. There was death in his eyes.

He rose to both knees, then to his feet, and dropped the cudgel.

"You come with me."

He stood waiting for me to gain my balance, then lifted the lamp from the ground.

"We'll find out who they were."

"How?"

"You'll see."

He led the way to the campsite, which was soundless and black as pitch, and then lit only by the lamp he carried.

If we were seen or heard by the drovers who lay in their blankets, they gave no indication.

Riker motioned me to stop, then set down the lamp and leaned close to one of the men, I couldn't tell which of them it was. He reached out and felt the throat of the inert drover for a pulse. In a moment he was satisfied and moved on.

Riker's thumb and forefinger were at the throat of another man, who woke and started to move, but Riker quickly covered the man's mouth with a hand and raised a finger to his own lips as a sign for silence.

As Riker started to rise, I made out movement from one, then more of the drovers, first Leach then Smoke and then simultaneously two or three of the others who jumped at him.

"Wolf!" I cried out, but too late.

Fist struck against flesh, again and again. The men flailed and piled onto Riker—with curses, grunts and yells.

"I got a knife!" I could tell it was Leach's voice. "Hold him!"

The knife struck in and out of Riker's side.

But in spite of his wounds and the ordeal in the quicksand, with his great strength, his fists smashed at his attackers. No other man could have done what he did. He picked up the lamp and swung it, hitting Leach and Smoke. They staggered and so did two more. Nearly blind with blood leaking into his eyes, he struck with lamp and fist felling Leach, Smoke, Latimer, and anyone within striking distance.

Riker dropped what was left of the lamp and disappeared while I stooped paralyzed, a short distance from the dazed and unconscious men at the campsite.

"Now we're in the barrel!" someone said.

"How'll he know which was which, unless someone peaches." Another voice.

"Blood!" Leach looked at the blade on Cookie's knife, then wiped it with his thumb and forefinger. "I knew I stuck him! Shoulda been his heart!"

"How'd he get outta that quicksand?" Smoke gritted.

"Because he's the devil!" Dogbreath spat out a mouthful of blood.

"He's a man and we'll get him next time," Leach said. "He needs us for the drive."

"Mr. Guthrie!" Pepper's voice. "The boss wants you."

A momentary silence as the men looked at each other.

"He ain't here," Leach answered.

"Yes, he is," I said. "I'm coming."

"No, you ain't," French Frank moved toward me. So did Smoke, and both grabbed hold of me.

"I've seen nothing. My word on it. This is between you and Riker."

Smoke still held on.

"Let him go," Leach nodded.

"Why?" asked French Frank.

"What're you gonna do, kill him? Besides he

don't like Riker no more than the rest of us . . . or
do you?" Leach looked directly at me.

"I'll not say anything about this. My word," I repeated.

Alan Reese, who had not participated in the
attack, spoke quietly.

"Leach is right. No good will come of doing
him harm."

"Let him go," Leach commanded again. "I said
it before . . . we might need him."

Smoke unloosened his grip.

"Guthrie!" Pepper called out once more,
louder.

"I'm coming." And I started to walk. The last
thing I heard was Simpson's voice.

"Leach, give me that knife."

I wondered what they would have done if they
knew it was I who pulled Wolf Riker out of the
quicksand.

CHAPTER XLIX

By then the rest of the camp was aroused.

Pepper, Dr. Picard, Chandler, and Flaxen stood close to each other, and Cookie was not far from them.

Wolf Riker stood at the entrance to his wagon.

"Doc, Cookie, Guth, you come inside."

Flaxen looked at me and trembled.

"Christopher . . ."

"I'm all right. Get to your wagon and lock it.

"But . . ."

"Just do it."

"God . . . you look awful."

"God . . ." I smiled, "You look beautiful. Now, go ahead."

She nodded and moved away.

Pepper looked at me and almost smiled.

"I must be growin' old—or gettin' deef—or

both. What you done out there . . . for the boss . . . he told me . . . mighty good."

The three of us, Dr. Picard, Cookie, and I, were inside the wagon with Riker. Riker had stripped to the waist, wiped his body with a towel and tossed me one as well. Picard had brought his medical bag and went to work on the wounds on Riker's head and body. I was surprised, considering what happened during the attack at the quicksand and the ferocity of the fight near the campfire, that Riker was not in much worse condition than was apparent.

There was some blood from his head, but with the exception of the knife wound, the rest were bruises and lacerations.

"You're a lucky man," Picard noted. "That knife could have done much more damage."

"Just nicked the fat," Riker said.

But it was evident that there was no fat, not on that iron hard body. Knots and ridges and mounds of muscle writhed and bunched under the skin.

Dr. Picard continued his ministering as Riker lit a cigar and puffed.

"Mr. Guthrie, would you care to smoke?"

"No, thanks."

"And I suppose you expect thanks from me for what you did."

"My expectations are . . . limited. Not what they used to be."

"Good. Then you won't be disappointed. You saw it all, Mr. Guthrie. Who was it? Who stuck me?"

I didn't answer.

"You know, don't you?"

Again, no answer.

"And they know you saw who it was, still they turned you loose. Why?"

"It was either turn me loose, or kill me. They decided to turn me loose."

"But why? Did you make a bargain with them? A promise? To spy for them?"

"I don't think you believe that."

"But you won't tell me. Cookie, do you know why you're here?"

Cookie smiled and nodded.

"Of course you do. Cookie'll find out, won't you, Cookie?"

Eustice Munger nodded again.

"That I will."

"I want a list of every man who was in on it."

"Good as done," Cookie wasted no time answering.

"Then good night and get out of here. You, too, Doc."

"But I haven't . . ."

"You've done enough . . . good as new. Now go ahead, I want to talk to Mr. Guthrie."

"All right," Picard shrugged and closed his

medical bag. "But go easy for a while, unless you want those . . ."

"I'll go easy, Doc. Now you and Cookie just go."

Cookie held the door open and indicated for the doctor to precede him, then closed the door from the outside.

Riker moved toward the shelf, then with bottle in hand poured brandy into two glasses, pointed at them, then at me.

"Sit down, Mr. Guthrie. Let's have a drink."

We both sat. He lifted his glass as casually as if we had just taken a stroll to a pub.

"What shall we drink to?"

"Confusion to the enemy."

"Excellent."

I also lifted my glass and we each drank, he deeper than I.

"Ah, but sometimes," he said, "the point becomes knowing who *is* the enemy . . . as in this situation . . . this drive . . . this night. True?"

"I'm not sure I . . ."

"Of course you do. Friend or foe? Earlier tonight you came to my aid. I might have got out of that quicksand or . . ."

"I don't think so."

"But that's exactly my point. In any case at that point you were friend, put yourself in danger, maybe even risked your life. How many times have you done that? Risked your life for someone else. Rarely, I imagine."

"Go on."

"But a little while later, when I was attacked, you just stood by, for all I know, maybe even hid in the dark, so your presence would not be detected. What were you thinking then? What were you hoping? That I would win, or lose? Be killed? Or escape?"

"I did cry out a warning."

"Did you? I didn't hear you and neither did they. At any rate you did not *act* in my behalf . . . friend. Still later, you came to some understanding with those conspirators—so they let you go. What was that understanding? There must have been some negotiation. Part of it obviously was that you would not identify those who conspired—"

"That was the only part."

"—to kill me. Now there is a different approach. Assume that everyone is a foe—until proven otherwise. So, where do you stand, Mr. Guthrie? Friend or foe?"

"There is another category."

"What?"

"Neutral."

"No such thing. Not in this situation . . . this drive. If not now, then sometime . . . and soon, you will have to decide—if you haven't already— the line will be drawn and you can't straddle it, otherwise you'll be caught in the crossfire, you and Miss Brewster."

He took another swallow.

"Of course, I know on which side of the line Pepper stands, as for the rest, including you . . . something to think about."

It was my turn to drink.

"There is another solution," he said. "An immediate solution."

"What's that?"

"Suppose I gave you a gun. There's one in this drawer, loaded. All you'd have to do is point it at me and squeeze the trigger and tear the life out of me. Would you do it?"

"No. That would be murder."

"Self-defense. There are no witnesses. You could say I attacked you. There are those on the drive who would be glad to testify on your behalf . . ."

"Pepper would kill me."

"You'll be their savior. The drovers would see to Pepper."

"Still it would be murder on my part."

He relit his cigar.

"Or maybe you think your chances are better if I stay alive. There's no telling what these bastards might do—to you and Miss Brewster—if . . ."

The cigar fell from his hand onto the table.

Both hands swept to his forehead as he leaned forward in pain.

"Mr. Riker . . ."

"Never mind. You can go now . . ."

"Let me help you, I . . ."

"I don't need your help . . . and don't say a word to anybody, or I'll . . ."

"I won't say anything. Good night, Mr. Riker."

I lifted the still lit cigar from the table and stubbed it out in the ashtray.

CHAPTER L

I had sworn that I wouldn't say anything.

First to Leach and the conspirators—that I would not identify the attackers—then to Riker, that I would not reveal he suffered a different kind of attack, one that rendered him vulnerable and nearly blind.

But before that, he had posed a provocative question. When the line was drawn, and a decision had to be made, a decision of life or death, perhaps of many lives and deaths—where would I stand, and how far would I go?

Instinctively, I had come to his rescue at the quicksand—but at the campfire, whether by instinct, self-preservation, judgment, or cowardice, I took neither side.

And I'd played enough poker to know a bluff when confronted by one, such as Riker's volunteering to provide me with a loaded gun and sit still while I squeezed the trigger and tore the life

out of him. He knew that would never happen—
and that he never would allow it to happen.

Something else he said struck home. In spite of
his unpredictable, pitiless brutality at times, and
in light of his confiding in me concerning what I
was writing about him, were Flaxen and I better
off if he lived and succeeded, or if Leach and the
other "mutineers" prevailed by any means, including murder?

Weighing the scale of survival, on which side
was our salvation?

For that matter, at this time on the drive, who
was on what side? It was apparent, at least to me,
who, and how many, would strike against Riker—
those who already had—Leach, Smoke, Dogbreath, French Frank, Latimer, and Simpson, who
now possessed the knife that Leach stole from
Cookie. All it would take would be for one of
them to strike a fatal blow. But easier said than
scored against Riker, who probably would take no
more solitary walks at night, and with Pepper
always on alert.

Beside Pepper, who else would remain, if not
loyal, at least not mutinous? Dr. Picard, Chandler,
and probably Reese, the unfrocked priest. As for
Cookie, in spite of his "good as done" spy mission,
I wouldn't trust him as much as a rattlesnake. At
least a rattlesnake gives warning.

As for Morales One, Morales Two, and the rest
of the drovers, they probably had more to gain,

even with the odds against it, finishing the drive and collecting top wages from Riker, than risking their lives going against Riker and collecting nothing. The drive never could be finished without Riker's discipline, determination, and domination.

The other alternative was desertion—for the drovers who were becoming more and more obdurate—and that might eventually be the course for Flaxen and me. But desert to where—and what?

Hostile Indians and craven Comancheros in uncharted territory.

And so, weighing the scale of survival, for the time being, for Flaxen and me, the better course was to put our trust in Wolf Riker.

But it was a thin crust of trust.

CHAPTER LI

On a Sunday afternoon I was saddling Tobacco to do a little exercising for the both of us. As I mounted I saw a sight I had never seen before.

A rider on a roan reined up next to me.

The rider was Pepper. And the expression on my face was a giveaway.

"Why the eye-pop look on your pan, sonny? It ain't that I can't ride, it's just that I don't favor it—except for certain occasions."

"What's the occasion?"

"Just follow me."

We rode along for over a mile, nearly two, into a narrow tree-lined gully.

"This'll do," Pepper said. "Unmount."

I did. It wasn't easy for Pepper, but so did he.

"We're far enough out of the sound of gunshots from them beeves, and it's about time you learned a little sumptin' about that iron on your hip."

By then I had realized what he had in mind.

He unstrapped his saddlebag and pulled out a couple of containers.

"I brought along plenty of cartridges. Now, there's them that keep the hammer on an empty chamber. I'm not one of 'em, might need that extra cartridge. Now, the most important thing is . . ."

For a moment I couldn't help thinking about how Pepper had taught Dirk and Wolf Riker his rudimentary rules of drawing and firing a gun—but only for a moment. Pepper was a masterful tutor and I became an eager pupil of his "Hook. Draw. Fire." tutelage.

A couple of hours, and one hundred or so cartridges later, I was not exactly a pistolero—but then, not exactly a pilgrim either.

In the next few days the ground became firmer and the drive moved faster. Almost fast enough to please Riker. At least he was not displeased.

Riker said nothing more, to me or anyone else, except maybe Pepper, about the quicksand incident and what followed.

Simpson continued to recover, even to the extent of resuming his duties on horseback—but maintained a solid silence and avoided eye contact with Riker.

Cookie scurried about more than usual, talking, listening, even bantering, with Leach and the others.

I made it a point to thank Alan Reese for putting in a favorable word for me before Leach and company had decided to set me free. Reese's only response was a slight shrug.

And one evening I did get the chance to spend some time with Flaxen.

I told her about my conversation with Riker and his latest seizure in the wagon—that I had weighed our prospects, if and when Leach and the others made their move against Riker—including the possibility of the two of us bolting the drive and taking our chances in the Indian Territory—and concluded that, after weighing the chances, it was wiser to stay with the drive so long as Wolf Riker was alive and well.

"He may be alive," she smiled, "but I'd hardly say that he is well. After some of the things he's done I'd say that he was at least borderline crazy."

"There are things you don't know, Flaxen, things that he's told me, about what's happened in the past and what this drive means to him . . ."

"Christopher, no matter what's happened before, and what it means to him, you can't condone his . . ."

"I'm not 'condoning' anything, Flaxen. He's a cold-blooded, callous brute . . ."

"That we agree on."

"But if anything happened to him, such as what might have happened with the quicksand, would we, you and I, be better off with the rest of them—or taking our chances . . ."

"Christopher, if it weren't for you I wouldn't be alive, so do you want to hear my conclusion— what I think?"

She went on before I could say anything.

"It's my conclusion that it's best you do the deciding. I'll stay or go—with you."

After supper, but before total darkness, Wolf Riker approached and extended an empty cup.

"Let's have some more of that swill."

I poured.

"Have you been thinking about our conversation the other night?" he asked.

"I've been thinking about a lot of things— including our conversation."

"Good. I want to . . ."

"Excuse me, Mr. Riker," Chandler moved up next to Riker. "I'd like to go over a couple of things about tomorrow. There's something I'd like to show you before it gets any darker, if that's okay."

"All right. Let's walk and talk. You come along,

Mr. Guthrie, and we can continue our conversation after that."

Cookie started to say something, but Riker's look put an end to it, and the three of us, Riker, Chandler, and I, moved away.

"I don't like the looks of some of the horses in the remuda, and . . ."

"Chandler, before you say anything more I want to tell you that you've done a good job, considering your experience, or the lack of it."

"Thank you, Mr. Riker."

"And when we finish up in Abilene there's going to be a sizeable bonus coming to you."

Both Chandler and I were pleasantly surprised.

"Well, sir, I do thank you."

"You could use some extra cash, couldn't you?"

"You bet. My wife and I've had our eye on a little spread along the Brazos and . . ."

"WOLF!"

Pepper's voice cried out a warning.

It happened so fast that I wasn't quite sure how it happened.

Riker dropped his cup and it seemed he sprang aside while shoving Chandler as a knife raced through the air and struck deep into Chandler's chest.

At the same time Pepper's Bowie whistled in another direction and penetrated almost to the hilt into Karl Simpson's midsection.

Twenty feet apart, both men, Chandler and Simpson, dropped to the ground.

Riker looked toward Pepper.

The rest of us stood frozen, all except Dr. Picard, who walked quickly and bent over Chandler whose eyes were locked open in death. Picard, with his fingertips, gently closed Chandler's eyelids.

Then Picard moved toward Karl Simpson. Pepper was already there pulling his Bowie out of the fallen man's body.

Picard went to his knees leaning over the quivering form as Riker came closer.

The doctor looked up at Wolf Riker.

"He's alive."

"Make sure he stays that way," Riker said—to everyone's surprise, until he added—"because I'm going to hang him."

CHAPTER LII

The same words beginning with—"The Lord is my shepherd; I shall not want. He maketh me to lie down in green pastures."

And ending with—"Surely goodness and mercy shall follow me all the days of my life: and I shall dwell in the house of the Lord forever. The Lord giveth and the Lord taketh away. Blessed be the name of the Lord."

Spoken by the same man, with the same unopened Bible in his hand.

But at a different gravesite. Not the bank of the Red River—but at the side of a hill in Indian Territory.

And for a different decedent, not for the soul of a cowboy lost in the surge of an onrushing current—a drover known only as Drago.

But for a buried cowboy named Chandler, killed at the hand of a fellow cowboy with a knife intended for another human target.

This time, Wolf Riker, the intended victim did not interrupt the service by shouting "put an amen to it." He stood silent until Alan Reese had finished the sermon, then stepped closer to Reese, paused for a moment, looked around at the mourners and spoke.

"The trail boss is dead. This drive needs a new trail boss and I'm going to appoint one here and now. From now on, if I'm not around you're all to take orders from him. The new trail boss is Alan Reese."

The drovers and the rest of us silently reacted to this unexpected announcement from Wolf Riker.

"That's all," he concluded, "we'll move out in half-an-hour."

The mourners started to disperse, all except Riker and Reese.

"Mr. Riker," Reese spoke softly, "I have something to say to you."

"Go ahead and say it. And, Mr. Guthrie, don't go away. I want you to hear this . . . if Mr. Reese doesn't mind."

"No, sir, I don't mind."

"Go on then."

"I appreciate your offer, but I can't accept."

"Why not?"

"Because . . . I'm not . . . qualified."

"That's for me to decide. Chandler thought he

wasn't qualified either, but he did a damn good job and so will you."

"The men won't listen to me."

"They will because I told them to."

"I don't want to be put in that position."

"I didn't want to be put in this position either. But I am, and now so are you. You want this drive to succeed, don't you?"

"Yes."

"Then do your part. And as trail boss you'll get the bonus that I promised Chandler."

"I can get by without the bonus. But Chandler's widow, who doesn't know she's a widow, can't. She needs it. Give it to her. That's your good deed. A worthwhile gesture, don't you agree, Mr. Guthrie?"

I looked at Reese.

"Mr. Riker doesn't need advice from me. He has to answer to himself and . . ."

I purposely didn't say anything more.

"I'll take the job, Mr. Riker."

"Good. From now on you're trail boss, Mr. Reese."

"About Karl Simpson," Reese added, "if he survives . . ."

"I said you're the *trail boss*, Mr. Reese. I'm your superior. *I* make that decision."

Wolf Riker turned and walked away.

"You did the right thing," I said to Reese.

"We'll see." He put the Bible in his pocket.

* * *

The drive went on.

Pepper had immediately retrieved his Bowie from the wound he had inflicted on Karl Simpson and replaced it in the sheath on his side. Cookie was also quick to reclaim his kitchen knife from Chandler's lifeless body—and to go on with the "good as done" mission for Wolf Riker.

I knew that Leach and his fellow conspirators would not give up. Another attempt on Riker's life was likely. But how? And when? Either that, or they would leave the drive—disappear in the dark of night and head back across the Red River to Texas. But it was also likely that they would await the outcome of Dr. Picard's effort to save Simpson's life. Likely, but not definite.

Once again, Flaxen was at the side of Dr. Picard, and once again Simpson's life was in the balance—this time in more ways than one.

I had taken two plates into the wagon for Flaxen and Picard, and once again asked the inevitable question.

"It's a fascinating situation," Picard said. "Pepper's knife went deep, and Simpson's lost a lot of blood. But that Bowie didn't decimate any vital organs. I might be able to save his life. But why?"

"Your oath is why. The Hippocratic Oath."

"But Wolf Riker didn't take that oath. He swore

another oath. He's going to hang Simpson. Is that what I'd save him for?"

"Doctor . . ."

"Have you ever seen a man hang, Christopher? I have, and it's ghastly."

"Doctor, you're ahead of yourself."

"What do you mean?"

"I mean save him first, after that anything can happen."

"Such as what? A thunderbolt from above striking Riker dead? Or a sudden clarion call of conscience cleansing that warped brain? Never, my friend."

"Do you think that Leach and the rest of them who attacked Riker that night are—"

"You mean that night that you saved him?"

"—you think they're going to help, or stand idly by, and let Riker hang Simpson?"

"You're right about that," Picard nodded, "One way or another, there's going to be some casualties."

"That's what I mean by being ahead of yourself. Do everything you can to save Simpson, after that . . ."

"After that, what?"

"So will the rest of us."

"Christopher's right," Flaxen said. "And I don't think you even thought of doing anything else . . . *Doctor*."

Picard shrugged, then smiled.

"Of course. I just wanted to hear it from somebody else. But there is something we have to do first."

"What?" Flaxen asked.

Picard pointed to the plates.

"Eat."

I had seen Cookie scurry toward Riker's wagon, knock, then enter.

I waited for what I thought was long enough— but not too long—walked to the entrance past Pepper, and knocked.

"Who is it?" came Riker's voice.

"Christopher Guthrie."

"Come in."

I did.

Riker was seated at his desk holding a piece of paper. Cookie stood nearby, the cat who swallowed the canary on his dirty face.

Wolf Riker glanced up at me.

"I'll be with you in a minute." And he went back to the paper.

I nodded, turned and looked once again at the "unsurrendered sword" on the opposite wall.

It was less than a minute when I heard Riker's voice.

"All right, Cookie—you can leave now."

"I said 'good as done,' didn't I?" Cookie grinned. "Well, it's done. All the names . . ."

"I said you can leave now, Cookie."

Eustice Munger walked past me cackling and mumbling as if I weren't there.

After the door closed I turned toward Riker. He, too, was looking at the sword, then down at the paper still in his hand, then at me.

"Well, Mr. Guthrie, I wonder why you're here?"

"Do you?"

"To give me a report on the condition of Dr. Picard's latest patient, the would-be assassin? Or to plead for his life in case he survives?"

"He may survive."

"The hanging?" Riker smiled.

"Mr. Riker, in the name of heaven . . ."

"Heaven! But we're not in heaven."

"Nor in hell, or are we?"

"What about justice?" Riker waved the paper at me. "These men tried to kill me and so did Simpson. There's such a thing as retribution, and justice."

"You need those men. If you hang Simpson, or try to, they'll take retribution on you. I repeat, you need them. Indians. Comancheros. Border Raiders. God knows what else. Why should they follow you? You'll never finish this drive. They won't fight for you."

"They'll fight and finish the drive—for their own greed."

"Not if you hang Simpson."

"I have a surprise. It'll make a good chapter for your book."

"What surprise?"

"You'll see tomorrow, along with the rest of them."

Wolf Riker folded the paper and put it in his pocket.

"Life is full of surprises, Mr. Guthrie."

CHAPTER LIII

Wolf Riker said that he wanted all of us to be there.

"But a lot of the cattle will stray," Alan Reese said.

"Let 'em stray. We'll gather 'em up later. I want everyone to hear what I have to say."

We were all there. All except Simpson.

Riker stood on a box and lit a cigar as his eyes swept across the assembled drovers, Pepper, Cookie, Dr. Picard, Flaxen, and me.

I had never seen him more confident, calm, and composed. Rather than harshness, there was humor in his voice and attitude.

"Good. All of you step closer. Mr. Guthrie, Miss Brewster. That accounts for everyone except Simpson. We'll get to him later.

"First of all, I want to talk to you about mathematics, among other things.

"More than half of you have worked or ridden with me before—some in uniform, in good times and now in not so good. But there could be something good—better than we've had in a long time—in Kansas.

"I think I can count on that half, I know that most of you have some complaints—well, so have I—but for the most part, we'll stick together and see it through to Abilene.

"But there's a handful among you that wants to see me dead. We'll put that aside for a minute, because as I told Mr. Guthrie last night, I have a surprise in store for all of you—everybody that's here.

"It's true that our supplies are low, too low—flour, sugar, dried beans, coffee and the rest of it, and you haven't got two dime neighbors in your pocket—and even if you did, there'd be no place to spend 'em 'til we get to Kansas.

"Well, the surprise is that there's a place where we can get flour, sugar, beans, coffee, and something stimulating to drink, and the money to fill all your pockets, and then some—and it's not far from here—a damn sight closer than Kansas."

There were shouts from the drovers.

"Where?"

"How close?"

And more.

Riker continued, sangfroid as before, between puffs.

"Fort Concho. That's where. There are some maps in my wagon and only Donavan knew about them. How many of you noticed that we've been veering west the last few days?

"That's because I've got a contract to sell a hundred head of cattle at ten dollars a head to Major Randall Wagner of the U.S. Army—some of them for the Indians and some for the soldiers at the fort."

There was a favorable reaction from most of the drovers, but not all of them.

Leach called out through his perpetual snarl.

"Why didn't you tell us about this before?"

"Because I saved it for just such an occasion, when spirits were low and everybody needed a boost. Well, you're getting that boost now.

"And that's not all. A hundred head at ten dollars a head, speaking of mathematics, you know how much that is? One thousand dollars coin of the realm.

"And do you know how much of that I'm spreading among you? All of it! I'm not pocketing a dime until we get to Kansas."

This produced an even more positive reaction, even from Leach.

"After Concho, it'll still be rough going 'til we

get to market, and there'll be trouble along the way, but we'll make it and you'll go home rich.

"Even with five thousand head at twenty dollars a head that's a hundred thousand dollars.

"I'll keep two-thirds, and the rest is split among you. You figure out how much that'll be—enough to buy a whole hell of a lot of Texas."

At this point there were even cheers. But not from Leach, whose snarl was once again evident.

"How do we know you'll do it?"

"I've been called a lot of things by some of you. But nobody's ever called me a liar. Even so, I intend to put it in writing—today.

"But before I do—about those of you who've already tried to kill me . . ."

He removed a slip of paper from his pocket and unfolded it.

". . . I have the names of those conspirators on this piece of paper."

This time there was a nervous, uncertain reaction.

"Now do you know what I'm going to do with them?

"Nothing. Not one blessed thing.

"And something else. I'm not going to hang Simpson. I'm going to free him . . . after I tear up this paper and forget about it."

Riker knew he had them, all of them, as he

smiled and tore the paper in half, then again and again—and let the pieces flutter to the ground.

"But I have to tell you something else. You've got to be more careful. There's a spy among you . . . an informer."

There was a momentary silence, a pause, as Riker drew on his cigar and allowed the revelation to sink in.

Leach, Smoke, French Frank, and some of the other conspirators all cast their eyes toward me.

I was uneasy to say the least. With Wolf Riker you never knew where you stood, or what he was going to say, or do, next.

"I see you're glancing at Mr. Guthrie. No, gentlemen, not Guthrie. He made a bargain with you and kept it. I tried to persuade him, but he wouldn't inform."

Riker looked at Cookie who was abashed at Riker's breach of trust as Riker went on.

"The spy is Cookie. I can't abide a spy."

By then, Cookie was terrified.

"You have my permission to repay him for his treachery."

That's all they needed. Lead by Leach, Smoke, French Frank, and Dogbreath, they chased after Cookie, who already was trying desperately to scramble out of reach as the pursuers shouted after him.

"The son of a bitch . . ."

"Dirty squealer . . ."

"Get a rope. We'll drag the dirty bastard . . ."

There were other epithets, more purple and descriptive, as they chased after the cursing Cookie, dodging and ducking. But the pursuers came from all directions.

Riker stepped down from the box grinning. Flaxen, Dr. Picard, and I were jolted by Riker's machinations. Pepper stood seemingly unaffected.

A couple of the men grabbed ahold of Cookie, who flailed with both fists and even managed to draw his knife, but it was quickly taken away as he was swarmed over, whining and gibbering, his mouth flecked with bloody foam, while he was brought down on the ground. In seconds a rope circled his wrists, and bound them tight. French Frank appeared on horseback and threw out the loop end of a lariat.

The men fastened it under the shoulders of the quivering and screaming victim.

"Drag him!" Leach commanded.

French Frank needed no encouragement. He spurred his mount until the rope snapped tight and jerked Cookie off the surface of the ground but only for a moment. He landed hard and was bobbing and bouncing through the torturous terrain tearing at his hurtling body.

But French Frank did not want to deny the drovers the sight and satisfaction of their revenge.

After a couple hundred feet or so, he whirled his horse and started back toward the onlookers, this time at a slower pace, still dragging and punishing the hapless man across the rugged tract through chuckholes, mesquite, and rocks.

But the drovers wanted more, shouting at French Frank to speed up again. He reacted favorably, spurring his mount.

But as the rider and horse began to bolt, Riker reached out his hand and Pepper lodged the handle of the Bowie into Riker's palm, who with one sure stroke severed the taut rope, and Cookie lay on the ground, barely conscious, twitching and cursing.

The drovers, most of them, obviously were disappointed that Cookie's travail had come to such an abrupt conclusion, surprisingly by the hand of Wolf Riker. But then, Wolf Riker was full of surprises that day. He looked at Flaxen, whose face was white, her eyes dilated with distress as she turned away.

"Man play, Miss Brewster," Riker said, drawing on his cigar. "It could have been much worse. He'll be back to his pots and pans soon enough, won't he, Dr. Picard?"

Picard was already leaning over Cookie. So was Alan Reese, cutting away the ropes that still bound the battered and contused Cookie.

Riker handed Pepper his Bowie, and looked at me.

"You see, Mr. Guthrie, I told you they'd finish the drive."

Then Riker turned and walked away, followed by a trail of cigar smoke and Pepper.

CHAPTER LIV

After that we were on the Hallelujah Trail to Fort Concho—or so the drovers thought.

But for Flaxen and me it would be the end of the trail. The end of this trail—and the beginning of a new one. That's where the two of us would bid *adiós* to Wolf Riker.

From Fort Concho there had to be a safer passage West, and Flaxen and I would book that passage.

After Wolf Riker's surprise speech, and Cookie's ordeal, there was almost an air of celebration along the way.

Picard, Flaxen, and I told Simpson that Riker had pardoned him from execution by hanging. He understood what we said, but reacted as if he had something else in mind. And as Riker predicted, soon after Dr. Picard's ministering to the cuts and bruises, Cookie was back among his pots and pans again. During the interim, Morales One and Morales Two filled in with an assist from me, and the cuisine was much improved.

The drovers, anxious to get to Fort Concho, drove the herd and themselves hard. At the end of each day men and animals were near exhaustion. But there were no complaints—not from the men.

On a couple of occasions there were even songs around the campfire—Lorena, Shenandoah, Bringing in the Sheaves—and Morales One and Two serenaded the moon in Spanish.

One night Wolf Riker invited me into his wagon for a cigar and brandy. When I entered he was going over his maps and looked up with a contented smile.

"Well, Mr. Guthrie, tomorrow or the next day we should be within sight of Fort Concho."

"Have you been there before?"

"No," he said, "but I know a little something about it. Years ago, to protect the wagon trains and stagecoaches moving West, the government set up army posts in the territory, but those outposts fell like a dark shadow over the Indian way of life. When the war broke out the Union Army needed all the manpower it could get, especially if that manpower had already been exposed to the ways of war. Much of that manpower was in the West. Some of the forts were abandoned. Others had to make do with reduced ranks. One of those was Fort Concho. All I know is that it's still there among the Kiowas, Comanches, Cheyenne, Cherokees, and a whole lot of other tribes—some of them sided with the Union and some with us. At any rate, I've got a deal to provide the army with beeves. We'll find out more when we get there."

And we did, much more.

From a distance it looked tiny—almost like a toy—anchored in a sea of sand.

And even closer it was still small—too small, it seemed, to make much difference in such a vast expanse.

We could sense that there was something wrong.

An unreal quietness.

No guard was posted. No colors flew from the staff. The gates were open, but nothing stirred. No living sound came from within.

And an uneasy quiet fell over all of us until Wolf Riker barked his commands.

Leach and Smoke were to stay outside with the herd.

The rest of us, including the wagons, were to follow Riker through the gates and into the fort.

Once inside it didn't take long to realize our worst fears.

Fort Concho had been attacked and wiped out.

In the center of the compound the ashes and remains of a huge pyre—a crematorium for the dead and wounded—from which came the odor of burnt flesh and bones—the smell of death.

Even those who had been battle hardened during the war had never seen anything to compare to the sickening sight and smell within the walls of Fort Concho.

We were stunned into silence—for how long I'm not sure—but only until that silence was ruptured by gunshots.

CHAPTER LV

They were at the gates—then inside the gates.

Indians. Some with rifles, others with lances, bows, and arrows.

How many, it was hard to tell. But too many.

And with them Leach and Smoke, bound by leather thongs and with blood leaking from a wound at Leach's head.

Carrying a coupe stick, the Chief was on the biggest horse, a piebald. His age, indeterminate, but he was no longer a young man. His eyes, two hard, narrow streaks. His face, worn, dark, and broad.

Next to the Chief, a younger warrior, the Goliath of the tribe, bigger even than Wolf Riker, with mounds of muscle bulging from his bare chest and arms. And on another mount, an Indian with a bullet-torn, and bleeding shoulder. The Chief spoke.

"I am Satanta."

"And I'm Wolf Riker." He stepped forward. "I know of Satanta, who was once called The Great Orator of the Plains"—Riker pointed to the pyre—". . . and now butchers and burns instead of speaking words of wisdom for his people."

Satanta's gaze went to the pyre and then to Riker.

Satanta dismounted, so did some of the other warriors, including the giant. Satanta took a step forward carrying the coupe stick in his left hand.

"You are called Wolf?"

"That's right, Wolf Riker."

"Wolf Riker, like other white men, you are quick to condemn . . ."

"So were you when you butchered and burned the . . ."

"No!"

"No, what?" Riker pointed at the pyre again. "There's the proof."

"That is not the act of the Kiowa. That is not why we came here."

For once I saw the look of puzzlement in Wolf Riker's face. He scanned the ground and picked up an arrow. He held it up toward Satanta.

"What's this?"

"Again, you are quick to condemn."

Riker walked away from Satanta, close to Smoke, and raised the arrow near the black man's face.

It didn't take Smoke long.

"Cheyenne."

Riker moved back to Satanta, broke the arrow in half and dropped the two pieces to the ground.

"I haven't said this many times before, but I say it now so everybody can hear. I was wrong, Satanta—and I'm sorry I spoke as I did."

Satanta said nothing.

Riker looked at Leach, then at the wounded Indian.

"What happened out there? The shots?"

Satanta pointed to the muscular red man.

"Iron Hand will tell you, his brother . . ."

"I'd rather hear it from him," Riker pointed to Smoke.

"As you wish," Satanta replied, "for now."

Smoke, still bound, took a step forward.

"Leach and I were talking, speculating about the fort. All of a sudden we were surrounded— Indians pointing guns at us. I guess Leach lost his head, drew and fired, hit one of them. I tried to stop him, but too late. They jumped us, bashed Leach's head—and here we are."

Riker looked at Leach, who, still dazed and bleeding, bowed his bashed head.

"Once again, Satanta, I have to say it. I was wrong and I'm sorry."

But Satanta was now looking at Riker's midsection, at the CSA buckle on Riker's belt.

"You fought against the Blue Coats."

"That's right, Satanta, during the war you and I fought on the same side."

"But for different reasons."

"Maybe not so different. But then, why *did* you come to Fort Concho?"

"We were promised beef. Food for our people."

Iron Hand stepped forward, pointed at Leach, then turned to Satanta and spoke in the Kiowa language.

As he spoke I noticed that the expression on Smoke's face became grim.

When Iron Hand finished, Wolf Riker started to say something.

"Satanta, you know that we have many . . ."

But Satanta held up the coupe stick.

"There is something that must be done. It is Kiowa law."

"What is?"

"Iron Hand's brother, Running Bear, is wounded and could have been killed by . . ."

"We have a doctor," Riker said, and pointed at Picard. "He has medicine. He will . . ."

"We have our own doctor and our own medicine, but Iron Hand demands the Blood Rite, to fight and kill the one who did this. It is Kiowa Law."

Wolf Riker laughed. The rest of us didn't. Then Riker spoke, and once again we were surprised at what he had to say.

"He will fight a small, wounded man half his

size because of his brother? That small, wounded man is *my* brother. Let him fight and kill me if he has the courage."

And without warning, in a whip-like motion, Wolf Riker slapped the face of Iron Hand hard, back and forth.

Iron Hand had no choice.

And neither did Wolf Riker, once the Blood Rite was explained to him.

Riker and Iron Hand would be tied left wrist to left wrist by a leather thong six feet long. Satanta would throw a razor sharp knife into a wall twenty feet away. The two would start a no-holds-barred run to get the knife and plunge it into the other's heart.

Satanta's arm arched back and came forward in a single, swift motion. The knife flew fast and sure, stuck into the wall and quivered.

Riker and Iron Hand ran toward the knife, Iron Hand a couple of paces ahead until Riker stopped, braced himself and jerked back with all his strength against the thong and Iron Hand, who was halted abruptly. But Iron Hand looped the thong. It circled Riker's neck. They both spilled to the ground, twisted over each other's body. Riker's elbow exploded into the Indian's face, stunning him. Riker freed his neck from the encircling thong.

But the red man's right hand secured the

knife. Iron Hand lunged—Riker sidestepped and hammered his fist into Iron Hand's jaw.

Riker crashed into him. Both men fell to the ground. Riker grabbed the knife hand with his left and smashed the Indian with the other. Still Iron Hand raised the knife and plunged it down.

Riker moved just in time and the knife was buried almost to the hilt in the ground next to Riker's ear. In the same instant, Riker's right fist burst into Iron Hand's face, splattering bone and gristle, with blood spurting from his nose and mouth.

Riker made a tight loop around Iron Hand's neck and pulled hard, his other hand gripped the knife handle and pulled it away from the earthen sheath, then brought the blade close to the Indian's throat, slowly the deadly blade came ever closer. The red man's eyes flashed with fear and frenzy. The veins in his neck swelled into thick, throbbing cords as he tried in vain to hold back Riker's hand. In another instant the red man would be dead—all the pent-up power in those bunched up muscles drained in defeat, rendering him defenseless. But suddenly Wolf Riker's hand holding the knife moved in another direction, with one swift stroke, cutting the thong that bound his own wrist, freeing himself and relieving the pressure from around Iron Hand's throat.

Iron Hand fell back against the ground barely conscious, but helpless, and did not move.

Riker rose to his feet—knife still in hand. He walked to Satanta, turned the handle toward the Chief and extended it.

"Satanta," he said, "we're still on the same side. We'll cut out a hundred head of cattle to feed your people."

Satanta took the knife and nodded.

CHAPTER LVI

What the hell kind of a man was Wolf Riker?

There was no way to define him.

Not from the way he responded on different occasions to the Indians—and certainly not from the way, or ways, he reigned over those of us on the drive—with absolute authority—from calculated cruelty to unexpected guardsman and defender, as was the case at Fort Concho when he risked his life on behalf of George Leach.

During that deadly encounter, all eyes had been riveted on the two gladiators, those of the Indians and certainly, those of us on the drive, including me. But I couldn't help glancing momentarily, from time to time, at the drovers, at Picard, Cookie, Pepper, and Flaxen, who was the exception, and whose eyes were averted downward so as not to witness what seemed to be the inevitable and violent death of either Iron Hand or Wolf Riker—and what might have been the end of the drive and us. As the Blood Rite began and Riker and Iron Hand ran toward the knife, Flaxen took hold of my hand and squeezed. She did not let go or stop squeezing until Riker turned the knife over to Satanta.

The truth was, no matter how anyone on the drive had felt about him, Wolf Riker was our gladiator, our champion, and none of us would have had the inclination, grit, or strength to have done what he was risking his life doing.

But afterward, when the hundred head of cattle were cut out and gifted to the Kiowas, and the drive continued, we were no longer on the Hallelujah Trail.

Luckily for us the cattle had not stampeded at the sound of the gunshots, probably because they were too tired. But the Cheyenne had left nothing at Fort Concho except cremated corpses.

We were still in short supply. The bounty that Riker had promised did not exist—no flour, sugar, beans, coffee, or something stimulating to drink, and no thousand dollar bonus to split among the drovers.

The Hallelujah Trail had become the Helleluiah Trail—with no end in sight.

Wolf Riker had once again become his unyielding, resolute self, with one aim in mind—Kansas.

And the drovers, particularly the conspirators, reverted to a more discernible drumbeat of revolt. Even Leach, whose head had been tended to by Dr. Picard, was still working the drag, and for whose life Wolf Riker had intervened, was heard to snark:

"He didn't do it for me. He did it for his goddamn drive."

That didn't altogether seem to make much sense, but it also didn't altogether seem to much matter, as Riker pressed us ever harder.

What happened during supper two nights later didn't help.

"Hello, the camp!"

We—all of us, including Wolf Riker—reacted to the crusty voice out of the darkness. The voice was followed by an even crustier character emerging into the light of the campfire and carrying a Sharps buffalo rifle.

His face was crisscrossed with creases and a crop of spiky yellow-white hair under what went for a hat. He was dressed in faded buckskin that appeared almost as old as he did. The whites of his eyes weren't white, more orange.

"Who's on guard out there?" Riker wanted to know.

"Wouldn't matter." The man smiled. "Long time ago I learned to walk moccasin soft and leave my pony a far piece. Who's the high hicalorum?"

"I am." Riker took a step forward.

"Abner Twist." The man smiled wider, this time

revealing discolored, rutty, and absent teeth. "Buffler hunter."

"I never would have guessed," Riker said.

"I know," Twist nodded, "buffler hunters smell like old guts all the time."

And he did.

"Could you eat?" Riker asked.

"I could and I would. Been killin' what I et for the last three days."

"Cookie," Riker said, "fix Mr. Twist a plate and some coffee."

The meat and drink did not interfere with Abner Twist's loquacity.

"Mighty lot of beef you got out there, Mr. Kiker."

"Riker."

"Right. I say maybe six thousand head."

"More or less."

"Good coffee."

"Glad you like it."

"Where you headin'?"

"Kansas."

"That'ud be north."

"It would—and is."

"I wouldn't."

"Wouldn't what?"

"Head north."

"That's the way to get there."

"Maybe and maybe not."

"Why not?"

"Comancheros. Saw their handy work a few days back."

"Chew it finer, not the food," Riker said.

"Ever hear of a bastard named Corona?"

"No."

"You will if you keep north. Got a hideout in the hills, forty or fifty of the worst sons of bitches in the territory—hit anythin' comes through and trade with the Comanches and Cheyenne—be it goods, wagons, cattle, horses, or humans. This outfit 'ud make a mighty temptin' target for that one-eyed booger."

"Corona, you mean."

"That's him I mean. Wears a black patch to match his black heart, if'n he had one—'breed sonofabitch, part injun, part panther. I seen what he done to that wagon train up north."

"What?"

"I seen 'em hit them four wagons, massacre some humans, and carry some away—along with the wagons and everythin' worth takin'."

"Were you with the wagon train?"

"Hell, no. Heard gunshots—looked down from a hill at a safe distance and seen 'em swarm in. Stayed at a safe distance and watched the whole shebang."

"You *watched*?" Riker repeated.

"Hell, yes. My ma and pa only raised one damn fool and that was my brother, who's dead. I could'na made much difference except to get killet. Say, could you spare another cup of that coffee?"

"Cookie, pour Mr. Twist some more coffee," Riker said, as we all looked on, and at each other.

"Much obliged," Mr. Twist nodded.

"I don't suppose you'd care to join the drive," Riker said.

Abner Twist shook his shaggy head.

"Headin' west. Santa Fe's buildin' a railroad, and they'll need buffler to feed on. That's where me and my Sharps'll be. Killed many a buffler. If there's another world and them bufflers got ghosts, I got a heap of explainin' to do."

"I'd say you have, Mr. Twist," Riker nodded.

"And I'd say you and your outfit better not cross anywhere's near Corona's territory. Well, thanks for the grub. I'll be gone before first light."

And he was.

CHAPTER LVII

"Buffler hunter" Abner Twist and his cautionary account of Corona and the wagon train was just that much more of what Wolf Riker already had too much of—trouble.

If there is a mutiny aboard a ship at sea, the mutineers can take over the vessel, bind or kill the captain, and sail to some island.

But what do the mutineers do on a cattle drive with six or seven thousand head of balky beeves, if they overpower or kill the owner—and are unable to market them? One way, or another, they'd still have to get through Corona and his Comancheros. The other choice would be to desert and forgo any compensation for what they'd endured so far.

They would have to make their choice in the next few days.

One of them, Smoke, made so bold as to ask Riker what he intended to do about Corona.

Wolf Riker's reply was enigmatic at best.

"Trust me," he said, "I've got a way to deal with Corona."

But the drovers had little trust in what Riker said.

It was one thing to deal with Satanta, a Confederate ally—and fight Iron Hand mano-a-mano, it was another thing to deal with a cutthroat Comanchero who had no allegiance to anybody or anything except wanton pillage for profit.

"Here's a pot of tea Riker asked for," Cookie said. "Be a good fella and take it over to him."

"Why don't you take it yourself—or are you still suffering the effects of Riker's man play?"

"I don't want to ever get any closer to that sonofabitch than I have to. He'll get his soon enough, he will."

"Would you like me to deliver that message along with the tea, Cookie?"

A look of concern, of trepidation, came over the man's welted face, and he was sorry as soon as he said it.

"You won't say anything about what I just said, will you, 'cause if you do I'll . . ."

"You'll what?"

He didn't know what to say or do. He just stood there holding the tray of tea with a helpless expression, and the truth is, I even felt a modicum of sympathy for what had happened to him—but only a modicum.

"Don't worry, Cookie, I am not an informer."

The door to Riker's wagon was ajar. I knocked. No response.

I pushed the door farther open, entered, and placed the tea tray on the desk. I couldn't help but notice the set of maps—and I couldn't help wondering if one of those maps might hold the key to freedom for Flaxen and me.

The first was a chart of Texas and territory we had already passed through. No help.

The others were of more interest.

The Indian Territory.

Kansas.

Rough, but better than nothing. Much better. My finger began to trace a line . . .

"Have you developed a sudden interest in geography, Mr. Guthrie?"

Riker's voice cut through me like a lightning bolt. I had no notion what his further reaction might be—but once again—the unexpected.

Calm. Almost congenial.

"You must have heard some of the men conspiring to get rid of me, or of deserting, but then what would they do? Where would they head? For that matter, where would you and your fiancée head . . . besides, they wouldn't be very good company. Is that what you were trying to determine?"

I didn't know what to say or do, so I said and did nothing.

He walked closer and picked up the maps.

"There's a river crossing station about a hundred and fifty miles northwest, along the Cimarron, but you'd never make it, not the two of you."

"We'll make it . . ."

"No, you won't. Nobody's leaving this drive alive until I . . ."

"You know this is no place for her, those men are . . ."

"Your colleagues. My crew. Destiny brought you to this drive and here you'll stay. Both of you—"

Riker set the maps back on the desk and lit a cigar.

"—all of you. I'll need everyone."

"For Corona? Or . . . your brother?"

Wolf Riker's lips became tighter.

"For anything that comes." Then softer. "But in the meanwhile, we'll have supper together again. Just like the last time. You, your fiancée, Dr. Picard . . . and me."

CHAPTER LVIII

Not more than a half dozen steps away from Wolf Riker's wagon, Pepper stood lighting his pipe.

"How'd the two of you get along this time, Mr. Guthrie?"

"Oh, fine. Even got invited to supper. I wonder if it might just be the Last Supper."

"None of us can tell," Pepper puffed, "which'll be the Last Supper."

"Especially with Wolf Riker."

"I sometimes wondered the same thing—but then, I've had a lot more suppers than you."

"I'd like mine to be in San Francisco, or even Timbuktu."

"I know what you mean."

"Do you also know that it seems to me he reacted more when I mentioned his brother than when I mentioned Corona?"

"I wouldn't be surprised."

"In front of the bank that Wolf told me about— was that the last time the two of you saw Dirk Riker?"

"The last time Wolf saw his brother, but I saw him again."

"You did?"

"One more time." Pepper took another puff, a long one. "Come on over here. Let's sit on this log while I finish this smoke, and I'll tell you about it."

We moved to the log and sat.

"I was alone on a buckboard, comin' back from Gilead, gettin' close to the Double R and there was horses and riders—as big a roundup as I ever seen. And also there was Dirk Riker with another imposin' fella mounted next to him. That fella, he wore a red scarf 'round his neck, and Dirk, he greeted me friendly enough.

"'How you doing, Pepper?'

"'Leanin' forward all the way.'

"'Good. How's that roundup of beeves coming along?'

"'Good enough. Gettin' close to the seven thousand mark. Looks like . . .' I pointed '. . . you're doin' good, too. Never seen that many horses, maybe near a thousand.'

"'Maybe more. Good ones.'

"'Never seen so many riders either. Looks like a whole brigade.'

"'Not quite.'

"'Notice they're all wearin' red scarves—like your friend there.'

"'Pepper, this is Adam Dawson, late of General George Armstrong Custer's Michigan Red Scarf Brigade.'

"'Yeah, they was also known as Custer's Wolverines. I heard of 'em, guess everybody did—on both sides.'

"'Glad to meet you, Mr. Pepper.'

"This Dawson fella had a sunny smile for such serious eyes.

"'Ain't no mister about it, nor "sir," nor ol' timer—just plain Pepper. How far did you ride with Custer?'

"'Well, "just plain Pepper," nobody rode *with* Custer, we all rode behind him—from Chickahominy, Brandy Station, Falls Church, Gettysburg, Yellow Tavern, to Appomattox.'

"'Yellow Tavern, huh? Surprised you didn't meet up with Dirk's brother. He rode with J.E.B Stuart.'

"'Maybe we did, once or twice. Never did have time for introductions.' Dawson continued to smile.

"'Well, don't meet up with him around here.'

"'War's over, Pepper.'

"'Don't try tellin' that to Wolf Riker.'

"'Adam,' Dirk said, 'my brother hasn't beat his sword into a plowshare, and never will.'

"'That's right, Dirk. And do you mind if I give

you and your Red Scarf Brigade a little friendly
admonition?'

"'Wouldn't try to stop you, Pepper.'

"'Don't come too close to the Double R durin'
your roundup, or to Wolf Riker's herd durin' the
drive.'

"And that's the last time I seen Wolf's brother—
and the last time I want to see him 'til the drive's
over."

Pepper took the last long puff from his pipe,
then knocked the ash off on the log.

"Well, I guess that's enough for tonight."

"Yes," I nodded, "I'd say that's plenty, and, no
matter what happens, I'd guess you'll stick with
Wolf Riker."

"Till the wheels come off and the pissants carry
me through the keyhole." Pepper got to his feet.
"I hope you enjoy that supper."

CHAPTER LIX

Cookie begged off cooking and serving the supper, saying that he was feeling poorly. Morales One and Morales Two took over the task, much to everyone's satisfaction.

Dr. Picard reluctantly accepted the invitation, as did Flaxen.

Once again Wolf Riker was a charming host—at first.

And once again Riker broke out the brandy and cigars. Flaxen partook of the brandy, Dr. Picard of neither.

Through supper the conversation remained innocuous until Riker inquired—

"How's your patient, doctor? Will he be willing and able to resume his duties?"

"Able? I think so. Willing . . . ?"

"I'll take care of that part."

"I'm sure you will," Picard said.

"And you, John-a-dreams, how's the journal coming along? And your characterization of me?"

"Any characterization is incomplete until the end is known."

"Not always. Take Milton and his characterization of Lucifer . . . 'hurled into hell, he was unbeaten and was not afraid of God's thunderbolts . . . a third of God's angels he led with him . . .' Yes, Mr. Guthrie, 'better to reign in hell, than serve in heaven.'"

"What about Corona's thunderbolts . . . and the drovers' . . . and your brother's?"

"I have a few thunderbolts of my own. What do you and your kind . . . like Miss Brewster here, know about those of us who were not to the manor born?"

"My life," I said, "was a waste, a sham, but . . ."

"All you care about is your kind."

Then Riker looked at Flaxen.

"I'll wager that if you weren't a high born lady of refinement you wouldn't be engaged to Guthrie; he would not be your benefactor, your protector. If you were . . ."

"But I'm not."

"Not what?" Riker asked.

I motioned to Flaxen not to say or reveal anymore, but she ignored me and went on.

"A lady. I'm not a lady. I'm a thief. At least a thief's accomplice. He happened to be my father . . . but still . . ."

"And Guth, you . . . you knew this all the time?"

"Yes, he did."

Riker pointed.

"The ring . . ."

"His mother's. He placed it on my finger after . . . after we got here, and before . . ."

"But why? Ah, I see . . ."

Riker studied me for just an instant.

"You thought if the rest of us knew, we might treat her differently. Lucky nobody found out."

"Dr. Picard found out," I said, "but he didn't say anything."

"Another do-gooder." Riker looked at Picard.

Picard remained silent, but I didn't. I rose.

"Why not, Mr. Riker? If we have it in our power to do good . . . why not? And can't you see that?"

"Why should a wise man look upon fools and wish to be a fool? Why . . ."

Riker paused. I knew what was coming. First one hand, then the other went to his forehead. He tried to rise, but sagged at the hips. His great shoulders drooped and shrugged forward. He was in pain and nearly sightless.

I moved closer.

"Riker, let me . . ."

"There's nothing you can do."

"The doctor . . ."

"There's nothing any of you can do. Get out! I don't need any of you. Get out!"

We left him, his arms on the table, his head

buried in his palms . . . and closed the door behind us.

Pepper was outside and started toward the entrance.

"He doesn't want anybody with him," I cautioned.

"I ain't *anybody*," Pepper said, and went inside.

No sooner did the door to the wagon close, than a voice came from somewhere in the night. The voice was unmistakably Cookie's.

"Just a minute, friends. Don't be in such a hurry."

But from where?

Out he crawled from under Wolf Riker's wagon.

"We got somethin' to talk over," he said from an even grimier mouth than usual.

He moved nearer to the three of us and spoke in a cackling whisper.

"So the Wolf man's havin' another fit. Good! I hope he goes to hell in a hurry. No! Let the bastard suffer. Oh, excuse my language, lady, but then you ain't a lady are you . . . *missy*—that's right I heard it all," he cackled even nastier. "Bore me a hole under his wagon sometime ago and took advantage of it tonight instead of servin' supper; so now I know sumpin' none of them other rawhiders does, and that ought to be worth plenty to you and the . . . *missy*."

"Cookie, you are a reprehensible . . ."

"Never mind that, Guth. I can keep a secret . . .

for a price . . . say that sparkler missy wears on her ring finger . . ."

"If you say a word I swear I'll kill you."

"I believe you would if you could, but that'ud be too late and who knows what might happen to the *lady*. But I ain't in no hurry. I'll give you two, no, make it three days to think it over—then my tongue just might start to get . . . slippery." He pointed, "The ring'ud put the brakes on it—so think it over . . . pardners."

Eustice Munger walked away and left the three of us looking at each other.

CHAPTER LX

The three of us went directly to Dr. Picard's wagon. Karl Simpson was asleep, or unconscious. At any rate we knew he could not hear what was being said—and decided—in whispers.

I couldn't help admonishing Flaxen.

"Why did you tell him about yourself?"

"I couldn't stand his arrogant self-assurance any longer. I had to prove him wrong about something, and besides, I'm tired of trying to live a lie."

"Look, you two," Picard said, "never mind what already happened. The question is what are you going to do about it . . . and that rat Cookie?"

"You're right of course, doctor. And it's not only Cookie. We've got a madman in charge, a mutinous bunch that's liable to do anything— killer Comancheros ahead of us, and Wolf Riker's brother probably not far behind. It's a powder keg that could blow up anytime. We've only got one chance. The sooner we get away from here the better."

"Away?" Flaxen shrugged. "Where?"

"When Riker caught me going over his maps, he let slip that there was a crossing station along the Cimarron a hundred and fifty miles northwest."

"A hundred and fifty miles," Picard emphasized.

"It's a desperate gamble, but a better chance than staying here."

"What about the Comancheros?" Picard noted.

"They're less likely to spot the three of us than six or seven thousand head of cattle."

"That's true," he nodded. "But if you go—it's just the two of you."

"But why . . ."

"I'm old and weak. I'd only slow you down and you'd need more supplies. You're better off without me and you know it."

"What about you, Flaxen? Will you risk it?"

She smiled.

"Sometime ago I said you'd do the deciding. *'Wither thou goest, I will go.'*"

CHAPTER LXI

The next day I managed to secrete supplies in a burlap bag without Cookie, or anybody else noticing—or so I thought.

"Thinking of taking a little side trip?" Alan Reese said when the two of us were alone.

But to my relief he quickly added—

"Don't worry, Mr. Guthrie. Your secret is safe with me. I think it's the best course for you, and I'll even do what I can to help."

"Will you come with us, Flaxen and me?"

"No."

"Why not?"

"I broke an agreement once, actually a vow. I have no intention of breaking my agreement with Wolf Riker, no matter what I think of him."

"You said you are an unfrocked priest. Would you mind telling me why?"

"No, I would not mind. They say confession is

good for the soul. Years ago, when I was a young priest, there was this younger couple, both friends of mine, who had asked me to marry them. Of course I agreed. The night before the wedding she was brutally murdered. All the evidence pointed to him. Blood. The weapon. He was convicted and sentenced to hang. But another man who had coveted her, and was now himself sick and dying, came to me and confessed, to wipe the sin from his immortal soul. He knew I could not break the sanctity of the confessional. But I did. I could not bear to see that young boy hang for something he did not do. So I broke the law of the church in order to save his life."

"But surely the church wouldn't . . ."

"Wouldn't unfrock me? I don't know. I didn't wait to find out. But I knew that I'd broken my vow, so . . . I unfrocked myself. I took off my collar and ran away . . . to Texas, as good a place as any for a sinner to hide."

"I'm not of your religion, but I don't believe that being a priest has anything to do with a frock or a collar—or that you have any reason to hide."

"Then why is it I see a shadow on the wall, where there is no wall?"

"I don't understand."

"I hope you never do, Mr. Guthrie. I hope you

never do. Yes, Mr. Guthrie, I'm staying here. But I will help you."

And he did.

The next day was fraught with anxiety and trepidation.

Cookie kept casting glances at both Flaxen and me that he meant to be meaningful reminders.

And whether it was my imagination or not, it seemed to me that some of the drovers looked at her, also in a different light—Leach, Dogbreath, French Frank. I couldn't help wondering if Cookie might have voiced, or hinted at some implication regarding her gentility.

Wolf Riker spent most of the day aboard Bucephalus, without seeming to have suffered any residual effects from the previous night's attack.

Pepper uttered not a word to anyone, not even to the animals pulling Riker's wagon.

Unfortunately, Karl Simpson took a turn for the worse. Dr. Picard believed that an infection had set in, and there was nothing he could do except dose his patient with laudanum to ease the pain until the end.

Supper was nearly unbearable, and I did my best to suppress the telltale quivering fingers of both hands as I served the drovers for what I hoped would be the last time on the drive.

How we would have fared without the help of Alan Reese is impossible to say, or think.

He had both our horses, Tobacco and Bluebell, saddled and laden with canteens and supplies, waiting at a prearranged spot a couple hundred yards from camp.

As Flaxen and I mounted, I looked down at him and whispered.

"Thank you. And please . . . say a prayer for us, padre."

"It's been a long time since anyone called me . . . that."

"But not a long time since you prayed."

Then we rode in the direction I hoped was northwest.

CHAPTER LXII

As we rode slowly away in what might have been a romantic moonlight, but in this case wasn't, I couldn't help thinking it was tantamount to leaving a large ship in distress with a maniacal captain and mutinous crew on a storm-torn sea, and boarding a compassless dinghy in that same stabbing tempest.

And instead of a liquid horizon in an infinite horizontal track, we faced a vast uncharted terrain—an endless earthen patchwork quilt of soil and stone, mountain and meadow, hillock and crust.

It was as if the Creator couldn't make up His mind what to do with it, or what it should look like, so He let the pieces fall where they may in a helter-skelter patchwork of some of this and some of that.

It was no wonder that the government gave it to the Indians. The wonder was that the Indians accepted it. But for us it was not only nature's contention—God only knew what human hostility might strike, be it Cheyenne, Kiowa, Comanche, or Comanchero. And there was the possibility that Wolf Riker would dispatch a couple of his drovers to bring us back to face the consequences of desertion as an example of what would happen to anyone else with the same idea.

All that on one side of the equation; on the other, the fact that Flaxen and I were together and away from what might have been a grimmer fate due to Cookie's invidious tongue, the drovers' lust, and Wolf Riker's caprice.

We rode at a moderate pace to preserve the strength of the animals, fed them the grain I had taken with us, whenever and wherever there was nothing on the ground for them to graze on. And the two of us ate more sparingly than we had ever eaten before—and drank even more sparingly, until the canteens were less than half full and more than half empty.

On the third day and near night, just as a cold wind whipped across our sand-streaked faces, we came upon the first sight of shelter.

A cave.

A natural hollowed out portion of a rocky embankment not far ahead.

A few minutes later, after leaving Flaxen and the animals outside, I entered, gun drawn, and examined the gritrock floor and uneven walls of the miniature cavern.

No sign of life. No wolves. No coyotes. No bats.

And a short time after that, a fire with warmth enough for the unsaddled horses, and for Flaxen and me.

The cave was, to put it mildly, aromatic from previous tenants, probably wolves, coyotes, and bats, but under the circumstances, it suited us better than the not-so-great and oh-so-cold out-doors.

After a less than hearty meal, Flaxen moved closer, close enough for me to put my arms around her, and for her to return the favor.

"Then flashed the living lightning from her eyes"—a reflection of the pent-up passion in mine.

Each of us held the future in each other's arms—if we had a future. The only thing we really knew—we had tonight.

And we both knew that what happened after that was inevitable.

In a way, so was what happened the next morning—waking up to guns pointed at both of us.

CHAPTER LXIII

The guns were each in the right hand of George Leach and French Frank—and on their faces, grins—not of good will.

"Well," Leach said, "nice, cozy setup, while it lasted—but the gimcrack's over."

"I thought Wolf Riker might send somebody after us, but I never figured it'ud be you two."

"Oh, Wolf Riker didn't send us."

"He didn't?"

"Hell, no. We quit on him. Just like you did." Leach smiled at Flaxen through his perpetual snarl. "Well, not exactly like you, Guth. You got more companionable company than either French Frank or me—so far."

I did my best to ignore the remark.

"And you just happened to stumble on this cave and us."

"Not likely. You weren't all that hard to follow

after Cookie told us he heard Riker tellin' Pepper about that crossin' station to the northwest."

"Cookie, huh?"

"Seemed like a good idea—getting' outta there—better than meetin' up with them Comancheros."

"Then I'm surprised there aren't more of you."

"Hell, no. Figured it'ud be best to sneak off, just the two of us, better than a few more of us facin' Riker's guns and that son of a bitch Pepper in a showdown."

"Very judicious."

"What's that mean?"

"Smart."

"We thought so. Didn't we, Frank?"

French Frank didn't bother to answer. His eyes never left Flaxen.

"Oh, by the way, Guth," Leach went on, "you shudda seen Riker when he found out you was gone—like he had a face fulla crawlin' blue snakes. Thought he was gonna throw a fit. Could hardly keep from shudderin'. First started out in a whisper. 'Traitor—Traitor'—then he gritted his teeth and hollered 'TRAITOR!' There's nobody I can trust!'—then he seen Pepper lookin' at him and he sorta calmed down some; but, did he get his hands on you, I wouldn't want to stand in your boots, bub. Come to think on it—I wouldn't want to stand in your boots right now—'course, I do imagine you had some good times with the *Missy* here—with your boots off."

Leach was the only one laughing. French Frank's attention was still absorbed by Flaxen Brewster.

While Leach laughed, I was gratified that I had remembered something Pepper had once said.

"And," Leach's laugh had dissolved into a grin again, "when ol' Doc Picard told him that Simpson was dead, he commenced to smile, then laugh. 'Good! Good!' he said, 'there is some ret . . . retrib . . . bu . . .'"

"Retribution?"

"Yeah, that's it—ret-rib-you-sion. Then that short-bit trail boss, Reese, asked about buryin' Simpson. 'I don't care what you do with him,' Riker says. 'But this outfit moves in fifteen minutes.' And we did, but some time later, French Frank and me, we moved in a different direction— and here we are—all nice and cozy, right Frank?"

"Right." For the first time French Frank's look turned away from Flaxen and aimed at me. "And I ain't forgot that fast one you pulled on me when I took that tumble, you bastard, and now it's my turn to pull somethin' on you, somethin' you'll remember long as you live and that ain't gonna be long."

"Sure, Frank," Leach said, "he'll get his, but first . . . there's one other thing, Guth, that Cookie told us."

"What's that?"

"About her. She ain't your 'fiancée.' Are you, *Missy*? She's your floozie."

"Leach . . ."

"Mighty greedy on your part, Guth. Keepin' her all to yourself instead of sharin' her . . . favors. We're part human, too, you know."

"Are you, Leach?"

"Sure I am." He winked at her. "And you know which part, don't you, *Missy*?"

"Leach, I swear . . ."

"You won't be around long enough to swear to anythin', pretty plug. All right, we've had enough talk. Now then, *Missy*. Take it off." He pointed with the gun. "The ring . . . his mother's ring." Leach laughed. "Take it off."

"I tried before," Flaxen said, and pulled at the ring. "It's too tight."

Then she put the ring finger in her mouth, licked it roundly with her lips, and extended her hand toward him.

"You try."

Leach's eyes were locked on her, just as were French Frank's.

"Sure."

Leach moved the gun to his left hand and with his right began slowly to work the ring free.

He did. Savoring every moment, every movement, every touch. Then he put the ring in his pocket.

"Is that all?" She asked.

"Is that all, what?"

"Is that all you want to take off?"

A look of pleasant disbelief came across Leach's face as her body and face moved closer to him, until her lips almost touched his.

"Flaxen!" I started to move. "You . . ."

But she interrupted.

"*Les choses ne sont pas toujours ce qu'elles paraissent . . .*"

"What'd you say to him?" Leach gritted.

"It's French."

"So it's French. What's it mean?"

"Means he's a beached whale—all washed up."

Leach grinned as her face moved closer to his.

"That's right, Leach," French Frank said. "Take off her clothes. There's enough for the two of us!"

"No, there's not, George," Flaxen said in a hushed whisper. "You and me. I'll go with you, but just you and me." Her arms were around him, fingers caressing his neck. "We'll make up for the time you spent in prison."

"You won't go anyplace without me!" French Frank took a step forward, gun pointed.

But Leach whirled and fired, once, twice, and as French Frank buckled, Flaxen pushed Leach away and cried out.

"Christopher!"

The gun was already in my hand with shots echoing in the cave along with Leach's curse . . .

"You son of a bi . . ."

As he fell I didn't know whether he was cursing Flaxen or me . . . and I didn't care.

I was beholden to Pepper's long ago advice, which went something like:

"Either sleep with your gun or . . . or keep it handy."

CHAPTER LXIV

Maybe we should have left the two bodies for the buzzards, but we didn't—covered them with rocks side by side after I removed the ring from Leach's pocket and replaced it on Flaxen's finger.

"You know," she smiled, "this isn't necessary anymore."

"I know a lot of things. Say, your French is pretty good."

"Had a good tutor, and you're pretty handy with a gun."

"I had a good tutor, too, ol' Pepper, but you made me kind of nervous there for a while."

"Not as nervous as I was with that pug-ugly in my face."

"Yes, well, it could have turned out a lot worse."

"Not for those two fellows—I'm happy to say."

"I wonder how it's turning out for Riker and Pepper and the rest of them."

"You mean what's left of the rest of them."

"That's right, Flaxen, what with Simpson dying, Leach and French Frank deserting . . ."

"Speaking of deserting, Christopher, do you still think we did the right thing? Leaving them?"

"It was the wise thing, the only thing. You know how Cookie opened his dirty mouth to Leach and French Frank and maybe everybody else, about you and me. Still . . ."

"Still what?"

"I wonder how Dr. Picard and Reese are fairing. I just hope that Riker didn't find out Reese helped us get away."

"What do you think Riker would do if he did find out?"

"Who can tell? But one thing in Reese's favor is that Riker needs him—and everyone else, to handle that herd. And you know something, Flaxen? I hope that, somehow, Wolf Riker makes it to Kansas with that herd."

"Christopher Guthrie, you are a strange bird."

"Don't you? Hope he makes it, I mean. Whatever else about him—he's got guts."

"So does a grizzly, but I can do without either one of them."

We took the canteens and whatever supplies we could from Leach and French Frank's horses, turned the animals loose, and rode on.

The sun had topped out over the eastern ridge

and barely broke through the still sullen sky. As we made our way north, a hot nomad wind whispered around smooth boulders and through forlorn trees and jagged rock. And somehow, it seemed to me that that wind was also whispering a warning. But I needed no messenger to convey such a signal—nor did Flaxen, although as I glanced across at her face there was not even a trace of trepidation.

It was as if we were out on a Sunday ride in Central Park. And when she looked across at me and smiled, it seemed as if her smile was in anticipation of a night at the theatre, with supper and champagne afterward.

Wolf Riker said that I had become her benefactor, her protector. But I wondered if, perhaps, at times, it was just the opposite—if it wasn't she who generated in me the grist to act as I had never acted before.

I, who had avoided the real hazards of war, where thousands were killed, and many thousands more were maimed and mutilated by bayonets and bombs. I, who enjoyed a charmed life with charming women and fey gentlemen in the rarified strata of society. Whose boldest undertaking was to sit on an aisle seat and criticize the portrayals of those who enacted drama and humor, classic and current.

Whose idea of adventure was to write about it

while sipping vintage wine and smoking expensive cigars.

A man who never had to make a hard decision. Who never had to choose between cowardice and courage.

A man who never acted—only reacted.

From the time of the attack on the stagecoach and becoming a part of Wolf Riker's cattle drive, I had never initiated an act of fortitude—I had only recoiled and reluctantly, or reflexively, responded in deference to my own self preservation. Even when I rescued Riker from the quicksand, it was at no real risk to my own being.

And at the cave with Leach and French Frank, it was Flaxen who took the initiative and made possible our survival.

Still, as I once again looked across at Flaxen, it was evident that she did have faith in me as her benefactor, her protector.

"Wither thou goest," she had said. "You do the deciding."

Her voice broke the silence.

"A penny for your thoughts." She smiled.

I said nothing.

"Well, then, I'll tell you my thoughts at no charge, Christopher. About what happened last night, and it was the first time it ever happened."

"I know that Flaxen . . ."

"Let me finish. I wanted it to happen. So, if we

get out of this, if we make it, you are under no obligation to . . ."

My hand reached out and took hold of her arm.

"Flaxen!"

From the rise where we were, I pointed.

In an expanse below.

Riders.

Thirty, maybe more.

We didn't try to count them. We stayed under cover, we hoped.

Comancheros.

Well armed with guns and rifles. And, from this distance, while we couldn't see the leader clearly, he probably was wearing a patch over one eye— and called Corona.

"Do you think they saw us?" Flaxen whispered, even though we were much too far away for them to hear.

"If they had, we'd know it by now."

"I guess you're right."

"But they sure as hell are going to see all those beeves, Riker and the drovers who don't have a prayer—and there's no way to warn them."

"Christopher, don't even think of trying."

"Don't worry, Flaxen. I'm not suicidal."

And then it hit.

CHAPTER LXV

It hit in the distance.

But it was not going to miss us—or anything close to us.

It hit like a tornado.

Because it probably was a tornado—or part of one—spreading as it whirled toward us . . . yes, this was what is sometimes called a twister—whirlwind—duster—tempest—sirocco—squall—dust devil—sometimes son of a bitch.

But whatever the nomenclature, it comes out of nowhere and wants to leave nothing, or little in its wake but devastation.

Luckily we saw it coming from a great distance, and I also saw in the far distance, in another direction, an outcrop of sizable rocks, which I indicated to Flaxen.

She nodded and we both kicked the animals toward what we hoped would provide some measure of protection.

Both Tobacco and Bluebell raced with hooves flying off the ground. A hundred yards, two hundred, half a mile, a mile and more.

The roaring maelstrom sounded like a freight train and struck like a spout out of hell—seething—churning—swirling—pitching—plunging—roiling—penetrating—but it was our good fortune to be on the outer perimeter, rather than the midmost of the holocaust.

Still, we were peppered with dirt, dust, sand, grime—nearly blinded, but we managed to make it to what shelter the outcrop of rocks provided. We slid down off our saddles and dove to the ground with the horses hunching close to us behind the craggy cover.

My arms were wrapped around Flaxen and my body pressed against her, with our heads coupled near the ground.

We were both beyond exhaustion, drained and flagged, but still alive and together—and we stayed that way until both of us lost track of time. Time was a clock with no hands as we fell into a black pit. It had no bottom—we were swallowed by oblivion.

For how long, neither of us knew, but we had dissolved into another world, a surreal universe of silence—until voices penetrated that universe.

First I, then Flaxen, became aware of those voices, then saw what appeared to be giant figures looking down on us.

CHAPTER LXVI

I could not determine what the voices were saying. They seemed like echoes in a far away canyon.

The figures, at first, were blurred, out of focus, then slowly I could distinguish a red scarf on one of the giants—and the features on the other face were faintly familiar, but younger, better put together—and without a scar on the forehead.

Both Flaxen and I were now conscious and thankful to be alive. The sky was a clean, clear blue, the air calm.

We both endeavored to rise.

"Take it on the easy, you two," said the man without the scarf. "You're a very lucky pair."

"The storm," I said, "it . . ."

"Gone. Those devils disappear as fast as they strike. But we were luckier than you. Missed us and the herd by a slender margin, Mister . . ."

"Guthrie. Christopher Guthrie, and this is my fiancée, Flaxen Brewster."

"Pleased to meet you."

"Not as pleased as we are . . . Mr. Riker . . . isn't it?"

He didn't conceal the look of astonishment on his face.

"Yes, but . . ."

"And the other gentleman, with the red scarf . . ." I added, "Adam Dawson, late of Custer's Wolverines?"

"Mr. Guthrie," Adam Dawson said, "are you by any chance some sort of fortune teller?"

"No. Just a friend of a fellow named Pepper— and a recent acquaintance of a relative of yours," I looked at Dirk Riker. "I'll tell you all about it."

"Tell us after we get you to camp," Dirk Riker said. "I'd be most interested to hear . . . 'all about it.'"

Dirk Riker's camp and crew were a pleasant contrast to that of his brother's.

Flaxen and I had refreshed ourselves and were treated to a tasty meal while Dirk Riker told us how they happened to find us.

He and Dawson were scouting ahead when they came across two saddled horses that were out in the open seeking to graze after the windstorm. Horses that led them to the outcrop of rocks— and Flaxen and me.

"Now then," Dirk leaned forward, "let's hear about the two of you and my brother's cattle drive."

I looked at Flaxen, took a deep breath—and began.

It was an abbreviated, somewhat abridged version, but close to the truth, close enough—from my first awareness of Wolf Riker and his callous reaction to the death of his trail boss, Donavan—his treatment of Dr. Picard and indifference to the survival of Flaxen—the capricious abuse of the drovers—and yes, my astonishment at his collected literary works, and his credence of Milton's line, "better to reign in hell, than serve in heaven"—his obsessive determination to drive the herd and men through rain and river—his brute strength, leaping on a crazed steer and killing it with Pepper's Bowie knife—and in marked contrast, his respect and deference to Pepper, and his concern and care for Bucephalus—how he negotiated with one tribe and challenged the strongest warrior of another—the attack and attempted murder at the pit of quicksand—the savage beating of Simpson—all of this and more—all a part of the journal he encouraged me to record, regarding his life and the cattle drive to Kansas—then, a somewhat varied version of Flaxen's and my decision to take our chances making it to the crossing station—and of course,

I addressed his brother's more frequent attacks of blinding pain.

"And Pepper told you how that came about . . . that it was I who . . ."

"He did . . . and the circumstances that led up to it."

"Wolf changed after that," Dirk said. "And I tried . . ."

"We all change, Mr. Riker, some for the better and some . . . like your brother. But as I said to Flaxen, I hope he makes it to Kansas."

"Someday," Dirk Riker smiled, "I'd like to read what you've written about my brother."

"Every story's got to have a finish. This one doesn't . . . not yet."

"From what I just heard," Adam Dawson said, "I wouldn't bet against him finishing that drive."

"Except for one thing . . ." I started to say, but didn't finish.

By then most of the camp could hear the pop-pop tattoo of faraway shots—see and hear a rider approaching.

A rider wearing a red scarf—and the way he rode and waved an arm telegraphed trouble.

"Riker! Mr. Riker!"

As he slid his horse to a stop and sprang from his saddle, scores of other men of the camp came close by to listen.

"What is it, Mantee?" Dirk Riker took a step near him.

"A raid! Slaughter, it's . . . it . . ."

"Take a breath," Dawson said.

"I'm okay, But they're not. Cattle drive, up ahead. Hit by ambush—more than a couple dozen—cattle stampeded—the whole outfit, what's still alive—takin' cover behind the wagons—gettin' shot to pieces . . ."

"Wolf." Dirk Riker looked at Dawson.

"Mantee," Dawson asked, "Indians?"

"Comancheros," I said. "That's what I was about to tell you. Twenty or thirty. Flaxen and I saw them, but they didn't see us, before the storm . . ."

"Can't last much longer," Mantee shook his head. "They ain't got a chance."

"Maybe they have," Dirk Riker said.

"Yea, maybe they do." Dawson smiled.

"Are you thinking what I'm thinking, Adam?" Dirk also smiled. "They could hit us next you know."

"Not if we hit them first."

"That's what I'm thinking."

Dawson looked around.

"What about it, Wolverines? Remember what Custer always said . . . *'Ride to the sound of the guns!'*"

"Let's ride!" someone shouted, and the rest took up the cry, including Mantee.

"You're not going," Dirk said to him.

"I'm not?"

"Well, are you?"

"Not 'til I get a fresh horse."

"Adam!"

"What is it, Mr. Guthrie?"

"Mind if I ride along? I want to finish that journal."

"No, I don't mind." Dirk Riker pointed toward Flaxen. "Not if she doesn't."

"Christopher . . . you don't have to . . ."

"Flaxen, this is my chance to do something I don't have to do."

Flaxen kissed me.

"Then do it."

CHAPTER LXVII

The bursts grew louder as we rode to the sound of the guns.

And as we rode, there were hundreds of cattle spread across the terrain, cattle that scattered even more at the sound and sight of the charging horsemen.

Guns drawn and hooves pounding, we topped out over a rise, where down below the Comancheros were circling Indian style, shooting and screaming, around the beleaguered wagons. One of the wagons was on fire, the others, riddled with bullets.

Bodies of drovers and Comancheros lay in twisted patterns on the ground. Smoke rose from the burning wagon and the rifles and revolvers of defenders behind cover, and attackers on horseback.

"Ride, you Wolverines!" Dawson cried, his red scarf flowing from his throat, accompanied by dozens of other red-scared riders spurring their mounts toward the melee with gunfire ripping through the air, and much of it finding human targets.

The attackers were attacked—not by civilians and cowboys, but by ununiformed cavalry, except for the fluttering red scarves—seasoned veterans of Chickahominy, Brandy Station, Falls Church, Gettysburg, Yellow Tavern and Appomattox, determined and disciplined, who had defeated the valiant ranks of mounted Rebel brigades.

The Comancheros were caught between the gunfire of the defenders and the onslaught of what they must have thought were riders from hell.

The toll mounted as one after another was hit and fell. I rode next to Dirk Riker and Adam Dawson, each of us with reins in one hand and guns firing with the other.

It was fulfillment I had never felt—especially when I saw one of the Comancheros, who was wearing a black eye patch, struck by a bullet, twist off his mount, and fall hard and lifeless to the ground.

I wasn't the only one who saw it. The Comancheros, those who were still on their horses and able, turned and rode away in all directions.

Dirk Riker and his men let them ride.

* * *

Flaxen rode in after we had all dismounted and began to see what we could do to assist those who had survived the attack.

Dirk and I, followed by Flaxen and Dawson, moved toward a group who had taken cover around Wolf Riker's wagon, some still alive and others not as fortunate.

The bodies included those of Smoke, Cookie, and Dogbreath.

Among the more fortunate, but badly shaken, Dr. Picard. Next to him Alan Reese and nearby, Morales One and Morales Two.

But there was another body on the ground close to Wolf Riker.

Pepper, still with a gun in one hand and the Bowie knife in the other, and blood smeared on his lifeless body.

We knelt close to Wolf Riker, wounded at his right side, but breathing—his eyes staring vacantly, seemingly blind.

Dirk Riker leaned closer.

"Wolf . . . Wolf . . . can you see me? It's Dirk . . ."

"I knew . . . it would be," Wolf Riker rasped.

"Doctor . . . ?" I looked at Picard who had already started to probe at Riker's wound.

"I've seen worse," Picard said.

"You sound . . . disappointed." Wolf Riker tried to smile.

"Wolf," I said, "you're indestructible."

"Is that you . . . Guth?"

"Yes . . . and Flaxen."

"You made it, huh. Good."

"You're going to make it, too, Wolf," Dirk Riker said. "But your cattle's scattered from here to breakfast."

"*Our* cattle . . . I never took your name off the land grant."

Dirk Riker reached out and touched his brother's face.

"Why didn't you tell me?"

"I don't know . . . maybe . . . I just figured . . . you'd find out sometime . . . one way or another."

"Wolf," Dirk said, "we'll get those beeves to Kansas."

"Sure we will."

"And Wolf," Dr. Picard, took a breath, "about Pepper . . ."

"I know." Wolf Riker barely nodded.

"Too bad," Picard looked from Wolf to Dirk Riker, "Pepper didn't live to know about this."

"He knows," Alan Reese said.

EPILOGUE

I'm finally finishing the journal and the story of the Range Wolf Cattle Drive.

Wolf Riker turned out to be a different man from who I thought he was—even a different man from who *he* thought he was.

Since Horace Greeley likes a happy ending, I'll do my best to provide one without tilting the truth, or the odds, too much.

Dr. Miles Picard still hasn't taken a drink.

Alan Reese once again is wearing a white collar.

The cattle drive did go on to Kansas, and the Double R, now one of the biggest spreads in Texas, or anyplace—where Bucephalus grazes contentedly in well earned retirement—once again stands for Riker and Riker.

Morales One and Morales Two, relatively rich, sank spur and rode south to Durango, Durango.

Wolf Riker, who now neither reigns nor serves, is about to have an operation in St. Louis, and the doctors say the odds are fifty-fifty that he'll see again.

And speaking of odds:

Flaxen has just entered the room and, as I write this, is looking over my shoulder. I think our odds are much better than fifty-fifty.

We are living quiet, peaceful lives in the City by the Bay, and Flaxen soon will give birth to a little boy or girl whose hair will be as yellow as Alabama butter. Our family physician is Dr. Picard.

We expect to continue living quiet, peaceful lives for a long, long time—with many *Veltio Avrios*, better tomorrows—that is, barring floods, fires, earthquakes, and other natural disasters.

"Right, Mrs. Guthrie?"

"Right, Mr. Guthrie."

And, Mr. Greeley, I'm still going to vote for Ulysses Simpson Grant.